SHORT CUT TO SANTA FE

SHORT CUT TO SANTA FE

MEDORA SALE

Charles Scribner's Sons
New York

Maxwell Macmillan Canada
Toronto

Maxwell Macmillan International
New York Oxford Singapore Sydney

Copyright © 1994 by Medora Sale Ltd.

Charles Scribner's Sons
Macmillan Publishing Company
866 Third Avenue
New York, NY 10022

Maxwell Macmillan Canada, Inc.
1200 Eglinton Avenue East
Suite 200
Don Mills, Ontario M3C 3N1

Macmillan Publishing Company is part of the Maxwell Communication Group of Companies.

Library of Congress Cataloging-in-Publication Data
Sale, Medora.
    Short cut to Santa Fe/Medora Sale.
        p.   cm.
    ISBN 0-684-19680-8
    I. Title.
    PR9199.3.S165S48   1994
    813'.54—dc20   93–47422   CIP

Macmillan books are available at special discounts for bulk purchases for sales promotions, premiums, fund-raising, or educational use. For details, contact:

        Special Sales Director
        Macmillan Publishing Company
        866 Third Avenue
        New York, NY 10022

10   9   8   7   6   5   4   3   2

Printed in the United States of America

For *Harry*
who was there
and *Anne*

ACKNOWLEDGMENTS

I would like to thank Layne Vickers Torkelson, Carolyn Kacena, and all the rest of the generous people from New Mexico who cheerfully and patiently answered my many questions, especially on things meteorological. Oddities and errors spring from the author's wild imaginings, as do all the evil characters and one large, interestingly shaped mountain. I would also like to thank Richard Owen, who chose the ideal light aircraft for a crew of villains to perpetrate their villainy in.

SHORT CUT
TO SANTA FE

CHAPTER 1

Inspector John Sanders stood in front of the white-painted door and gave his tangled bunch of keys a dispirited examination. He was shivering with cold in the gray, windswept May afternoon, but he shied away from the doorway like a horse facing a burning stable. There was nothing sinister about it. Open that door and he knew he would face five days' worth of garbage, unwashed coffee cups, dust, dirty shirts, and solitude. He had put Harriet and all her gear on a plane last Thursday and discovered that without her in it, their apartment had become unbearable.

He had sent her off with an air of martyred goodwill that she had treated with the contempt it deserved. "John," she'd said as she moved along the endless passages of Toronto's Pearson Airport, apparently unimpeded by at least forty pounds of photographic equipment, "if you don't stop looking like a spaniel that's just been kicked, I'll throw something at you. You haven't been home for more than six hours at a time for weeks now—you won't even notice I'm not there."

"The hell I won't," he'd said, matching his long stride to her slightly shorter one. "I always notice when you're not there."

"You promised when you moved in that you wouldn't mess with my work. Remember? And this is work. I've wanted to do this Kansas project for more than a year and now is the perfect time. Days are getting long, shadows aren't bad, and by the time I've finished you might have wrapped up your case." She had stopped and turned to him, her face grave and her green eyes intense.

"But what if—"

"Don't say it. Don't even think it. I'll be fine. I can look after myself. You'd think I was flying to Beirut, not Kansas City." Then her stern voice had melted into husky laughter, she had grinned, put down her gear, and wrapped her arms around his neck. "But I sure as hell will miss those six hours you are at home," she had murmured lasciviously and kissed him. "I'll call you from Kansas City. Don't forget to leave the machine on when you go out," she had added, picking up her gear and preparing to do battle with the airport's security equipment. "And eat something besides doughnuts and hamburgers."

He pushed open the door and stooped to gather up the mail. Under the bills and the advertising flyers lay an envelope with Harriet's cramped scrawl on it. He ran up the stairs to the living room, dropped the rest of the mail on her desk, and ripped open her letter.

> Lawrence, Kansas
> Thursday.
>
> John darling,
> I decided that I was never going to telephone at an hour when you were home (how is the case? Active, I assume, since I couldn't reach you tonight), and so I'm

attempting the old-world expedient of writing. I'd fax, except that I don't want all those louts in your department snickering over my letter.

So far, the trip has been fine. I picked up the van in Kansas City—almost new, and at last, something big enough for my equipment—and set out westward ho. I didn't get very far, as you could tell if you knew anything about this part of the world. I was planning to drive a hundred miles or so but was stopped by Lawrence—it's a university town with some very tempting houses and streetscapes. I can't help it. I promised myself I'd stick to industrial buildings this trip, but there is so much as I go along and who knows when I'll get this way again.

Abilene, Kansas
Friday

Very slow progress. I keep stopping to grab silos and such against the sky—which, by the way, is wonderful. Like an Irish sky, in the rapid shift of sun and cloud. Spring is here, and everything is green and growing. The world is defined by trees. A single tree standing in an empty field. A line of trees defining a river. I am in danger of becoming a landscape freak. All right—I'm becoming a landscape freak. So far, no tornadoes, no gray landscape. What was Dorothy talking about?

Saturday

I've been in Abilene since yesterday afternoon. It's an old railroad town, with a fabulous mill and grain elevator.

How goes the case? Have you nailed the husband yet? It must be the air out here, but all sorts of fresh ideas occur to me. Have you considered that you're having trouble proving he did it because, just maybe, he didn't? Hard as it is for me to admit it, women are killed by people other than their husbands or lovers.

Anyway, so much for today's insight. I'm planning on leaving here tomorrow very early in the A.M., in time to catch several places on my list before the sun gets too high. I'll spend tomorrow and the night after in Kansas wherever I can find cheap motels in interesting towns, and then into Denver to see Kate Grosvenor. I called her today, and managed to lock myself into spending two nights at her place. She's in rougher shape than I realized. Apparently (although you probably know this) bullet wounds in the shoulder are nasty things, highly disruptive to bones, ligaments, cartilage, and all that, and it's taking her a hell of a lot of time to recuperate from this one. She is beginning to feel that there are better ways of earning a living than photojournalism.

Anyway, my love, this dreary recital of my itinerary all has a point. I was thinking of leaving Denver on Thursday. Even if I just loafed down the highway, stopping whenever I felt like it, I could get to Santa Fe—or wherever the nearest airport is—on Friday, and pick you up. Get it? Then we head north again on Friday or Saturday or Sunday to Taos. I think we both need a few days off, and Kate says—I'm not sure why—that there are places near Taos that she thinks I might be able to photograph. Fax me in Denver? Or telephone? You'll find the numbers on the Rolodex under Grosvenor.

I am assuming that when I left, you were at the darkest-before-dawn point and that I can't reach you because you are wrapping up the case. If you're still up to your ears, then let me know and I'll rearrange my plans. But I won't be happy about it. Life seems very curious without you turning up at least once a day. I'm startled at how used I have become to your toothbrush in my—or now our—bathroom. I thought that I had acclimatized myself so completely over the years to living alone that I would find a few days of solitary bliss a relief. It isn't. I miss you, damn it, in more ways than I thought I would. Away from you for three days, and my treacherous body thinks you've been gone for a month. I keep storing up little things to tell you at dinner and then I dine alone. So come and meet me if you can.

All my love,

Her familiar signature, awkward and spiky, was scrawled across the bottom of the page. He sat down abruptly. It brought her voice, and her solemn mocking green-eyed look into startling proximity and juxtaposed it to the horror of the day.

Harriet had been right in her diagnosis of his case; it had not been her husband who had killed Mrs. Novak and their two daughters. John had been contacted that morning as soon as the body and the confession had been discovered, and he'd reached the pleasant house on its prosperous street before the scene had been tidied up. The shattered head, the blood-soaked bedding, the heavy assault rifle made a fitting final chapter to a history steeped in so much blood. Only the main character seemed insanely out of place. Slumped on the bed lay a frail, skinny fifteen-year-old child, dead by his own hand.

The weapon on the floor would almost certainly turn out to be the one used on Gail Novak, Seana, thirteen, and Erin, eleven, on the night Roy Novak had been on a business trip to Edmonton. And from that moment, Sanders and his team had participated in turning Novak's life into a living hell. They had searched every cranny of his existence, looking for a mistress, or a large insurance policy on his wife, anything that would motivate a prosperous, sober businessman to slaughter his family. Because who would have thought that the boy who had lived four houses away for less than a year, and had never—as far as anyone knew—spoken to either daughter, had owned a weapon like that and was crazy enough to use it to avenge a fancied slight and an imaginary broken heart.

That's what he had said. He loved Seana Novak, his letter said, and she had refused to go out with him. But he had seen her talking to another boy and that was when he had decided to kill her. Now he couldn't live without her. He was going to kill himself and wanted to be buried in the same grave with her, like Romeo and Juliet, he said.

His mother had sat in the living room, smiling politely, as if Sanders had come for morning coffee. "What is he talking about, do you know, Officer?" she had asked, with a puzzled frown. "He's been studying *Romeo and Juliet* at school. Maybe his teacher knows." She grasped nothing. Not his death, not the murders, not her loss.

"Where did your son get that rifle?" he asked.

"He must have bought it," said his mother brightly. "He has a job after school three nights a week. And he still has his paper route. He's had that since he was eleven. He saves every penny he earns to buy himself things he really wants."

Like enough firepower to wipe out the neighborhood, thought Sanders. Sweet, hard-working kid. "Did you ever worry that your son might be violent or disturbed?" he asked at last. "Did he get upset easily?"

"Oh no." She shook her head in amazement. "He was always the quietest, nicest boy," said his mother. Her voice was becoming thick and her eyes were drooping at the corners. She blinked him back in focus.

Coked to the gills. Some doctor's been at her. Sanders smiled gently and got himself out of the room, abandoning her to the protective armor of shock and little white—or whatever color they were—pills.

"Is there any doubt he did it?" asked Sergeant Ed Dubinsky, his partner. They had stood outside, on the lawn, removing themselves from everyone's way.

Sanders shook his head. "Everything he says in the letter fits the physical evidence. No one else could have known. He did it, all right."

And that was it. The case was over.

He put Harriet's letter down on the desk and headed for the shower. He couldn't talk to her before washing the blood off his soul.

John toweled himself as if he were trying to remove his skin along with the water, and then slipped into jeans and a sweatshirt. He looked in the refrigerator, shook his head, took out a beer, and headed for the telephone on the desk. He hated the flippant voice on the answering machine at Kate Grosvenor's and slammed the receiver down.

There was a fax waiting for him as he approached his desk. It was demurely addressed to "Inspector John Sanders," and had no doubt been read by everyone in the sprawling room by now. He spread it open.

> Dear Inspector Sanders,
> Arrived in Denver. All is well; trip uneventful, but please call me at Kate's. It's important.
> > Harriet.

"But not from here," said John, and was rewarded with a suspicious look from someone rushing by with coffee and a sandwich. He shrugged and went over to fax his carefully worded reply to Harriet's first letter.

"This one is for you," said Kate Grosvenor, as she came out of the study. "A fax addressed to Dear Harriet with no cover page."

"John," muttered her friend, snatching the page out of her hand. "That was a superb lunch. Thank you. Do you mind if I—"

"Go ahead. Find a comfortable spot in the living room and I'll get us coffee."

Kate's house was tall, and longer than it was wide, built of red brick and in the Victorian manner, and ornamented with stained glass. It had been divided into two apartments: Kate's took up the first floor and part of the second;

a silent tenant lived above. Harriet shivered as she walked into the living room. An air of uninhabited desolation seemed to hang over all the rooms except the little study just inside the door, where Kate's battered oak desk and spring-backed chair occupied every inch of floor space. Ominous quantities of dust lay over every surface in the darkroom. Kate had stopped working some time ago.

Harriet resolutely curled up in a large chair to read John's fax.

Dear Harriet,

Yes. I'm exhausted and I miss you and I don't give a damn if all we do is meet in Chicago or Tulsa or Dallas and spend four days in an airport hotel, sending out for soggy pizza and hamburgers. Although Taos sounds good, too. It's cold here and miserable but the good news is that as of a few hours ago I can get away. Thank God.

The case is solved, if you can call what happened a solution. Ended is maybe a better word. I'll tell you about it later, except that you're right. It wasn't the husband. It was a neighbor.

Meet me at the airport in Santa Fe at five-thirty Friday. I'll call you tomorrow at your friend's place at five Toronto time to confirm.

Love,
John.

"So—what's up?" said Kate. She was standing in the door-way with two cups of coffee and no color at all in her serenely classical face.

Harriet leaped to her feet and grabbed the coffee cups before they crashed to the floor. "Are you all right?" she asked, although the most stunned observer could have seen that she wasn't.

"Jesus—who can tell?" said Kate, her voice rather hoarse. She walked carefully over to the sofa and lowered herself into it. "I'm fine and I feel great and then suddenly this pain grabs me in the shoulder, runs across my torso, and charges down to my wrist. It happens when I use the arm, usually, although sometimes it happens when I don't." She laughed, a nasty, short little laugh. "I hate whining about it, but I'm not used to being in pain. It unsettles me. Could you reach that bottle of Scotch over there?" she added. "Help yourself and pass it on."

Harriet reflected on the bottle of wine they had split over lunch and shook her head, silently passing the bottle over to her friend. "Are you sure?" she asked.

"Yes—I'm damn well sure," said Kate. "It's about the only thing that helps." She rummaged in her jacket pocket and came up with a small plastic container of pills, shook out two, tossed them in her mouth, poured a dollop of Scotch into her coffee, and washed down the pills with the mixture.

Harriet opened her mouth to object and closed it again.

Kate settled back and gave her a crooked smile. "So tell me about John whoever-he-is. Couldn't you have found someone with a more original name? What does he do? What does he look like? Is he good in bed?"

She's drunk, said Harriet to herself, and God only knows what's in those pills. "None of your business, Kate Grosvenor. Besides, would I be messing around with any-one who wasn't? Anyway, he's a cop, believe it or not, and . . ." As her voice droned on, she studied the woman sitting across from her. She had met Kate four years ago at an advanced seminar on architectural photography in Rockport, Maine, and had been impressed, in spite of herself, by her energy and self-reliance. And cockiness. All packaged with long legs, a thick mane of wavy hair, and an oval face punctuated by sharply intelligent blue eyes.

Kate was the oddity in the group. Most of the participants worked in the field, and spent their time swapping information on subjects like the costs, benefits, and agonies of running your own color lab, and whether the trouble and expense involved in changing format from four by five to five by seven was worth it. Kate was so typically the risk-taking, hard-driving, as-it-happens news photographer that Harriet would have dismissed her as a rank amateur who'd picked up the jargon from the movies, except that she worked for a major newsmagazine and her photo credits were everywhere. She had scooped Harriet into her circle, and one night over a late, late beer admitted that she had always wanted to do architectural work, to have the luxury of fiddling for hours over a single shot, instead of the snatch-and-grab stuff she was doing at the present. Harriet had laughed, thinking of Kate's prestige and probable income compared with her own.

Then she had received a painfully scrawled postcard a few weeks ago. Kate had been sent to do a background piece on the current state of affairs in south Lebanon. As far as Harriet could make out, she had been wounded in crossfire. She was going home to Denver to recuperate, she said, and begged Harriet to come and visit.

Kate lived alone. By choice, surely, Harriet had long ago decided, considering how funny and lively and incredibly good-looking she was. The world couldn't be that short of possible mates. The only man Kate had mentioned was a

Dutch photographer with whom she had shared this house for a while after she had inherited it from her grandmother. "Anyway," said Harriet, who had completely lost the thread of her narrative, if it ever had one, "that's about all I can tell you about John. Oddly enough, we get on very well. And he's tall, fairly thin, with dark hair going gray and a long, thin face. Quick-tempered, thoughtful, generous, and he likes me."

"I should bloody well hope so," said Kate.

"No—you don't understand," said Harriet, frowning in intensity. "Anybody can love someone, but John actually likes me as well."

They were sitting in Kate's tiled kitchen with the remains of take-out Mexican spread over the pale wood table. Kate had helped herself and then pushed at her food, nibbling a mouthful once in a while. She finished a token beer and returned to coffee laced with Scotch. "I've been thinking of going back to south Lebanon and doing a study of what's left. While it's still there. You know. The aesthetics of death. Rubble as beauty. Sort of après–bomb art. Too gruesome?"

"More like too dangerous," said Harriet. "The next one might land a little closer to a vital organ."

"Now there's an argument for booking the next flight to the Middle East," said Kate. "Anyway, so much for me in this ten-minute time slot. Have you given any thought to Taos?" She bent forward, her clear blue eyes fixed on Harriet intently, as if her answer were terribly important.

"Some," said Harriet cautiously.

"You have to go," said Kate. "You've never seen anything like it. You have to go and take your equipment. As for me—all I can shoot in Taos is the tackiness." She grinned lopsidedly again and refilled her cup. "I've done some terrific studies of that—hard-edged and vicious, sort of Arbus-like. But the real stuff eludes me."

"What do you mean?" asked Harriet. "The real stuff. And how does it elude you?"

"You'll see when you get there," said Kate vaguely. "It's funny, though. Sometimes it's physical. Like—I get set up and clouds whoosh in from nowhere. I step back to squeeze the shutter release and someone runs by and hits the tripod. Or I stumble and hit the tripod. I've had totally reliable equipment jam. It's weird. I walk into that place and I'm all thumbs." This time her laugh was almost real. "A friend who's into crystals and all that kind of shit says that war and hatred have darkened my soul and prevent me from penetrating the atmosphere up there. But you might have the right genes or background or whatever it takes."

"You're crazy, Kate. You're just working with equipment you're not that happy with."

She shook her head. "No—it's real. Look," she went on, leaning over the table. "I don't know when you have to get back, but if you can spare a few days, we could go to Taos together and I'll show you around. Unless you think I'm a jinx." Her eyes burned with a drug-and-booze-sodden intensity that Harriet found profoundly disturbing.

"For God's sake, Kate, you're not a jinx. You're wounded. You can't work with a four by five yet. Too heavy and cumbersome. Laying off the booze and pills wouldn't hurt, either."

"It's not that. It started before I was hit. It began—" Her pale face froze and she stared off into the corner. "It began years ago when—Harriet, do you know about *la noche oscura del alma*? The dark night of the soul? Well, I'm in it and I'll never reach dawn. I didn't tell you how I got this, did I?" she said, touching her shoulder gingerly. "I mean, the real reason. I didn't tell anyone. It wasn't random violence, the luck of war, or whatever you call it. I was taking a picture of a dead child when a sniper got me. She was just a little girl, maybe four or five. I'd been watching her play on the road. One of those really beautiful dark-eyed children, and she had a thing over her head, a scarf, to cover her hair, only it was coming down because she was concentrating so hard on whatever it was she was playing with. One of those perfect shots you sometimes get with kids, you know? Deserted, war-torn street, contrasting perfect innocence and domesticity. A career picture. An essence of the conflict picture. I spent a few extra seconds framing the scene and all that crap, and just as I released the shutter, she was shot in the head. And killed. And I walked up to her and took a picture of her anyway. Beautiful dead children also sell well. Then I was shot from the other side of the street. It makes me sick to think of it." Kate's hands were trembling and she tried to steady them around her coffee cup. "Who could kill a child like that? It can't have been an accident—there was no one else to aim at. So it was some bastard on one side or the other who cold-bloodedly decided to shoot that little girl because a well-known photographer was standing close enough to take a 'war is hell' picture. I killed her," she said. "By being there. And her father or her brother shot me because he knew I was responsible." She paused. "But, Harriet, that wasn't the first time that someone died for my benefit, let me tell you—only I never let myself think about it before. Any time I wanted to get a particular angle on something, all I had to do was appear. They're all hungry for media attention—everyone knows that. I have blood on my hands, Harriet, a lot of blood, and I can't get rid of it."

"You don't know that," said Harriet. Profoundly shaken, she began to clear the take-out containers and dirty dishes off the table as briskly as she could manage.

"Yes I do. Would you mind if I went Taos with you? Jesus, I hate whining like this, but it means a lot to me. I can't go by myself."

"Nothing I'd like better," said Harriet, lying bravely. "The only problem is that I'm picking John up in Santa Fe first." She tried to form a mental picture of John Sanders and Kate Grosvenor sitting across the table from each other. And shuddered. "If you could meet us there," she added, with a sinking sensation in her gut, "it would be great. But no—you'd never be able to drive all that way, would you?"

"Sure I can," said Kate. "It's not far. And I know a neat place to stay. Slightly scruffy, but very comfortable—with fireplaces. Do you want me to get us a couple of rooms?"

"Yeah, sure, Kate," said Harriet weakly. "Sounds great." She leaned over and grabbed the Scotch bottle. "Just lay off this stuff or it'll finish you off before you get there, Kate," she added grimly. "Especially if those are pain pills you're taking with it."

Kate's perfectly shaped face was devoid of expression.

CHAPTER 2

Harriet finished off her *huevos rancheros*, and turned her attention to the road map and brochures she had picked up the previous afternoon. After a moment's consideration, she ordered a sweet roll and asked for more coffee. After all, who knew when she would eat again? For two days she had been watching Kate play with her food as if every bite could be the one the wicked witch had injected with poison. And she'd brooded over John's reaction to sharing his brief holiday with a neurotic semi-invalid who drank her meals. The experience had done serious damage to Harriet's appetite and sleep patterns. That disordered state hadn't survived crossing the state line into New Mexico, and arriving at a peaceful motel in Raton.

The big decision was which route to take to Santa Fe. Via Taos or Las Vegas? Harriet had started in on this momentous piece of planning last night over dinner in the motel restaurant. On the principle that getting local input was always good, she had asked the waitress about the roads. They were, of course, just fine. All of them. Just fine.

"Listen, honey," said a woman from the next table, "if you're thinking of that road through the mountains, don't. We just came that way and we're lucky to be alive. Aren't we?" There had been a chorus of agreement from the other three people at her table. "We don't have roads like that in

Missouri, and we don't have people who drive like that on them either. Take your life in your hands, and that's God's truth."

"Is it pretty?" Harriet had asked. First things first.

"Who knows?" her friendly adviser had said. "I had my eyes shut tight all the way. You stick with the other road."

"It's beautiful," the waitress had declared firmly.

"That road's not dangerous." A man who was sitting at the counter eating a steak with french fries joined the fray. "Lady knows how to drive she won't have trouble."

"That's right." Someone from the table closest to the door added his opinion. "You can't hardly call that a mountain road at all. It's these people doing twenty miles an hour make it a problem." He had glared at the foursome from Missouri, as if he suspected them of being prize members of the slow-driving fraternity. Then he had winked at Harriet.

Harriet weighed the claims of the opposing parties over her coffee and thought how extraordinary it was to have an entire restaurant fall into general conversation. Did it happen all the time in Raton, New Mexico, or had it required the catalyst of the table from Missouri? Perhaps the merry foursome from the plains wandered through the world, causing these tiny events, believing that everywhere people were chatty and concerned and helpful. She folded the map so that the right sector was visible, and decided on the mountain road.

And in another dining room, miles away, on a spacious piece of property close to Dallas, more travel plans were being finalized over breakfast, with even greater delicacy. Victoria Deever picked the coffeepot off its elaborate warming stand—pot and stand a present from some grateful beneficiary of Carl's generosity—and filled her tiny flowered cup. It was difficult to tell if Carl Deever noticed the shaking hand, and the telltale splashes of coffee that had found their way onto the tablecloth. But he seemed to be concentrating on a briefcase filled with documents that had arrived for him that morning. And frowning. Her anxiety level eased slightly as she watched him go steadily through the material, thick black pencil in hand. The more work he had, the less time he spent thinking about what she was doing. She took a deep breath to slow her racing heartbeat and counted to three before trying to speak.

"Carl, honey," she said. "Can I get you more coffee?"

He made an indeterminate noise that could have been yes or no and held out his cup.

She took it and poured. More carefully this time. "Carl, honey—" she started.

He took the coffee cup, added sugar, and stirred vigorously to cover his surprise. "You said that already. What do you want?" She had never been an early riser, and he hadn't expected to see her at breakfast that morning, of all mornings; he fixed his expressionless brown eyes on her while he tried to figure out exactly what she was up to. Besides attempting to put one over on him. She was wearing the red silk negligee with ruffles around the neck and wrists that he had given her for Christmas. The one his secretary had found and paid a packet of his money for. It was worth it. The strong color turned her blond hair to ash, and left her looking pale and elegant without her makeup. Once more he congratulated himself on her pure class, from her modulated vowels to her graceful bearing. She was worth every penny he spent on her. Even if he'd rather sleep with other people.

"Could I have Ginger to drive me to the airport this morning? Or do you need him?"

"The airport? Why in hell do you want to go to the airport this morning?" Deever's eyes narrowed, but his wife was too far into her scenario to notice or halt.

"But, Carl—don't you remember? I'm going to New Orleans with Jessica. Just for a week. You said you were going to be so busy you'd hardly be home and this sounded like fun. You know how I hate being alone in the house. I told you about it—at least three times."

"What in hell are you going to do in New Orleans, for chrissake? It's dead right now."

"But, Carl, that's not true. It's never dead. Jessica has a wonderful little hotel she stays at. She says the food is terrific. Not touristy at all and very quiet and private. If it's as good as she says, maybe we could go there for a weekend sometime. I'd have invited her here for the week, but I know you can't stand her." A steel edge that was new to him crept into her voice. "I've already paid for a week at the hotel and the plane tickets aren't refundable."

"Oh well—in that case, if the tickets aren't refundable, by all means, leave me by myself for a week." Then he smiled to show that he was teasing her. The smile that reminded her of a piranha. "And you're right. I'll be very busy. But I'm afraid you can't have Ginger. Not this morning. He's already left on some urgent business for me."

"That's okay," said Victoria, who had watched him drive away as she packed and was not surprised. "I'll call for a limousine."

"You do that, Vicky sweetheart." The discussion was over. He returned to his documents; Victoria Deever clenched her teeth, picked up her coffee cup, and headed for her bedroom to finish packing.

As soon as he was alone, Carl reached for the phone connected to his very private line and jabbed his finger down on one of the preset numbers. "About that project," he said. "Get going."

Then he punched in another number. "Scotty," he said. He sounded almost jovial. "Vicky's going on that trip after all. This morning."

"No shit," said Scotty. "I'll believe it when I see it."

"Report back to me as soon as you have anything." Carl Deever's wife didn't travel much these days, and when she did, it was rarely without an escort. Whether she knew about it or not.

In Washington, D.C., a promising young federal agent whose vacation plans involved leaving work before lunch was standing in front of the head of the division, mutinous thoughts hidden behind a mask of deference.

"He has *appendicitis*?" said the agent, overwhelmed by anguish and disbelief. "You're sure it isn't just a world-class hangover?"

"Look, Cathcart—I know you were hoping to get away today—"

That killed it. That verb. Hoping. Emphasizing that agents with only four years' experience are not supposed to think they can make definite plans. Not in this division. "Yes, sir, I was. The Santa Rosa file is finished at this end and my background report is written and on your desk, sir. And I have tickets, reservations, all those things that you get and pay for in advance."

He shook his head. "That wasn't very bright, Cathcart. You should know better by now. But there's no question about it. We need someone to keep a close and unobtrusive watch on the subject. You can pick up Hendricks's tickets, instructions, reservations—all those things we arrange and pay for in advance. And identity."

"Do I know where I'm going with these tickets? Sir?" asked Cathcart.

"Dallas, in the first instance. Where you pick up the subject. And if all goes as currently planned, to Santa Fe and a bus trip. You, of course, stay with the subject."

"A *bus* trip? Is this some kind of stupid joke?"

"You know me, Cathcart. I don't make jokes. They tell me it's a very interesting tour. First class all the way and educational. Right in your line of things. I'm sure you'll do an even better job on this than Hendricks . . ." He added this last comment in his trailing, noncommittal voice that promised untold wonders of promotion and glory, but since everyone who had worked in his department for more than two weeks was only too familiar with it, it had no effect on the distinctly irritated agent standing respectfully in front of him.

The mountain road seemed a good choice, initially, although it proved difficult to drive and concentrate on the landscape at the same time. As Harriet climbed, more and more patches of snow sat on the dark evergreens that crowded the road from the uphill side, dark, brooding, and ominous even on a day that elsewhere was sunny and warm with spring. Then suddenly the road twisted, plunged, and leveled out into spaces that looked almost tame and domestic before making its next climb. Here and there, shiny cabins clung to the side of the mountains, like boils on a neck. On sudden impulse, Harriet pulled off the road, dragged out all her equipment, and began to set up a shot.

An hour and a half later she packed up her equipment, almost satisfied with what she had done, and settled it neatly back in the van. Just as she was about to pull onto the road, an elephantine RV lumbered past her and headed doggedly for the hills. At twenty miles an hour. A military convoy would have been easier to get around. A herd of moose would have been more responsive to the common good. Harriet honked, swore, dropped back, and resigned herself to a scenic drive.

When the procession neared Taos, the RV lurched away to attend to its own little concerns, leaving the road to Harriet and the fifty cars that had collected behind her. As she pulled onto Route 68, she glanced at her watch and was overwhelmed by a panicky sense of haste. It was almost four. She had little more than an hour to drive seventy miles and find the airport in Santa Fe. She hadn't left Raton until noon, determined not to spend hours pacing up and down in the airport, imagining all sorts of disasters occurring on John's flight. She had planned on a late, unhurried lunch in Taos and a peaceful drive to Santa Fe. Now she was haunted by visions of construction, accidents, and freak storms stopping her for hours. John arriving, exhausted and miserable, and no one there to meet him. There was no time to stop for lunch. What if she couldn't find the airport? "For God's sake, Harriet," she muttered to herself, "there'll be signs to the airport. And if you can't find any, you can ask at a gas station." Forty-eight hours with Kate Grosvenor and she was turning into a helpless neurotic. She stopped at a grocery store, bought sandwiches, cheese, crackers, fruit, drinks, and some ice, thought a moment and added beer in case John got off the plane hot and thirsty. She removed the film holders from the cooler, dumped in the bag of ice, and put the cheese and drinks on top. She set off on the road south again, puzzled and beset by a nagging sense that all was not right.

As soon as she approached the city, the same wave of uncertainty washed over her again. Why hadn't she checked the map and found out where the airport was? Because she was going to do that over lunch, only she hadn't stopped for lunch, and— "What is wrong with you, Harriet?" she muttered to the trip odometer. It was approaching the eighty-mile mark. Suddenly a vast sign with a tastefully executed airplane on it pointed her toward the next exit. She darted across three lanes of traffic, slowed, and pulled off, into the middle of ill-tempered, ill-regulated late Friday afternoon traffic. She looked at her watch. It was six-ten. An endless succession of car dealerships and shopping malls later and she was on top of another tasteful sign—so discreet she almost missed it—pointing her to the next left. She forced her way into a line of cars headed left.

She drove on and on and on, through piles of red earth, construction sites, desolation, and demolition. All the horror of the urban sprawl. Not a whiff of an airport. But as she searched the horizon, she actually saw a tiny plane circling in the sky. Evidence. There was an airport. Over the next slight rise she caught another glimpse of the plane as it began its orderly plunge toward earth. One more sign, one more left turn, and she had made it, just as the little plane touched ground and began to taxi gently toward a low building ahead of her. It was, as airports go, slightly grander than the two-hangars-and-a-shack variety, but no O'Hare. And that meant she shouldn't have any trouble finding John. She glanced at her watch again, her heart sinking. She was an hour late.

She pulled up behind a small but very elegant bus, dark

blue in color, that was identified by the logo discreetly displayed on the door as from Archway Tours. Surely John hadn't come on a charter—of course not. She glanced at her watch; he should be standing outside, furious with impatience. She peered into the waiting room; no John. Then his plane was late, too. Very late. She grabbed a small camera and jumped out of the van. Whenever trivial events in her life threatened to turn into overblown, crisis-ridden nightmares, she had always found that examining them through a viewfinder had a wonderfully steadying effect on the nerves.

While she was working her way around the building, people were crowding into it from the landing field. She concentrated on a young woman standing in the doorway, wearing a navy blue skirt and white blouse that shrieked "tour guide" in every stitch. Rapidly switching to a wide-angle lens, Harriet caught her in a continuum that started with the bleak doorway, followed the low sweep of the building, and ended with the tail of the small plane, looking very much as if it were growing out of the terminal. She grinned cheerfully, temper restored. The guide gave her an annoyed look of the you're-the-last-thing-I-needed-today variety and began to speak. "If you could all just identify your luggage, please, then we'll have it put on the bus. Unless you prefer to carry it yourself. There is room inside the bus for hand luggage. Larger pieces go in the hold."

A uniformed man was hurrying about the room, snatching up bags and putting them on a trolley, muttering, "Archway Tours, miss? Sir?" and adding to the frantic, uneasy air of the whole operation.

It occurred to her that there must be someone in that building who might know how late John's plane was likely to be. Harriet kept well back until the man with the bag-

gage came sweeping through with his load; the group
began to straggle along after him. Impatiently, she moved
forward toward the waiting room. "Excuse me," she said
firmly as she tried to push her way past a large, brown-
haired man with sulky eyes who had the air of an athlete
beginning to run to fat and booze. "I'm trying to get in, if
you don't mind."

"You the person who's taking pictures of everyone?" he
said. "What goddamn business is it of yours who's on this
tour?"

"I'm not," said Harriet crisply. "I'm taking pictures of
the planes and the buildings. I could not be less interested
in the people getting on that bus if I tried."

"For God's sake, Brett, watch where you're going." The
sharp, annoyed voice seemed to come from nowhere. "Let
the woman get inside."

Brett muttered something that might even have been an
apology and stepped aside. The disembodied voice had
come from a woman who had been hidden by his bulk,
brown-haired, freckled, and thin, with sharp blue eyes and
a basic expression like a lost and hungry kitten.

Beyond her, Harriet could see a child in jeans, a man in
uniform, and a tall, thin man wearing a beige raincoat and
a tired, uncertain expression. John. Her heart lurched; she
forgot her annoyance and the frustrations of the day.
Harriet raced over and flung herself at him. "My God, but
it's good to see you again," she said finally, loosening her
grip. "But why were you on that plane? It looks like a charter for a tour."

"That's the choice. Charter or buy your own plane.
Most scheduled flights land in Albuquerque. You didn't
know that, did you? But your word is my command. You
said you'd meet me at Santa Fe, and Santa Fe it was. Never

mind, it was an experience and you look terrific," he murmured. "And smell—mmm. Tangerine soap, grapefruit
shampoo, with an overlay of sweat, road dust, and—I
know. Garlic. You have no idea how sexy it is."

"You're so romantic, John. And I'm sorry. It never
occurred to me you'd have trouble getting a flight into
here. I didn't even check."

A soft voice interrupted her. "Excuse me, ma'am.
Could you—"

Harriet turned and saw the skinny child in jeans. She had
long, lank, dirty blond hair and a long, very serious face,
and looked to be about eleven. Her pale blue eyes were
growing alarmingly large and moist, and her pale cheeks
were beginning to blotch slightly. "What can we do for
you?" asked Harriet quickly, crouching down slightly to
adjust to the difference in height.

"Are you with the tour?" she asked. "Because I can't find
our luggage and I can't find my brother either, and we have
to catch the bus or we won't be able to get home. My
mother is supposed to pick us up—" She paused, unable to
go on.

"No problem," said John efficiently. "I think I saw your
brother on the plane. What's his name? And just to keep it
official, how old?"

"Same age as me," she said. "Eleven. We're twins. I'm
Caroline. He's Stuart."

"That's easy. We'll have him for you in a second." And
he was gone.

"Is he—" She looked worried.

"He's a policeman," said Harriet. "You couldn't have
picked a better person to ask." She saw him emerge from
the men's room, shake his head, and start for the door that
led to the landing field. Meanwhile the area had emptied

of extraneous humanity. "Are you on this tour?" asked Harriet.

"Oh no," said Caroline. "But our parents know Mr. Andreas. He owns the tour company. Mum and Dad run a hotel near Taos and Mr. Andreas is one of their biggest customers. He's nice," she added doubtfully. "I guess. We don't know him very well. Stuart and me, I mean. Anyway, if there's room on the plane from Dallas he lets us catch a ride. And then Bert, he's the bus driver, takes us to where our road is. He drops us off at the intersection and Mum comes and picks us up. Otherwise she'd have to drive all the way to Albuquerque and back to bring us home and that isn't very convenient. It's already a long way from our place to the road."

Harriet could hear the self-justifying voice that Caroline was unconsciously imitating. If she were mother to this pleasant child, she thought, she wouldn't leave her to find her way on her own to an intersection on the highway, and there to wait to be picked up. But still—who knows what sort of difficult life the woman might lead? "Were you visiting people in Dallas?" she asked, desperately trying to keep up a conversation to hold those imminent tears back.

"Oh no," said Caroline. "We live near Dallas with Aunt Jan. It's because of school, you see. We go to school there and we come home a lot for the weekends. We've been doing it since September," she added. "It's sort of fun traveling. And Aunt Jan is nice." She looked a little doubtful, as if "fun" were too strong a word to describe the situation.

"I see," said Harriet. "Where does the bus go after it leaves your place?" she asked, looking impatiently around for John. She was running out of topics.

"To Taos. I don't know where it goes after that."

"That's where we're going tonight," said Harriet. "And I

hope it doesn't take us as long to drive up there as it took me to get down here. I'd like to arrive before dark if I can."

"Then follow us," said Caroline. "Bert knows a really fast way to get onto the road north from here. Otherwise you have to—"

"Yes, I know. The long way. That's how I came in. It sounds like a very good—"

She was interrupted by an excited burst of conversation behind her. Coming in the door from the landing field was a man in a captain's uniform, his hand resting lightly on the shoulder of a boy who could only be the twin brother of the grave Caroline. John stalked behind them carrying two suitcases.

"I found him discussing the finer points of aircraft design with the captain. He had picked up the luggage and left it just outside the door when he went to investigate."

"Stuart, the bus is going to leave without us," said Caroline, "if you don't hurry up. Thank you for finding my brother, sir," she added graciously, turned and ran, just in time to see the bus driver climb aboard, close the door, and pull away from the curb.

In the hot, dry, sand-and-rock-filled gully at the foot of a tree-covered mountain, a crow was first on the scene, investigating a heap of pallid flesh, lying face down, dressed in navy-blue socks, striped boxer shorts, and a white T-shirt. He screeched and flapped his wings. The passenger in a pickup truck traveling along the road above the gully, a young, sturdy blonde, was pointing out things of interest to distract her tired and hungry toddler. "See, sugar," she cooed, "there's a big, black crow down there, and he's— Oh, Jesus. Billy," she went on, trying to keep her voice as steady as she could. "Sweetheart, I think you'd better stop. There's something down there ought to be seen to."

He caught the tone under her cautious words and brought the truck screeching to a halt on the shoulder.

Her eyes narrowed in disgust as she got a closer look. "There's nothing down there," she cooed once more at her baby. "Look, darling, up there. It's an airplane. Look up in the sky. A great big airplane. Not down there. The nasty old crow's gone. There's nothing to see. Look up in the sky."

"Looks like someone killed him for his clothes and money," said the state trooper, staring at the partially clad corpse. He pointed at the bloody depression in the back of the head. "Knocked him out and undressed him and just dumped him off of the road. Left him to die. Look at that—you can tell where the poor bastard tried to crawl for help. Take a look around. Maybe we'll see what he used to hit him with and save everyone a lot of time."

"Pretty risky," said his partner, shaking his head. "What if he'd survived? Then he could describe the guy who hit him."

"Probably thought he was dead. It's not that easy to tell, sometimes. That's why people get buried alive," he added with relish. "Anyway, you get bashed on the head hard enough, you don't remember much. That must've been what happened to you," he snickered, poking his partner in the ribs.

"Yeah, well, thanks a hell of a lot," said the partner, looking a bit green.

"Probably stole his car, too. A hitchhiker, I'd say. We'll check on hitchhikers. That's it for now," he said loudly. "I'd like to thank you folks for stopping and contacting us.

Ginny, Billy. And say hello to your ma for me, Ginny. We know how to find you and we'll be in touch if we need to." The young couple and their baby climbed back into their pickup. The crow watched from a distance, sitting disconsolately on a bare branch.

CHAPTER 3

"Damn," said Harriet. "How could they do that? They could have waited thirty seconds for us."

But John was no longer standing beside her. He was on the other side of the room, deep in conversation with a sour-looking individual. "And thank you so very much for all *your* help," he was saying in a voice thick with sarcasm. "In that case, we might as well take the children ourselves and drop them off."

The answer was inaudible.

"Do you know your intersection when you see it?" he asked.

"I do," said a very white-faced Stuart. "And I'm sorry—"

"No time for apologies," said Sanders. "Just follow that bus."

The four of them ran as fast as they could, weighed down with one huge suitcase and two gym bags, and scrambled into the van.

The assistant airport manager watched them disappear down the road. A twinge of guilt, quickly replaced by anger, caused his forehead to tighten. He shrugged and prepared to finish up for the night.

*   *   *

Harriet slung the gym bags in the backseat, the children scrambled in after them, and by the time John had the suitcase in back and the door on the passenger side closed, they were moving down the long approach road from the airport. "Which way do we turn up here?" she asked.

"I'm not sure," said Caroline nervously, "but— There it is. It's got its left-turn light on."

"Then left it is," said Harriet.

"I hope this isn't out of your way," said Caroline. The cares of the world seemed to be piled on her thin shoulders.

"That bus goes to Taos and so do we," said Harriet. "And you said the driver knows the fastest route to Taos. So it can't be out of our way, can it?" They had reached the intersection and Harriet squeaked in between a car and a truck to make one of the world's fastest left turns. "Buckle your seat belts and prepare for warp drive, Lieutenant."

The children giggled and Harriet flew down the road after the dark blue shape ahead.

"It's not that I'm nosy," said Harriet, once the gap between them and the bus was narrow enough to keep it in sight, "but what did you put into that suitcase? Granite blocks? Light artillery? It weighs a ton."

"Only following orders," said John. "Warm clothes for the mountains, light for the desert. I brought an extra pair of jeans and a sweatshirt. The rest of the space is filled up with your heavy sweater. After all, I wouldn't want you to get cold."

"All right—one point for you. How did you know we'd need heavy sweaters?"

"Research, my beloved Harriet. Research and inquiry.

It's the foundation of all great policework. Not your line at all."

"Research? You?"

"Using my highly developed detecting skills, I called a travel agent and asked what the mean temperature was in Taos in early May. She told me to bring a sweater."

"Smartass," murmured Harriet, ducking his fake punch. He turned it into a condescending pat on the head. "It's been pure hell not having anyone around to fight with."

"What about your friend, Kate?"

"At the moment, she's too neurotic to fight. Or too drunk. You can have a very solemn and serious discussion with her—usually about Kate's world view or Kate's problems—or you can put her to bed. Those are the choices. She's at a rather self-absorptive point in her life right now. Did I tell you she'll be meeting us in Taos?" added Harriet, with enormous casualness.

"You intimated something of the sort. Delicately. Sounds interesting," he said.

"Do you mind?" Anxiety clutched at her again. "I'm sorry—I got cornered—trapped into inviting her. I can call her tonight and tell her it's impossible for us—"

"Harriet, darling—what's wrong with you? What in God's name are you apologizing for?" John shifted around in his seat and studied her taut shoulders and unhappy expression. "When did you ever worry about dumping me into the middle of your neurotic—or unneurotic—friends? I'm a grown-up, Harriet. Don't worry about me."

"I don't know what's wrong with me." She pushed the hair off her face with nervous fingers. "All day I've been suffering from a sense of impending doom. Every time I approached a curve on my way down here, I had a vision of a huge truck thundering along the road the wrong way, in my lane, coming straight at my front bumper. There are a lot of curves in that road, too." She tried to laugh, unsuccessfully. "It kept me busy. And in between, I'd imagine that your plane had crashed into a mountain, or that I'd get to the airport so late that you'd given up and caught the first flight home."

"You were wrong. I don't fly on planes that crash, and I would have waited all night if I had to. I wouldn't have been very happy about it, but I would have waited." John gave her a reassuring squeeze of the shoulders. "Anyway, I'm relieved. I thought you'd turned into one of those creatures who hover, wringing her hands and worrying about what I think. And then apologizing for everything that goes wrong. I don't think I could stand that."

"Clown." This time the laugh was real, and the anxiety faded off into the distance. "Anyway, Kate will probably behave herself around you. She is, after all, an intelligent and rational woman. She doesn't normally wander around like the ancient mariner, grabbing total strangers and pouring her life story into their unwilling ears. She's simply been using me as an echo chamber," said Harriet firmly. "A therapeutic device."

"You don't sound very convinced. But it doesn't matter. Kate and I probably have more in common than you realize. We'll sit around boozing, exchanging horror stories, and showing each other our scars. By the way, is that blue thing that's making the left turn ahead the bus we're following?"

Karen Johnson, the guide for the Archway Tours "Mysticism and Magic in Old New Mexico" special package, watched her clientele handing over their heavier pieces of luggage and heading toward their places. She exuded something less than the cheerful enthusiasm people on such an expensive holiday ought to be able to expect from the help. At the moment, she was staring with a perplexed frown at a note paper-clipped to the annotated passenger list. "Karen," it said, "the kids are nonpaying passengers. Be nice, but don't waste too much time on them. They won't expect it."

What kids? She had eight passengers on her list. There were eight passengers and two male employees of the tour company on the ground outside. Inside the airport, as far as she could see, a family was gathering itself together—a man, his wife, and one child. In fact, the man seemed to have been on the flight with the rest of her passengers, but was definitely not part of her group. Maybe the note was supposed to go on someone else's passenger list.

Karen, twenty-three, nervous, and absolutely new at the job, felt she was guiding this tour under false pretenses. It was true that she was an embryonic archaeologist, and that was what Archway had advertised for at the student job center. Unfortunately, her field was underwater archaeology—not usually much in demand in the mountains—and she had left the rocky shores of Maine, many thousands of miles to the east, less than eight months ago. So far in her life, she had been on two wonderful diving expeditions off a tiny Greek island, but except for flying to Texas to begin graduate school, her out-of-state explorations in her native country had consisted of a few trips to Boston and one holiday in North Conway, New Hampshire. The result was someone who felt quite confident on the subject of Mediterranean classical pottery, but was ashamed at how poor her grasp was of the history, geography, or mystical sites of New Mexico. To her astonishment, however, the management of Archway Tours, Inc., seemed to feel that an underwater archaeology student was an archaeology student. Not only were all archaeologists interchangeable, but they were equally useful, except perhaps for minor differences in appearance and temperament.

Karen was being paid five hundred dollars and her room and board to shepherd these eight passengers for the next ten days. Her job was to make sure that nothing—absolutely nothing—troubled their existences while she was in charge. And since she had just been thrown out of her miserable room over a matter of unpaid rent, and was facing a moneyless stretch until next September when her student grant came in, ten days' room and board and five hundred bucks were not to be sneezed at. But she did have a distinct feeling that she didn't know what she was supposed to be doing. And that nothing was happening the way she expected it to.

First of all, the person heaving suitcases into the hold as though they were so many shovelfuls of dirt was not the driver of the bus. That shouldn't have surprised her, she realized, since he was behaving more like a longshoreman than a bus driver. After telling him sharply—and to no effect—to treat the luggage with more care, she had climbed aboard to arrange the seating and discovered the actual driver, uniformed and in control, sitting behind the wheel. He had described the suitcase handler as the relief driver—of whose existence no one had warned her—and had pointed out rather menacingly that the jacket, gym bags, and tool kit tossed on the first pair of seats on the right-hand side belonged to them. Karen opened her mouth to object to this cavalier takeover of the best seats on the bus, looked at the surly face she was going to have to deal with for almost two weeks, and retreated in defeat.

And the next passenger to board, a gray-haired woman with sharply observant eyes and a vague smile, declared that she intended to sit next to Karen in order to have someone interesting to talk to. "Rose Green," she said, pointing to her name on Karen's clipboard. "Silly name—but just imagine, I knew a Joe Garden when I was in school, and if I'd married him instead of Wilf Green—but never mind about that. I'm used to it now. I'm on this trip because my sister, Ruth, died and left me all the money her husband left her. Isn't that strange? Carter was such an unpleasant man, too. What he wouldn't say if he knew his money was paying for my holiday. My daughters—I have two daughters, Joy and Wendy—they said I had to do something fun with the money, but my son and his wife wanted to invest it all for me. . . . He's a stockbroker, you see. But why should I invest it? I'm seventy-nine years old and everyone in my family dies from heart trouble before they're eighty-five. Look at my sister, Ruth. Energetic as a six-year-old until the day she died and went just like that. Eighty-four. Anyway, they were so shocked when I told them that I went and booked this trip. I told the travel agent I wanted a comfortable, interesting tour, and I didn't want to be half-dead from jet lag or run off my feet all the time, and he said this was the one. It was booked solid past June when I called last month and then they said they were putting on an extra tour in May, not advertised, to cope with the demand. They said they never take more than eight people and I liked the sound of that. I'm not sure it sounds like fun, exactly, but it'll be more interesting than shopping." As she spoke, Mrs. Rose Green was stowing her possessions above her head, under the seat, and in a net thoughtfully attached to the partition between passengers and driver.

"Happy to have you with us, Mrs. Green," said Karen weakly.

A knot of four people were waiting to get by Karen, and as soon as she turned, the largest of the men pushed the rest out of the way and spread himself triumphantly across the double seat behind the relief bus driver. He threw his name at Karen as if it were a small dog biscuit, designed to keep her quiet for the moment. She checked him off and decided that she was not going to like Mr. Kevin Donovan.

The rest of the passengers filed on more or less peacefully. A tall, elegant blonde slipped into the double seat across the aisle from Mr. Donovan and gave her name as Teresa Suarez. She didn't look like a Teresa Suarez, thought Karen, but this was a day for the destruction of preconceived ideas. She looked more like a Diana Morris, who was also on the list. Then two couples, Brett and Jennifer Nicholls, and Richard and Suellen Kelleher, meekly filled in the next two seats. Finally, a small, dark-haired woman in her twenties, with intelligent dark eyes and a warm complexion, introduced herself as Diana Morris, and slipped into the last double seat on the left-hand side.

"Good evening, ladies and gentlemen," Karen Johnson began. "Welcome to 'Mysticism and Magic in Old New Mexico.' Archway Tours hopes that you have a very pleasant ten-day journey into a world that will stretch the boundaries for you. My name is Karen, and my job is to make sure that your visit to New Mexico is as pleasant as it can be." A snigger from Mr. Donovan made her blush self-consciously. "Our first stop will be Taos. Since we'll be there in less than two hours, we'll be having dinner at our hotel, but in the meantime, your bus is equipped with a small galley, and as soon as we are under way, I will be serving drinks, coffee, tea, and snacks. The rest room is at the very back of the bus," she added, on an anticlimactic note. "Behind the galley. Does anyone have any questions?" she asked, praying as fervently as she ever had in her life that the response would be negative. She had been lifted from a waiting list for the job only yesterday, the regular guide having failed to appear, been flown up to Santa Fe this morning on the company plane, and her training had been nominal, at best. Most of the background material on the tour had been handed to her an hour ago, and she had been planning on using this evening's light schedule to digest it all.

"I do," said Donovan, with a leer. "Just how pleasant can we expect you to make the trip? And is it extra, or does it come with the godalmighty high price we've paid already?" He laughed and looked around him for the applause that he felt his wit deserved.

Karen's frosty look—much practiced—was one of her most effective skills; she was pleased to note that it seemed to dampen him slightly. Without a doubt, Mr. Donovan was a jerk. And drunk. She would make sure that damned little of the company's free booze went in his direction.

The hatch to the hold was slammed shut, and the surly-looking relief driver climbed into the bus. He moved his tool kit over and sat down next to the aisle. Surely the company didn't send an emergency mechanic on every trip, thought Karen. Surely not. Or did you need a mechanic on a trip into a world that stretches the boundaries? And exactly what boundaries were going to be stretched? And how, not to say why? If the rest of the patter she had to memorize made as little sense as this, she was going to rewrite it. Maybe this job wasn't going to be worth five hundred bucks and all you could eat.

"Jesus, Gary," said the relief driver. "Let's git the hell outta here."

With a clash of the gears, Gary threw the idling bus out of neutral. It lurched forward at an astonishing rate of speed, barely negotiating the turn at the airport gate, and tore in the direction of the setting sun like a charging rhinoceros.

"Isn't Taos somewhere north of Santa Fe?" asked John.

"Mmm," said Harriet. "Definitely north, and somewhat to the east, I think."

"Then why do you suppose we've gone from driving straight into the sunset to heading south?"

"To avoid all the crowded suburban roads running between the interstate and the airport? I really don't know," said Harriet irritably. Doubt was creeping into her voice as she spoke. "You know—longer but faster. There. Look—the bus is turning right up ahead. We'll probably connect with the road to Taos any minute now. Why don't you check the map and see if you can figure out where we are."

"I always get the impossible jobs. Why can't I chase the bus, and you try to work out where we are?"

"Because it would be tricky to change drivers in mid-stream, so to speak. And if we stop, we'll lose them. They're moving at a hell of a clip. I trust they know more about the location of radar traps and all that than we do. How are the kids doing? By the way—there's food in the cooler right behind you. I'm famished. Did you eat on the plane?"

"Are you kidding? I value my life and health more than that," said Sanders. "How about you two?" he asked in a muffled voice as he searched through the cooler sitting between them on the seat. "Anyone feel like a sandwich? By some stroke of luck, we seem to have four sandwiches here—they all appear to be ham and cheese on dark bread with lettuce and pickles and stuff. In addition, there's cheese, piles of fruit, and things to drink. Coke?" he asked, passing out the wrapped sandwiches. "Here. And in the paper bag at your feet is the world's most enormous bag of cheezy things. Really, Harriet. I begin to doubt your taste and refinement. Also four boxes of crackers."

"I was hungry," she said. "So I bought lots. Is it still cold?"

"Very," said John. "An extremely efficient cooler you have. Have a sandwich." He unwrapped one and gave half to her.

"Gorgeous. Hang on a minute, though, they're speeding up again, and the road is getting worse. I hope you kids don't get carsick."

A muffled chorus from behind declared their immunity from such childish ailments.

And indeed, the van, admirable though it was for transporting large amounts of photographic equipment, was not designed for high-speed chases over bad roads, and at the moment it was rocking and bouncing like a small boat on a choppy sea. Suddenly, in a terrific crash of sound, the bus made a rapid right turn and disappeared from sight.

There was a worried exclamation from behind.

"I'm sorry," said John, turning toward the backseat to hear better. "I didn't quite catch what you were saying."

"We said that he's turned the wrong way." Caroline was

speaking softly, as if she were afraid to voice her concerns out loud. "Our regular driver never goes this way."

"And he isn't the regular driver?" asked John.

"No. The regular driver's Bert, and Lesley's the regular guide on this kind of tour. Lesley does historic sites and Susie does desert flora and fauna. That's plants and animals," added Caroline politely, in case their traveling companions didn't have a scientific bent. "Someone at Dallas said that Lesley was sick today, but Bert never gets sick. He always drives. He's nice. We really like Bert."

Her brother nodded.

"I hope he isn't lost," said Caroline. Her voice was carefully neutral. "I hope he drives past our road."

"Don't be stupid, Car—of course he'll go past our road. He's just been heading around the city a different way." Underneath his bravura tone Harriet heard the panic of a small child lost and far from home.

"Okay—what if we don't drive past your road?" interrupted Harriet. "Let's consider the possibilities. What do we know? Two things. The bus driver is new, and the bus is leaving the city—or has left the city—via a route unfamiliar to you. In these situations one begins, always, with the worst-case scenario. The new driver is just taking what he thinks is the best and most rapid route to Taos. Let's say it doesn't intersect with your road. When we get to Taos, we call your parents, who will be very pleased to know you're okay. Then we whisk you down to the hotel."

"Do you work for the CIA?" asked Stuart. "You sound a little like a CIA operative."

"Stuart asks everyone that," said Caroline. "Our dad says he has a friend who works for the NSA, but he won't tell us who it is, in case we drive him crazy."

"Or her. We love spy stories," added Caroline.

Harriet shook her head. "I'm a photographer. Not nearly as exciting, is it?"

"A news photographer?"

"No. I only photograph buildings. But I have a good friend who's a news photographer. She's had pictures on the covers of *Time* and *Newsweek*," she added. "Do you read magazines?"

"Of course we do," said Stuart. "Hey—what's the bus doing now?" he asked.

"I think it's probably turned north," said Harriet. "Toward Taos. Not a very good road."

Karen Johnson was in a quandary. Her instructions were to start serving drinks and snack trays—cheese, crackers, nuts, veggies, and two very small sandwich quarters—as soon as the driver was well on his way. She had somehow imagined that they would be gliding smoothly along a broad, well-tended road surface, instead of bucketing down a series of desperately bad secondary roads. Perhaps she should start with the food. It, at least, couldn't spill. She extracted herself from the history of Rose Green's late husband's unhappy business ventures, to which she had been devoting perhaps a tenth of her attention, and headed unsteadily along the aisle to the galley. Coffee and tea were imprisoned in urns; there was a tiny sink and a burner, although she couldn't imagine trying to cook anything under these conditions. She unlatched the door above the sink and discovered a refrigerated compartment with trays neatly stacked on wire shelving, close together. She counted them. Twelve. Eight passengers, two drivers, one guide. Eleven people on the bus. A wave of relief passed over her. If they had been expecting more passengers, they would have loaded more trays. She wedged herself into the corner, grabbed a tray, unwrapped it, and gave it to Diana Morris. "It's a bit bumpy for drinks," said Karen. "But there are things in cans that probably won't spill."

"I think I'll risk a soda," said Diana. "Anything cold and wet."

The Nichollses declined both food and drink, and Karen's spirits lifted. She was starving. Food had been in short supply in her life lately and she felt faint from hunger. She took the few steps back to the galley, put down the two trays she was carrying, ripped the plastic film off one, scooped up the two little sandwiches, and consumed them with the rapidity of a starving dog. They were astonishingly good. Smoked salmon on whole wheat bread, and some kind of exceptionally tasty pâté on thin rye. She was impressed. Perhaps this tour really was worth its exorbitant price. She grabbed a carrot, looked hungrily at the sandwiches on the second tray sitting in front of her, then, with heroic resolution, picked it up intact, added another tray for the other hand out of the refrigerated compartment, and headed back down the aisle.

The Kellehers turned out to have notions about food. Suellen loathed fish of any kind, she explained to Karen, although she might eat the pâté if it weren't too rich or too spicy. Karen suggested leaving the smoked salmon; Rick thought he might be able to eat it, although he didn't particularly like the idea of hors d'oeuvres an hour or so before dinner. Suellen offered to share a tray instead of taking two; Rick pointed out that they had paid for two trays and might as well get them. Suellen countered with a proposal to take one now, and another a little later, if they were still hungry. Never had so much brainpower, thought Karen, been expended on such a useless topic. After all, in an hour or two, everyone was going to be sitting down to a huge meal. Prepaid. Taking matters into her own hands, she set a tray in front of each Kelleher, very firmly.

The relief driver had been crouched over his tool kit, fiddling with something, with his back to the aisle. But the interminable discussion over the Kellehers' snack trays had finally aroused his curiosity, and when Karen looked up, he was peering down the aisle to see what was going on. It was evident that something other than the snack tray imbroglio had captured his complete attention. He seemed to be staring past her, through the back window; then with a muttered word that Karen didn't quite catch, he heaved himself out of his seat, grabbed onto the two uprights that marked the beginning of the aisle, crouched down, and said something directly into his co-worker's ear.

The sudden increase in speed startled them all. The Kellehers lost their dual snack trays on the first bump. Diana Morris's cola can bounced onto the floor and rolled, dribbling dark liquid as it moved. "What in hell is going on?" said Kevin Donovan in a surprisingly clear and sober voice. He slid over to the aisle and tried to get a look at the road ahead, but he was hindered by the bulk of the relief driver and the fast-gathering dark. "What do you bastards think you're doing?"

"Deal with him, Wayne," said the driver.

"Shut up." There was an edge of panic in the relief driver's voice. "And sit down." He swung himself around, achieving stability in the crazy lurching environment by looping an arm around the pole and wedging his feet against the steel dividers. With a wary eye on Donovan, he bent over to recover something from his seat; when he straightened up again, he was holding a huge and cumbersome weapon.

The only noise to be heard was the bus bouncing over gravel—the only movement that of the passengers swaying in spite of themselves from the mad careening of the bus. Donovan was half in the aisle, hanging onto the back of the relief driver's seat, staring down at his weapon; Suellen Kelleher had shrunk into her corner, with her husband protectively in place between her and the gunman. Teresa Suarez watched it all without expression. Someone behind her gasped.

Then everything happened at once. Donovan yelled, "Put that thing away, you fucking idiot." The bus lurched violently to the right. Arms grabbed Karen from behind and toppled her to the floor. There was a burst of gunfire, agonizingly loud in that confined space. Hot air exploded beside her head and she heard a startled "oof" from behind. By now she was flat on her face on the carpeting that ran between the seats of the Archway Tour bus, bouncing painfully on the hard surface.

Dizzy and confused, she lifted her head, knowing only that she had to be on her feet. She was in charge. That was her job. But the scene in front of her made no sense. Kevin Donovan was kneeling with his feet sticking out into the aisle, his torso flat down on his seat, very still. Ahead of him, the relief driver waved his weapon back and forth, in harmony with the swaying of the bus. Donovan raised his head, looked back at the relief driver, and began very slowly to resume his sitting position. How could either one of them have thrown her to the floor with so much violence? And as far as she could tell, she hadn't been hit by a burst of gunfire. Then the sound of distressed breathing reached her and she turned her head to look.

Diana Morris was crawling on her hands and knees toward the back of the bus. The pool of blood she'd left

behind her was soaking into the carpeting. More dripped
from her as she struggled. Karen scrambled along the aisle
in a hunched position, picking up bruises as she was flung
against the metal sides of the seats, until she was beside the
wounded woman. "Where are you hurt?" Diana Morris
fell over on her side, her hand pointing down at a huge,
bleeding wound in her thigh.

"You could have killed us all, waving that gun around,"
said an incisive voice. It was Mrs. Green. An invigorated
Mrs. Green. "You've certainly hurt that young woman. We
can't leave her like that. Here—just a moment." She
reached into a capacious bag that was slung in the net in
front of her and produced a plastic case with a red cross
emblazoned on it. Then, rummaging farther, she pulled out
a plastic bag containing a number of pastel scarves. "I'll just
make her a bandage—"

"No. I'll take care of her." This was a new voice, controlled and calm. "Get out of my way, Brett, will you?"

"The hell you will." His voice was strained. "Stay where
you are."

"Brett—don't be a fool. Let me out. Unless there's someone else in the bus who knows what he's doing?" Silence.
"Right. I'm a nurse and I've seen my share of gunshot
wounds. Now let me out."

Jennifer Nicholls's husband seemed to have turned to
stone. She sighed and crawled past him into the aisle.
"Excuse me," she said to Mrs. Green, "but if that's a first-
aid kit—"

"There's one in the galley, too," said Karen.

"Good. I can use both."

"What in hell do you think you're doing?" The man with
the weapon seemed to gather his wits together again at last.

"I'm keeping this woman from dying. If I were you, I

wouldn't try to stop me, not unless you'd like to face a charge of first-degree murder."

"Huh?"

"As it stands, you fired that gun because the bus lurched. But if you stop me from helping her, and she dies, you'll have murdered her."

"Is that true? Can he get away with calling it an accident?" whispered Karen as she knelt down beside Diana Morris with the second medical kit.

"Shit, baby—I don't know," whispered Jennifer in return. "And with any luck, neither does he. Open that thing up, will you?"

The bus felt as if it were gaining momentum in spite of the fact that it still seemed to be climbing. Karen's fingers were struggling unsuccessfully with the clever device that kept the kit safe from small children, when an alarmed voice boomed over the noise of the engine and of wheels racing over rocks and gravel. "Shit, Gary, look out!"

The driver hit the brakes, the bus skidded on the loose surface and came to an abrupt halt, nose in to a very steep slope.

"What is going on?" said Harriet. "The bus has disappeared. Just like that."

"Don't be silly. It can't have disappeared. It's turned off somewhere up there."

"Into what? In case it had escaped your notice, on your right we have what you might call an upward precipice. A cliff. The steep side of a mountain. It would be a clever bus that drove up that thing."

"Then there must be a break in it, with a road. Slow down, Harriet. We'll miss it."

"I can't see why we want to find it. If one thing is clear, it's that the lousy bus is more lost than we are. I don't believe in a rapid short cut that goes straight up a mountain. Jesus! There it is." Harriet brought the van screeching to a halt and then began to reverse.

"I thought we didn't want to find it," said John. "I call your attitude a trifle inconsistent."

"We might as well try it for a mile or so," said Harriet. "If a bus can make it, then this thing can, too."

It turned out to be a narrow canyon with a very rough track running along it, its entrance half-hidden by brush. "Not the best-marked road, but what the hell," she said, putting the van into forward and heading into the blackness ahead.

CHAPTER 4

Kate Grosvenor pulled into the gravel drive of the motel with a deep sigh. What aberration of mind or spirit had forced her into her car and made her drive all the way down here? Just to spend a couple of days with a chance professional acquaintance and her fascist cop boyfriend? Because no matter what Harriet might think, all cops were fascists under their skins, even the ones who went around giving talks on community involvement and minority rights and all that sort of shit. Besides, she hurt. Everywhere. Last night's Scotch—its grip unsoftened by a kindly lunchtime haze—was still exploding in her temples. Her shoulder throbbed, her arms were trembling, her neck and back were stiff and sore from the unaccustomed driving. Her body had turned into an alien entity, screaming for anesthetizing drink and pills. At least she hadn't been stupid enough to dope herself while she was driving; but after all this time she was unable to deny the desperation in her need.

The motel was very Taos. Adobe, with units scattered around a grassy courtyard, sheltering under broad cotton-woods backed by towering pines. She stepped out of the car and shivered in the chill wind. Inside the dark little office, she rang the bell on the counter with an impatient slap of her hand and called out: "Grosvenor. Kate Grosvenor. Two rooms."

"Hi, Ms. Grosvenor." The proprietor appeared around the curtain that shielded his living quarters from the public. "Rooms twelve and fourteen." He pushed the inevitable little chunk of cardboard at her.

She began to fill out the bare details of her existence—how many thousand times had she done that—and stopped, as always, to check her license plate number. "My friends arrive yet?" she asked.

"Not yet, Ms. Grosvenor. You want me to call when they come in?"

"Sure. Thanks." Her mouth stretched in a smile she didn't feel and she picked up the key.

The room was rustic, heavy with rough wood furniture. It was also damp and chilly, but supplied with both a heater and fireplace and abundant quantities of wood. It wasn't "great country inns of the world" elegantly rustic, merely comfortable and solid. Under normal conditions—whatever they were—it was the sort of place she liked, one that numbed her pain, lulling her with memories of a childhood in the mountains.

She dumped her suitcase on the bed, turned on the heater to take the damp out of the air, and collapsed in the big, soft chair in front of the empty hearth. Where in hell were Harriet and her fascist friend? She had expected them to be here, expected them to drag her resentfully out of her lassitude and misery, to force her out to a restaurant to eat, and, in short, to make her decisions for her. She had been fully prepared to be irritated and angry and uncooperative. Not to be alone. It was almost nine o'clock and they hadn't dragged their asses up from Santa Fe yet. She'd give them thirty more minutes to get here, and then forget about them. She stared into the dark fireplace, exhaustion and despair keeping her immobile, preventing her from taking the bottle of Scotch from her suitcase, the painkillers from her bag. It hadn't been clever of her to make the drive in one day, just because she always used to and only a wimp—even injured—would do it in two. In spite of the throbbing in her head, and the throbbing in her shoulder, Kate dozed off, soothed by the smell of pine and the cool air and the strange quiet.

"Thank God we've stopped," said Jennifer Nicholls briskly. "Makes it a bit easier. Open up the other first-aid kit, would you? I need more gauze. As much as you can get me." As she spoke, she kept on working at a rate that astonished Karen. Using the cheap, tiny scissors from Mrs. Green's kit, she had already cut and ripped away the material from the area of the wound, mopped up the blood, and swabbed the surrounding skin with disinfecting pads while Karen struggled to open the first-aid kit supplied by the tour company. "Quick," said the nurse. "Those things on the right-hand side are what I need. Come on, she's bled enough already."

Karen fumbled through the supplies, trying to figure out which things she wanted; Jennifer ripped out several pads and pressed them into the wound. "Give me your hand," she said, grabbing it and cleaning her fingertips off with a disinfecting pad. "There—now press down gently right here while I see what else we've got." There was a gasp from the woman on the floor as Karen's fingers settled on the mass of gauze pads. "Gently," Jennifer repeated. "You're only keeping those things in place. Not wrestling her to the floor." The nurse sat back on her heels and looked at the wounded woman. "We'll have to roll her on her side," she said at last. "That's an exit wound we're dealing with."

"It's bleeding," said Karen, as she watched the gauze darken and felt the blood ooze up between her fingers.

"I know. Just a minute." She settled more pads under Karen's fingers and looked over at Mrs. Green. "I need those scarves," she said, grabbing them and tying them over the collection of gauze on Diana Morris's leg. "We're going to turn you on your side," said Jennifer briskly. "It'll probably hurt like hell, but there's nothing for it."

Ms. Morris's olive skin had turned to gray, but she nodded and allowed herself to be turned.

"Two rounds," said Jennifer Nicholls. "One is still in there, one we dealt with." Karen glanced down and turned her eyes rapidly away. She could see nothing but blood and Jennifer's rapidly moving hands. She had been swabbing quickly as she spoke and setting pads on the cleaned area, taping them down with the inadequate materials in the kit. "Give me the rest of those scarves," she said, and began to wrap the leg firmly. "You'll do for a while, sweetheart," she said to the woman on the floor. "And, by God, do you have guts."

Up at the front of the bus, the two drivers were whispering vehemently together. While Jennifer was still speaking, the lights flickered and went out.

The bus had turned onto a track, rocky and very narrow, that climbed steeply up the side of the mountain. Darkness had rolled in around them, unalleviated by the glow of cities or the pale emanations from clouds. Their headlights stabbed the night like a flashlight probing into black water. There was no moon. Harriet abandoned her usual driving style to crawl along the ruts ahead, feeling her way through the darkness.

"This is brutal," she said. "All we need to improve the situation is a bit of fog."

"Doesn't seem to be the place for fog, somehow," said John mildly. "May I ask why we are doing this? I'm not trying to criticize . . ."

"At the moment," said Harriet, in a waspish tone, but keeping her voice down. There was no point in alarming the twins needlessly. "At the moment, as I said, we're doing this because we're not sure that we would survive an attempt to turn around. Originally, we were acting on girlish impulse and curiosity. And stupidity, if you insist. Any more questions? As soon as I find a place where it is possible to reverse direction without hurtling down a hillside, I shall. Believe me. Because I doubt very much if the bus has really found a wonderful short cut to Taos. I can't imagine what they're doing on this road."

"They're lost?"

"Possibly," said Harriet and dropped her voice again. "Either that or trying to avoid us." The track shifted direction again and Harriet followed; brush scraped against the paintwork; the right wheel dropped into a hole. "Well—we've found the bus," she said brightly, and brought the van to a halt. Their headlights lit up a symmetrical pattern ahead: bus angling off to the right; road curving away to the left, with the rear end of the bus blocking their way completely. Harriet sighed and switched off headlights and ignition. "Now what?" she said. "This could be awkward. Definitely awkward."

The bus appeared to be in worse trouble than they were. Its left headlight lit up a steep slope only inches away; its right headlight seemed to be buried in something. "Stupid bastard plowed right into the side of the mountain," muttered John. "Did you bring a flashlight with you? For some reason, I neglected to pack my full kit, not realizing that we were going to be roughing it in the bush, New Mexico style."

"Don't be snotty," said Harriet. "Of course I have a flashlight. Two flashlights, actually. You want the big one?" As she began to open the door, John leaned over and closed it again.

"I wouldn't climb out on your side without checking the terrain," he said. "Let me get the flashlight. Where is it?"

"In the red knapsack, on top," said Harriet. She peered out through the open window into the darkness to her left.

At that point the lights that had been gleaming softly inside the bus went out. And the remaining headlight. A huge pillow of smothering darkness descended on the scene.

Harriet stared out the side window, trying to adjust her vision to the dark. It became more and more obvious that there was no warm reddish earth beside her, with its contrasting humps of brush and weed. The van had stopped perilously close to the edge, beyond which there lay only the impenetrable blackness of nothing. She undid her seat belt and moved carefully over to the other door.

"Are you awake back there?" she asked.

"Yes," said a tentative voice. "Are we lost?"

"More like slightly off course," said Harriet cheerfully. "Nothing serious. I have a pile of maps in here and all that. But the bus seems to have gotten stuck up there. Why don't you curl up and go to sleep? I'll move that cooler out of your way. We're going up to see if we can help at all."

There was a heavy, frantic pause. "We'd rather come with you," said Stuart. "It's not that we're scared to stay alone or anything, but we'd rather come with you."

"Sure," said Harriet. "Come along. Get out this side of the van. The other side leads to a steepish hill. John? Where did you get to?" she asked.

A light flashed on and off, close to the front fender of the van. "Over here," said John. His voice was loud in the silence.

"We're coming with you," said Harriet. "Why aren't you using the flashlight?"

"Batteries are low. Anyway, wouldn't it be better if you . . ." He stopped. The memory of a hundred quarrels on the subject of his overprotective nature sprang unbidden into his brain and he shook his head. It didn't look as if the bus was badly damaged, but if there had been injuries, Harriet's skilled hands and clear head would be very useful. And they couldn't leave the kids behind to be scared out of their wits. "Okay. Let's go."

They padded quietly along, using their feet to keep them on the track, turning on the flashlight only to check from time to time. When they reached the dark hulk of the bus, they followed it along the right-hand side, up to the front door. "I wonder where they hide the latches on these little things. I'm more used to standard-sized municipal buses," said John, running his hand along the side of the door.

Suddenly the door swung open and lights glowed on each side of the steps. They afforded just enough illumination to make it clear to John and Harriet that they were facing, not a grateful survivor of a bus crash, but a semiautomatic weapon that wavered uncertainly between them. "Back off," said a voice that sounded very local. "And git the hell outta here."

"You can't let 'em go, Wayne," said another voice in the darkness. It sounded almost bored.

"Why not, Gary?"

"Because if they're the ones who've been following us . . ."

"Oh, yeah. Inside," said Wayne. "Right now. Both of you. And turn that fucking light off. The kids, too. In you get."

The first intimation that something had gone wrong with Archway's "Mysticism and Magic" tour—their third most popular specialized tour, after "The Desert Blooms" and "Arts of the Indigenous Peoples"—should have come from the officers investigating the death of a half-naked, unidentified man, found shortly after 6 P.M. in a gully in the desert west of Santa Fe. And if Norbert Jones hadn't been on three days' leave in Phoenix to attend his son's wedding, he would have recognized the body as his friend Bert Samson, longtime regular driver for the Archway people. As it was, the slow process of identification had been set in motion, and the Albuquerque detachment of state troopers was waiting to see what it turned up.

The hysterical telephone call from the Rogers at 8 P.M. might also have set them looking for the bus earlier, if Samantha Rogers had been more coherent and precise when she reported the disappearance of her children.

The hotel had had a hellish night. The night clerk and the maître d' had been celebrating some obscure event in one of their lives, and by dinnertime they were incapable of standing upright. Joe Rogers took the desk and Samantha the dining room. Then the chef walked out of the kitchen before seven, yelling that if they thought they knew so much more about food than he did, then they could cook their own dinners. The sous-chef—a rather grand title for someone who, in this small establishment, was basically the salad maker—was in tears. Whenever she had taken over before, the menu had been carefully tailored to her lack of skills and Samantha had helped. Samantha dashed between the dining room and the chef's room, exerting her charm alternately on the annoyed and hungry guests and the furious chef. Without ever discovering who had questioned his capabilities and driven him from his post, she managed to cajole him into putting on his apron and hat, and taking up his duties. At this point she looked at her watch. It was seven-thirty.

The bus would have dropped the children off thirty minutes ago. She shrieked at her husband and tore out to her car. She reached the intersection in record time. No children were waiting. Night was closing in, thick and black, as it does on a moonless night in the country. She sat in the car, tears coursing down her cheeks, trying to imagine what they would have done when they discovered that she was not there, waiting for them. It had happened once before that she had been two or three minutes late, and when she arrived, they had already set out, panic-stricken, in the direction of the hotel. She had given them a lecture on following orders and having faith in their parents; they had been upset enough that they wouldn't do that again. Surely not. Would they have accepted a ride with someone? Her stomach tensed at the thought. Could they be hiding in the ditch, or under some brush, frightened, as an alternative to striking out on their own? She got out of the car and called their names, over and over again, hopelessly into the blackness. Why in hell hadn't she had a car phone installed in the station wagon? She needed to call the police; she needed to talk to Joe. But how could she leave here in case they were somewhere around? She drove back to the hotel.

It was Joe who suggested that they call Charlie Broca at the airport and ask if the children had arrived and caught the bus. Charlie stared at the telephone in absolute horror. "Your kids?" he asked at last.

"Yeah, Charlie, our kids. Did they come off the plane?"

"Sure," he said. "They come off the plane all right. I saw them."

"Okay. Did they get on the bus? The Archway bus?"

"Hell, Joe, what else would they do? Anyways, they sure as hell weren't there when I locked up, that's for sure." He laughed a forced, hollow laugh. "Is anything wrong?"

"Not so far," said Joe, sounding sick with worry, and Samantha called the state troopers.

She had explained that their children had caught the six o'clock bus from the airport, but they weren't waiting for her at the intersection where she expected them to be. It didn't occur to her to mention that it was an Archway Tour bus. Or, in fact, which airport she was talking about. The troopers instituted inquiries at the Albuquerque airport and headed out to the intersection to look for the twins.

The hotelkeeper in Taos whose seven previously booked rooms were not being occupied that night raised no alarm either. The reservations had been canceled long before the sun had set. He wouldn't have called in Linda to work on her night off if he had known earlier, but what the hell. Archway would pay anyway.

Kate Grosvenor woke up with a start. A noise had startled her—a car honking, an animal cry, someone speaking. She didn't know. She was only aware of her misery. Her neck, her head, her shoulder, her arm were all throbbing hideously. Somewhere within that pain, her stomach must have been growling with hunger, but its feeble cry was lost in the greater demands of the rest of her body. Her mouth was thick and sour-tasting with sleep. She forced herself out of the chair and stumbled over to her suitcase. She took out the Scotch, located her pills after much searching through her bag, shook two into her hand, poured herself a half-glass, and used it to wash down the painkillers.

With a gasp of pain as her upper body hit the quilted coverlet a little too hard, she curled up on the bed beside her luggage and plunged once more into oblivion.

It was clear who was in charge. Gary stood beside the driver's seat, apparently unarmed, looking at John and Harriet with interest. His stance and air of authority marked him as the leader. The other was on the step up to the passenger area, clutching the weapon awkwardly and nervously. It was not a good vantage point for firing on them, and for a moment—just one—John considered the possibility of flight.

Gary motioned the children onto the bus first. They mounted the steps, never taking their eyes off the man with the weapon. John grasped Harriet firmly by the arm, in case unwise thoughts of flight were running through her fast-moving brain as well, and followed the children.

Gary looked nonplussed at the sight of what looked like a perfectly ordinary family. Like someone who had ordered eggs in a restaurant and had been handed a live chicken. "Who in hell are you?" he said. "And why were you following us?"

"Were we following you?" Sanders said cautiously.

"Of course we were, darling," said Harriet, in cloying tones. "You were asleep again and didn't notice. He always falls asleep in cars, don't you, dear?" She turned to Gary and went on earnestly. "We were the other people at the airport, remember? You must have seen us. Someone said your bus was going to Taos and that's where we're going and I thought you'd know the way. We've just been following right along behind. You were so easy to spot. The children made a game of it. I did wonder when you turned onto this road, but I just assumed it was a short cut."

"Cut the crap, lady. I want to know what you're after. And give me that thing," he added, reaching for the flashlight. "See if they're carrying anything, Wayne, and then put them back there with the rest of them. And turn those goddamn lights on again."

Wayne paused in the face of so many instructions.

"Give me the rifle. Put the fucking lights on," said Gary. "Then check them for weapons and put them back with the passengers."

Wayne stumbled through the first two instructions; then with avid clumsy fingers he ran his hands over Harriet's body. Slowly and with great thoroughness. "Nothing," he said at last, disappointed.

"Then get on with it," said Gary. "And for chrissake, you're supposed to be looking for weapons, not feeling her up."

His inspection of John was cursory and much faster. "Okay—git back there and sit down."

But when John Sanders had moved up the two steps to the passenger area, his way was blocked by two women kneeling on the floor. They were bending over another woman, who appeared to be unconscious. As he moved forward, she opened her eyes and drew a deep, sobbing breath.

The slight woman with pale brown hair turned to him. "Can you give us a hand?" she asked. "We have to get her onto the backseat. Maybe this gentleman will help you," she added, pointing to Rick Kelleher, who scrambled at once to his feet. He was considerably shorter than Sanders, with a square, powerful build, black hair, and very blue eyes in a deeply tanned face. He looked strong and hard-working in the physical sense, like a rancher or a construction worker.

"Rick Kelleher," he said, with a fast grin, on and off. "How do we do this?"

Kelleher seemed a good choice, although John wondered for a minute why she hadn't picked on the man sitting right beside them, who was a good ten years younger, as tall as Sanders, and considerably heftier, but the woman looked like someone who knew what she was doing.

"What do you think you're doing up there?" said Wayne nervously. He had somehow acquired a pistol since John had last looked at him, and he was waving it about like a man unsure of what he had found.

"We're moving this woman to a more suitable position before she dies of shock," said the woman. "Any objections? Or would you rather do it yourself?" There was no response. "Right. She has a messy wound in her thigh," she went on, addressing her remarks to Sanders. "She's lost a lot of blood. I've done what I could but we want to get her back there and lying down as gently as possible. If the three of us pick her up at the same time and move back, keeping her level, we shouldn't do too much damage. The important thing is to keep her as level as we can."

"The three of us?" said John, looking down at her.

"I'm considerably stronger than I look," she said flatly, "and much more experienced at moving people who are injured than you guys are. Or does either one of you happen to be an ambulance driver?"

The question was rhetorical and Sanders accepted the rebuke.

"This lady is red hot," said Kelleher. "I've been watching her."

The move was agonizing—not just for Diana Morris, who bore it with so much stoicism that Sanders wasn't sure how conscious she was—but for the three bearers who felt every jolt and shift in position with her. After they eased her down on the backseat, Jennifer waved them away and crouched beside her patient.

There was a general shifting of seats. The twins slipped into Diana Morris's place since it was the only empty double seat. Teresa Suarez crossed the aisle and shifted Kevin Donovan over with a single glance, sitting down beside him and leaving her double seat free for Harriet and John. Everyone was behaving as if one man with a gun wasn't standing at the front, waving his weapon in the air.

"Sit down," said Wayne, his voice cracking and dying away as he spoke. His hands trembled visibly with the effort of holding his pistol steady.

"What my little brother here is trying to say," said Gary in a soft, reasonable, almost friendly voice, "is that we've had enough bullshit from the whole lot of you. Okay—we have our reasons for trying to keep the lady back there alive. At least for now. And it isn't 'cause we're afraid of the law, or 'cause we like you folks all that much. Understand?

The next person who moves or makes a noise without permission from me is dead and over that cliff. Nothing'll find you down there for at least five years. Nothing human, anyway. Everybody understand that?"

The loudest sound in the bus was the noise of the two brothers breathing.

"Now," he went on, "I want to know just who you are and what you're doing here. Don't ask why. Just believe me that it's important. At least it's important to me, and I'm the one who's armed. And you'd better be convincing." He paused to look the group over. "There's no hurry. We got all night. How about we start at the back, with you two kids?"

"Oh, but the kids are—" Harriet started.

"The hell they are," said Gary. "They were on the plane, weren't they? And that's more than you were. I'm beginning to find you more and more interesting, lady."

"I'm Stuart," said the boy, suddenly and loudly. His face was chalk-white, but he seemed to have a firm grip on his reactions. "Stuart Rogers. And this is my sister Caroline."

"Let her answer for herself. Is that your name?"

"Yes. Caroline Rogers." The girl stared at him the way birds are supposed to stare at snakes, but her voice was steady enough. "Our parents run the Hotel Sans Souci. It's between Santa Fe and Taos. When we come home we usually catch a ride with the Archway bus. There's always room because regular passengers never sit on those backseats. But this time we missed it, and these people gave us a ride. They were just trying to catch up to the bus, so we could get home."

"Is that true?"

"Yes," said Harriet. "I figured you'd pass by their intersection and they'd be able to recognize it. Then I could drop them off."

"Where were you coming from?" Gary didn't seem to be as interested in the story as in the twins.

"From Dallas. That's where we live."

"You said you were going home," said Gary.

"We are. Our parents live here," said her brother. "We live with Aunt Jan except during vacations. We go to school in Dallas. Our parents know the man who owns Archway and they let us fly home for the weekend on the Archway plane." The child sounded desperately tired and Harriet's eyes suddenly filled with tears for an instant, quickly suppressed.

"The hell you do." Gary's voice was flat and without expression. "That sounds crazy to me."

"It's not crazy," said Caroline. "We do it all the time."

"Your parents rich? Do they own the hotel?" asked Gary.

Stuart shook his head. "It's owned by the Marenda Corporation. They manage it for them."

"Shit. That's no use," said Gary, and lost interest in the twins. "Anyone know the woman back there?"

The sudden shift in topic caught them off-guard. There was silence.

"Who is she?"

Karen Johnson intervened nervously. "Her name is Diana Morris and she's from Virginia. That's all we know about her."

"She's a librarian," said Caroline Rogers suddenly. "We were talking to her at the airport and on the plane, and she told us she was a librarian. She said it wasn't a very exciting job but she really liked it. We were talking about books."

"A librarian? I thought this was some sort of posh tour," said Gary.

Teresa Suarez turned slightly in the direction of the gunman. "She told me on the plane that she was in lousy shape after a nasty divorce, and had heard that the mystic powers of the sacred places would heal her. A very chatty woman." The voice was low-pitched and cultured. "I said I didn't know about mystic powers, but I thought getting away from home would help. Clearly I was wrong."

"Who are you, lady?"

"My name is Teresa Suarez," she said. "I work for an advertising agency, I live in New York, I'm single, and I make enough money to afford a holiday like this. Does that answer your questions?" She managed to sound faintly amused by the situation and by the two men.

"You don't look like someone called Teresa Suarez," said Wayne, dragging himself back into the dialogue now that it had hit a point he was sure of.

"Don't I really? And what does someone called Teresa Suarez look like?" she asked.

"Like a Mex," he said. "More like her." He pointed back at Diana Morris.

"How fascinating," said Teresa, raising one perfectly shaped eyebrow. "I'm truly sorry. I have a nose very like my father's," she added, as if this would explain everything. "And his name is Pedro Suarez." Wayne stopped, baffled, like a dog who suspects that people are laughing at him.

Harriet looked at the disciplined blond hair, the cool blue eyes, and that long, thin, curved aristocratic nose with its flared nostrils and was impressed. Teresa Suarez was someone to reckon with.

Gary ignored his brother's discomfiture. He was looking

straight at Brett Nicholls, the man built like a football player, who returned his look with eyes hot with rage. But he sat quietly, and in a steady voice said he worked for his father's insurance agency, and that his wife, Jennifer, was the nurse. They were taking a vacation. Gary turned abruptly away from him, as if he found him a hostile species.

He wasn't interested in Rick and Suellen Kelleher either. Rick, who looked as if he could wrestle a bull to the ground, told them in his soft, unworried voice that he was a computer person, associated with a small software company, and that he worked at home in Amarillo, Texas. This trip was his and Suellen's fifteenth-anniversary present. They had left the kids with his mother and blown the bank account. He didn't go in for all this mystic sites stuff much, but if Suellen did, he was proud and happy to go along with her. She smiled in nervous agreement.

The brothers ignored Mrs. Green and Karen and turned their attention to Kevin Donovan. "Now you," said Gary. "You interest me. Who are you, besides a loudmouthed son of a bitch?"

"Not a particularly interesting person," said Donovan casually. "Not to you, anyway."

"What do you mean by that?"

"I'm just a tourist, along for the ride, watching what's going on. That's what I do. I watch things for people. I guess you could call me a consultant." He smiled, as if at some secret joke. "You know, I follow trends and see how people are behaving. I keep track of what's profitable and what's not for the people who hire me. And sometimes I watch to make sure their investments are safe. Not very interesting."

"What's he talking about, Gary?" asked his brother.

"Shut up and look after the rest of them. Now—who in hell are you two?"

"Tourists," said John. "From Canada. We flew—"

"The hell you did," said Donovan easily. "You were alone on that plane."

"I came a week early," said Harriet, quickly. "I flew in to Kansas City and rented a van. That's why it has Missouri plates. You can check if you want."

"Why?"

"I've never been this far west before. I wanted to have a look. John couldn't take that much time, so we met in Santa Fe."

"You got some sort of proof?"

"I have a passport in my left-hand breast pocket," said John carefully. "If you want to see it, I will reach into my jacket and get it. Your brother already checked that I wasn't carrying a gun—not that either one of us could have brought a gun into the country. Think about it. We were flying and had to go through airport security."

"Okay—get it. And no sudden moves."

John moved his hand toward his breast pocket. Slowly.

"Wayne, reach in there and get the passport."

John opened his jacket wide to display the inch or two of deep blue of the passport. "This it?" asked the younger man. Sanders nodded.

"It don't say what you do," said Wayne, after puzzling over the document for some time.

"They don't," said Sanders. "But it's got my picture and it does prove I'm who I say I am, and that I come from Canada and have nothing to do with anything here."

"What do you do?"

"I don't see what difference it makes, but I'm a—I'm in the—"

"In the professional accounting business," said Harriet quickly. "Now that everyone's finished their income taxes, poor John can take a holiday."

It didn't occur to them to ask Harriet what she did.

Gary stood looking at them in silence. He was holding his weapon across his body, in one of those relaxed but vigilant stances, and suddenly Harriet was swamped in flickering memories from her childhood. Memories of television news programs, with their images and words alternately boring and terrifying her. Men in camouflage dress, stalking through the trees, holding weapons just like that one; fires blazing up; and ultimately the terrible knowledge that this was real. The people on the tiny screen in her father's study were dead. Really dead. And then there were the nightmares. Ghosts in black and white with hands that burned reaching out to pursue her through the forests of her childhood and the comfortable streets of home. That was all that she had taken from the turbulent sixties, a nightmare, and it was standing in front of her right now.

"I just have a couple things I'd like to say right now," said Gary, in that soft voice that made her shudder. "We've heard a lot of words in here, all real interesting, and probably some of 'em even true, but I know at least one of you is lying, and I aim to figure out which one. My little brother here is going to go out and bring in all the bags stored in the hold and you're going to claim your own bag and then we're going to search it. Because someone on this bus is carrying something worth close to a million dollars, and that million dollars is owed to us, and we aim to find it tonight. And if we don't, we're going to start killing people. One at a time. Not that we specially want to, you understand. But it works. People are just a little more cooperative and honest when they think they're going to be next."

"And when you find it, whatever it is, then what are you going to do to us? I like to be prepared." This was Teresa, sounding almost bored.

"Don't you worry about that. We're just going to leave you here. It's not so far away from help. You can send someone back by the road. We have our own plans for getting out of the country, so we're safe. All we want is our money, in whatever form it's been turned into." His voice was silky and confiding, like a snake slithering along the dirt. "Anyone want to tell us, and save us all a painful search?"

CHAPTER 5

It was an evening of growing enlightenment for the state troopers called in to search for two missing children. The dawning realization that there was no need to find and interview a driver of a regularly scheduled airport bus from Albuquerque who had dropped two children off on the road to Taos came to them in the middle of a long and patient conversation with Joe and Samantha Rogers. With a certain amount of annoyance, directed silently at Joe and Samantha, and a professional embarrassment at being caught leaping to conclusions, the Albuquerque detachment called off the search for that nonexistent person, restructured their ideas, and returned the problem to Santa Fe. And Taos. Since the whole thing started here and went to there, so to speak.

"Why are you so sure the children got on the bus?" asked Ed McDowell. His grievances went beyond annoyance and embarrassment. He had been dragged away from his wife and family in Santa Fe, and Friday night movies with pizza, because his ability to coax information out of terrified and hysterical parents was legendary. "Just because they were supposed to catch the bus, and they're good kids? Because even the best behaved kids can miss planes, or not catch buses. And you know that kids never react the way we think they're going to. They don't worry about themselves. Not until it's way too late. They just worry about your reaction. Only it never seems to occur to them that you'll be frightened for them, not mad at them. You know—they stop to buy some candy, and there's a lineup, and bang—they've missed their flight." The soothing voice went on, giving them a chance to think, tossing up ideas for them to reject.

"Rodriguez," he called over to the man from Taos, "have we heard from Dallas? Did the kids get on the plane?" It was, after all, his district.

"I'll check," said Rodriguez.

"No, no—you've got it all wrong," said Joe. "I know our kids. They can do things like that—especially if both of them get interested in something. Usually Caroline keeps an eye on the time, but you can't count on it. But, you see, I called Charlie. Charlie Broca at the airport. We know him, and he knows the kids. He said they got off the plane and onto the bus. We have this arrangement with Archway Tours. If they have a plane flying in from Dallas and a bus going up to Taos—and they do Fridays—they'll take the kids along for free. There's almost always room, because they're hardly ever fully booked. On purpose. They charge so much that they don't want to crowd people into the bus. In return we give them a better deal on one of their special tours. And Bert—the Archway driver—he knows the kids, he knows us, everything."

"And Charlie said that he actually saw the kids get on the tour bus?"

Joe Rogers had stared at McDowell in horror. "Christ almighty," he'd said. "I never thought—"

"What?" What was left of Samantha's voice had come out in cracked whisper.

"He said something about what else would they do? And

they weren't at the airport when he locked up. I thought it
was a funny way of putting it." He had stared into the distance, like a man who sees hell opening up in front of him.
"He always tells us that he makes sure that nothing happens to the kids and that they get from the plane to the bus
personally. We gave him a pretty generous Christmas gift to
make sure he does."

Charlie Broca had been easy enough to find.

His wife had looked at the two men on her doorstep.
"Come in," she had said. "You wanna see him, go look."

The remark had had an ominous flavor to it.

It was a little house, with a dark hallway running straight
through to the kitchen, and a narrow staircase going up to
an even smaller second floor. Mrs. Broca ushered them
through a door on their left into a small, square living
room, where she had been sitting with a glass full of amber-
colored liquid and a pitcher of more of the same beside it,
watching the late movie. "Have some tea," she had said. "I
put mint and lemon in it. You'll need it." She had poured
two more glasses and handed them to the wary officers.
"Here."

McDowell took a mouthful and set the glass down.
"Thanks, ma'am, but we really have to see your husband."
He was quickly developing one of those suspicions that he
should have posted someone to watch the back of the
house while Mrs. Broca distracted them with tea. He listened hard for the sound of footsteps and of windows
opening, but the house was already noisy with what
sounded like faulty machinery.

"What's it about?" Mrs. Broca had asked. She didn't
sound upset or suspicious. Just tense and resigned.

"Two kids got lost, and we think they were at the airport for a while. We need to know if Mr. Broca saw them."

"The Rogers's kids? He saw them, all right." Then she had led them out of the living room into the narrow hall and through the next closed door to their left. She had flicked on an overhead light and revealed a dining room, with a polished circular table and chairs, and shiny cabinets filled with plates and glasses. Shoved up against a double door that led to the living room was an old leather couch.

The sound that McDowell had heard from the living room and dismissed as a faulty air-conditioner was now both loud and recognizable. It was someone snoring—a snore that was enveloped in such a wealth of disgusting smells that McDowell, caught unawares, gagged. Sprawled on the couch was the source of all the noise and stench. Rye, vomit, urine. This was Charlie Broca.

"I was going to clean him up tomorrow," Mrs. Broca had said. She might have been referring to a kitchen floor. "But if you want him tonight, I'll do it right away. We have a bathroom under the stairs. It has a shower."

She had turned abruptly on her heel and left the room. The sound of water running formed a pleasant distraction to the noises made by Charlie. The two troopers retreated out into the hall and stood awkwardly about. In a minute or two she had been back. "It's ready. Cool but not ice-cold. You can keep him in it longer that way and that's better."

Then she had walked over to the couch and slapped him across the face. Hard. "Get up, Charlie. Move."

He grunted and stopped snoring.

"Quick," she said, pulling him to a sitting position. "On your feet." And miraculously, she had yanked him to his feet. "Take one arm each and steer him into the bathroom. I'll go ahead."

Rodriguez looked disgusted, but grabbed one upper arm, McDowell got the other, and they shuffled him rapidly after his wife. She pulled aside the shower curtain and unceremoniously shoved him in. Clothes and all. "Stay in there, you miserable bastard," she yelled into the running water. "Stick your head under the water. You're filthy. You're absolutely disgusting."

She had turned back to them. "I don't know. He's pretty bad, but there's one thing, he got rid of a lot of it, so he should sober up faster."

"Is he like this often?" asked McDowell. If he was, then they were talking to some sort of saint. Or masochist.

"Never," she'd said. "That's why I was so shocked."

"But you seem to be so good at—" At that point it had occurred to McDowell that this was not a skill that most people want to be known for.

"My father was a lush," she'd said. "And so was my oldest brother." Suddenly a dam had broken, and her terse responses had expanded into an unstoppable flow of speech. "There ain't nothing in this world about putting drunks to bed that I don't know. I swore I'd never marry a lush, and I told Charlie that. I knew when I married him he wasn't a drinking man, and he's stayed that way, but tonight, I don't know what happened. He just opened a bottle someone gave us once and started. And he kept talking about the twins." She was leaning against the wall, looking exhausted and overwhelmed. "It's not what you think either. I know him, we're close. When he buys magazines and hides them in the cellar, they're all these huge-breasted cows, that's what they are. Not little kids. Whatever he knows about those kids, he never did anything to hurt them. Anyway, I drove out to pick him up, and we did the airport together—I often do that—and that was just after the twins would have left on the tour bus. He'd never have had time to do anything."

A gurgling sound was issuing from the shower. Mrs. Broca stuck her head back around the curtain. "Strip, you miserable bastard. Everything. Leave it right there."

A mumbling protest testified to the efficacy of Mrs. Broca's remedies.

"Do you think we're likely to get anything out of him tonight?" asked McDowell, turning to his partner.

"If we take him to the hospital, they can liven him up a bit," said Rodriguez. "Then we bring him back and start filling him up with coffee, we'll get something in a couple of hours, maybe. That's better than waiting until morning."

Mrs. Broca dragged the miserable creature out of the shower and began drying him off. "Hold him up," she instructed the two officers, and disappeared. She returned with a pile of clean, pressed clothes and in an amazingly brief period of time they were looking at someone with a white face, red eyes, and wet hair, but dressed in a clean checked shirt and jeans. He still wobbled, but he was capable of walking.

"I don't know how to thank you, Mrs. Broca," McDowell had mumbled, embarrassed. "And if it hadn't been so important, we wouldn't have done this to you."

"You'll bring him back when you're finished with him?" she'd asked. There had been the ghost of tears in her eyes. "Or call me and I'll come fetch him."

Neatness was apparently not a life priority for Wayne and Gary. Every suitcase, bag, canvas bag, and container belonging to anyone on the bus had been opened and dumped and searched through. The contents were spread over the seats, on the floor, and tossed over the seat backs. Wayne complicated the search by fastening triumphantly on every gold chain or dinner ring he came across, convinced that he had found the pot of gold and demanding that his brother assess his new find.

Gary lost his temper on the fourth chain. "For chrissake, Wayne, we are looking for something worth close to a million bucks, not some two-bit chunk of tin. Understand?"

"It looked real valuable," said his brother sadly. "Maybe what we're looking for was already on the bus when we got here," he suggested, eyeing the fabric of the seats.

"Wayne, maybe you gotta be stupid, but do you have to try to prove it to the whole goddamn world? Whatever it was came on the plane from Dallas, so how could it have been hidden in the bus?"

"Maybe someone got to the bus earlylike."

"Yeah. Maybe someone did. Remember who?"

Wayne subsided into silence. The passengers repacked most of their despoiled belongings and fell into a sullen lethargy. Diana Morris sank farther and farther away from the unpleasantness around her. Jennifer Nicholls sat on the floor beside her, holding a cup to her lips, and moistening them whenever she could rouse her to something close to consciousness. Her concentration on the woman was so intense that she seemed unmoved by their common danger. The children had collapsed into sleep, huddled against each other like wretchedly tired, cold puppies. Just after midnight, Gary snapped that he couldn't breathe, that there was no goddamn air in the bus, and Wayne opened the front door, allowing in waves of night air. Suellen Kelleher, who had also escaped into childlike slumber despite the commotion around them, stirred restlessly and burrowed in closer to her husband.

Then the lights began to flicker and dim. "Now what's happening?" said Gary.

"I imagine your battery's dying," said Kevin Donovan helpfully.

"Get the goddamn bus started again, Wayne," said his brother. "We got to keep the lights working."

"We're on empty," Wayne whispered. "I think we shoulda filled it before we got to the airport."

"Switch batteries. Use what we've got," said his brother impatiently. "There'll be some fuel in there, even on empty."

"I don't know how to switch batteries in this thing, 'specially when I can't see what I'm doing," muttered Wayne. But he started the bus. The sleeping passengers stirred and muttered and sat up again.

In fifteen minutes or so the engine spluttered and died. Soon the lights began to show signs of weakness. They dimmed, went out, glowed themselves into a temporary afterlife, and then, very, very slowly, faded away. They reminded Harriet of the Cheshire cat, disappearing and leaving nothing behind but a faintly illuminated filament.

"Stay where you are." Gary's voice penetrated the darkness. "We'll finish this search as soon as day breaks. And believe me, we'll shoot anyone who tries to get away. The rear door is locked and that means you'll have to climb over us to get out." He paused. "You might want to consider what we're looking for," he added, almost as an afterthought. "At sunrise, we take the first person out and shoot him."

Someone gasped and a frightened silence fell over the bus.

*   *   *

But the height of any emotion can only be maintained for a certain period of time in absence of outside stimulation; gradually soft rustling noises filled the night, as the exhausted passengers settled down in their seats again and—with some exceptions—fell into slumber.

It was close to 4 A.M. before they got a coherent story out of Charlie Broca. "I'm so sorry," he said at last. "Yesterday was an awful day. I always do Friday nights—I don't mind, usually—but last night everyone was yelling, and raising hell, and nothing was coming in on time. But you don't want to know all this, do you? Just that I was tired, and Helen was coming to pick me up, and I thought we'd go out for dinner somewhere—there's a neighborhood Mexican place—" He stopped again, as if he realized that no one was interested in his eating habits either.

"And then what happened?"

"The Archway Tours plane came in, finally. That was the last flight expected in. And there was a strange bus driver— but I didn't realize that at first. I don't know what's happened to Bert. He always drives. Bert's a great guy—" He blinked them into focus. "And I saw Caroline Rogers talking to this lady, and then finally Stuart comes in—they're a little late, but I'm not worried, because I know Bert would never leave without the kids. Of course I never knew it wasn't Bert. And then suddenly I see the driver get on the bus—and it was a guy I didn't recognize—and the door shuts and the damned bus takes off." He stopped dead, as if he suddenly wound down.

Rodriguez handed him fresh coffee.

"Thanks," he said. "Sorry. I just feel so— Well—I could

see us having to drive the twins to the hotel after Helen came to pick me up, because I couldn't just leave them there, could I? Friday nights at the hotel are always crazy— Joe and Samantha can't leave the dining room. And then this lady who was talking to Caroline, she starts going on about them missing the bus, and her husband comes over and asks me what in hell is going on, and I get mad and say something about not being responsible for kids playing around and missing buses, and he says since he's going to Taos he might as well take them himself. So he picks up his suitcase and she picks up the kids' suitcases and they all go off in his van."

"Mr. Broca, did you see the van?"

Charlie blinked. The lids dropped over his bloodshot eyes. His head drooped onto his chest.

"Mr. Broca—wake up. Did you see the van?"

His head snapped up and his eyes opened wide. "Chevy van, cream-colored, one, maybe two years old, Missouri plates. Didn't get the number. Guy was tall, wife skinny, about five six." His head fell onto the table, just missing the coffee, and he was out. The time was 4:25 A.M.

Karen Johnson had already been frozen into immobility when the lights when out for the last time and Gary uttered his final threats. She was, she had decided, beyond terror. It was the outrage of it all, the random outrage of it all, that had finished her. That by some vicious chance she—a fill-in, totally unprepared for the job—should have to cope with *this*. The unfairness of it had destroyed her, had transported her out of the bus into some other dimension, one ruled by strange laws, where she was enveloped not in air, but in some thick, muffling substance. Each breath she took had to be dragged into her lungs with deliberation; sounds came to her ears from very far away; people's movements were slow, terribly slow, as if impeded by a terrific force of gravity. But in here, in this gelatinous fog, she was safe, wrapped up, away from harm. As long as she didn't try to move, or speak, or think.

She reached for comfort toward the old lady beside her, and realized that she had fallen asleep. She had her own manner of fleeing the horror, and Karen decided that she had no right to interfere with it. There was nothing for it, then, but to sit here in immobile silence until daytime came and they started to kill. Tears she was scarcely aware of trickled down her cheeks.

From somewhere in the bus, she heard a voice whisper, "Grab the girl. We might need her." A huge hand encircled her arm and squeezed; she gasped and another hand was clapped over her mouth. She was lifted up out of her seat and pulled into the aisle; in a few stumbling steps she was out of the bus. The cold air felt like the water off Popham beach back home; clean, powerful, and breathtakingly frigid. She shivered.

"She's cold." Karen recognized Wayne's voice.

"Here—she can have this." That was Gary. And one of them placed a jacket over her shoulders and with great care and delicacy put her arms into the enormous sleeves. The jacket came down to her thighs, the sleeves almost as far. The same careful hands brought the zipper together and fastened it almost to her chin. It was warm, blissfully warm. A gust of wind blew against her face, and she realized she was breathing again.

"How fast can you walk?" said Gary softly.

"Pretty fast, except that these shoes aren't the best for walking. They slip on the dirt and gravel." This was her voice, speaking normal, intelligent things.

"Okay. We have a plane to catch, you might say, and we're taking you with us for insurance. You stay quiet and stay with us and nothing will happen to you. We'll make sure you get back to Dallas or wherever safely. Now let's move."

The two men walked with extraordinary speed and silence through the dark night. They were following the road farther up the mountain, around the bend that the bus hadn't managed to negotiate. Neither one spoke, and Karen was too concerned with keeping her footing and not losing her companions to want to fall into casual conversation. She was wearing elegant flat-heeled shoes that slipped up and down her heels and slid on every stone, making each step an adventure. At the outset, Gary had gone ahead, and Wayne had walked beside her, his hand on her arm, holding it, lightly. After twenty or thirty minutes, they were following along in single file. And either the sky was lightening somewhat, or Karen was developing eyes like a cat, because now she was able to see, more or less, where she was going.

They had been walking for hours, it seemed, most of it uphill. Karen had long ago pulled her neat, too-tight skirt up way above her knees, folding it over at the waist to allow her to take longer strides, but she could still feel the muscles in her calves and in her arches seizing up, preparing to cramp. She was seriously considering taking off her shoes, when suddenly Gary stopped and looked around him. "Did I miss it?" he asked quietly.

"Up ahead there," said Wayne, and the strange procession plunged on into the night.

Then the black shape that she had been confidently following disappeared into the trees.

A hand grasped her by the arm again. "Real quiet, now." She found herself turned onto a path that ran through absolute blackness. A hand reached back and found hers and placed it on his waist. Miraculously Gary continued to be able to see his way through the night, and kept padding silently on. They climbed steeply now; then the path twisted and they were on the lip of a cup, looking down onto a small, very flat mesa, about the size of seven or eight football fields, Karen estimated automatically. The area was lit up by what appeared to be a pair of enormous headlights, and one small searchlight, all emanating from a small plane. Two men were talking; they appeared to be shifting cargo. One laughed. After the silence of the night, it sounded obscene.

The searchlight swept around the circle of hills, picking out a narrow dirt road about a quarter way round. It rose briefly and crested at a dip in the rim surrounding the mesa. It was so clearly superior as a means of entering the plain where the plane was waiting, that clambering up the way they had come seemed perverse. Gary took her hand from his waist and pushed her back slightly, into the trees. He moved forward a step or two, silently, drifting along the rim, and then returned.

He beckoned to her to move down the hill the way they had come up and pointed at a little hollow, protected on three sides. She moved into it. He crouched beside her and murmured into her ear. "This is our plane, sweetheart. But we have to go down and get it from those two guys. You just stay there, very, very quietly. No one can see you if you don't move, remember that. We'll be moving slowly, so give us time." And he disappeared, if not exactly in a puff of smoke, then into the trunk of a tree.

For a long time she heard nothing but her own breathing. Then, somewhere, a chunk of earth and rock, loosened by a silent footfall, threw itself down the side of the hill.

Then silence.

Suddenly the quiet of the night was destroyed by the starting up of the little plane's engines. She heard a shout, an answering shout, a building up of noise as the engines increased their speed. Finally the noise began to fade, farther and farther. The plane was gone. They had left without her. They had left her here to perish.

Don't be stupid, she said to herself. They left you here within walking distance of the bus.

Slowly she stretched out her tight leg muscles and then silently pulled herself to her feet. She could see nothing but trees against the lightening sky. She moved up to the rim and looked over. The little airfield was quiet. She walked on, always keeping the airfield in view and to her right. This way she wouldn't get lost. She hoped. And then, about halfway between the proper road in and the path they had used, she saw a heap of clothes lying on the ground ahead of her. She walked up to it, and stared straight down into Wayne's slashed throat. She turned her head aside and gulped in some cold, clean air.

When she turned back, he was still there. And lying beside him was Gary, his throat another open wound. She turned and fled.

Karen took three steps, slipped, and fell, wrenching her ankle and bruising her knee. This was insane. She kicked off her shoes, pulled herself up very gently and began to slide sideways into the woods. She moved as quickly as she could, darting between trees, trying not to fall, until at last she realized that no one was chasing her. The silence of the night ruled once more, and she climbed back up to the top of the hill, slightly to the right, she thought, of the path she had been on with Gary and Wayne.

Once out from between the trees, she saw that the sky was turning from black, studded with stars, to silver, brilliantly lit by one or two. The mesa was empty, except for a couple of beer or soft-drink cans where the plane had waited. She perched on the rim of the enclosing mountain, shielding herself behind some brush, and searched for signs of life. There was nothing. She shuddered and moved along the top, staying away from the steep slope that led to the mesa in case she slipped and fell and broke something. It seemed to take her forever before she reached the entrance to their little path. With a sob she could not suppress, she began to run, stumbling, back toward the road.

"What time is it?" Harriet whispered the words directly into John's ear.

He raised his watch and flicked on the tiny light buried inside. "It's three forty-five," he said. He spoke softly, but well within the range of normal speaking tones.

Harriet jumped, startled. His voice seemed to echo across the valley in the silence of the night. "How long have we been sitting here in the dark?" she went on, still whispering into his ear.

"About an hour." John had pitched his voice low enough not to disturb other people, but not at a level of a man who expects to be shot if someone hears him talking. "I imagine Gary and Wayne are long gone."

"What makes you think that?"

"There's been a certain amount of movement back and forth, along the aisle," he said. "Maybe you didn't notice it from where you are, but I could feel people creeping by. I wasn't counting, but it's entirely possible that we're the only people left on the bus. Except for the injured woman and the kids. Did you say you had another flashlight?"

"Sure," said Harriet. "In my knapsack. I also have more batteries, as far as that goes."

"I wonder where they put our flashlight?"

"On the seat," said Harriet. "Gary's seat."

"It should have enough juice in it to take me back to the van. Stay here."

"You'll need the keys." There was a faint rattle as she extracted them from her pocket. "Here. Don't get shot."

And indeed nothing impeded Sanders's progress down the steps of the crippled bus. The batteries had regained a faint measure of their strength in the meantime, and the glow of the flashlight was enough to guide him to the van. It still sat there peacefully, locked and unmolested. The knapsack was open, as he had left it, and a second flashlight was lying close to where the first had been. Fresh batteries were neatly disposed in one of the outer pockets. When he replaced the used ones, he flicked on the flashlight and it lit up the night. Wonderful, organized Harriet, he thought, in a sudden surge of affection for her. She really always did things properly. He stretched luxuriously and strode back to the bus.

"Gone without a trace," he whispered to Harriet, "and the van is fine." Then stepping as lightly as he could, he made his way back to see if he could help the injured woman. There were indeed empty seats. Across from them, the cool Teresa had decamped into the darkness. And so had Kevin Donovan. The big football player was gone. Rick Kelleher was still there, wide awake, supporting his sleeping wife. Sanders leaned over. "They've gone," he whispered. "Are you all right?"

"We're fine," said Kelleher.

The children were sleeping, and in the back, Jennifer Nicholls was sitting on the floor, leaning her head against the seat, guarding her patient. She looked momentarily destroyed with exhaustion. "I brought you a flashlight," said Sanders. "I thought it might help. Is there anything else we can do? The brothers seem to have disappeared completely, taking their guns with them."

Nicholls pulled herself upright. "I hope they don't come back. Do you have the time?" she asked, yawning.

Sanders looked at his watch by the light of the flashlight. "About four."

"I wonder when it starts to get light around here," she said and yawned again. "You can begin to see it way before five at home, this time of year. When you're on night shift. I love watching the dawn creep in. Actually, I like working nights."

"You must be either crazy or a masochist," said Sanders with a laugh. "I always hated working nights."

"Working nights! That must be a weird firm of accountants you're with. What did you do? Emergency tax returns at three in the morning?" she asked, giving him a sharp look.

"You'd be surprised," said Sanders evasively, embarrassed at being caught in Harriet's lie.

"I think I would," she said. "But night shift is pretty lively at the hospital I work for. You feel like what you do makes a real difference. Of course, you lose a lot of people. All the worst things seem to happen at night. But you save a lot of them, too." She turned and looked out the window. It was still pitch black outside. "I guess dawn's probably later here. We're farther south." She accepted the flashlight Sanders gave her. "Thanks. I was going into suspended animation. You've yanked me awake again." She grinned. "I can't believe you're sticking with the bus when you could have left. You've got transportation."

"So could you," said John. "Lots of people have."

She grinned suddenly. "Naw. Habit. I couldn't have left."

"When it's light, I'll see about using the van. The road's narrow, but we can always back out. And we can make a bed for your patient."

"Where's that bastard I'm married to? Has he left yet?"

John was left openmouthed, trying to think of a tactful way of answering her question. "I didn't really notice—"

"He probably fell down the mountain," said Jennifer calmly, and turned her attention back to Diana Morris.

Sanders flashed the beam over the tiny galley and halted it on the shiny urn that said "Coffee." He located the cup dispenser, poured a cup, and brought it back to the tired nurse. "You want some coffee? It's black, and it may be cold, but I brought some sugar and a spoon." He emptied these out of his pocket and dumped them on her lap.

"You are a lifesaver," she said.

He filled two more cups, put lids on them, and began to work his way back to his seat. "I found us some coffee," he said to Harriet. "First come, first served."

"Do you think we should wake people up?" asked Harriet. "Let them know those guys have gone?"

"Why? The Kellehers are awake already, and so is the nurse. That leaves the two kids, and the pair in front of us. The rest have taken off. Anyway, there's not much we can do before daybreak. Let them sleep. Maybe some of the people who left went to find help. They might be back when it gets light."

"My God, are you ever filled with the warm glow of hope and charity," said Harriet. "The ones who left didn't strike me as the selfless and sacrificing types. If you want my opinion, they took off without a word before anyone could ask them to do something."

Harriet stared out the window into the blackness and nursed her cup of coffee. She tried to remember the exact route and times of last evening's journey. How many miles had they driven away from Santa Fe? And in what direction? The road had snaked a good deal at first, she remembered, and it seemed to her that they were heading southwest or even south as much as they were heading in any other direction. As soon as it was light enough, she'd get the map from the van and check what center of civilization they were likely to be near at the moment. If any. And check how close she had parked to the abyss down there. If it was really an abyss, and not just a slope. She yawned and started wandering down the slope, admiring the spring flowers . . .

"Don't spill that coffee," said John. "I'm not sure how much of it there is."

"I'm wide awake," said Harriet.

"Liar."

And then suddenly the bus seemed to be filled with cold gray light. Harriet wriggled her toes, stretched her spine up against the seat back, and drank the remains of her coffee. Small noises—birds, animals scuffling about—broke the silence of the night and she looked around. The remaining passengers were moving back and forth, energized by the returning day. The Kellehers, bright-eyed, were sorting out their belongings. "We're going out to see where we are," said Rick. "But we'll be back. We're hikers, and it might be that we can find a way to get help. Does anyone have binoculars?"

The remark drew nothing but silence. Rick shrugged his shoulders and headed outside.

"Let's get ourselves out there, too," said John. "I've had enough of the bus for the moment."

Harriet glanced over at the first seat and was disturbed to see that the tour guide had also left. Her unspoken question was answered before she had time to frame it. "I don't know, my dear," said Rose Green. "I must have fallen asleep—I found last night very tiring—those men, and all the mess. I was very upset and that always makes me tired and when I woke up again she was gone. I thought nothing of it at first. A call of nature, you know. That's what I thought. After all there were people creeping back and forth all night. I heard them, and you could feel the bus lurch and sway as they went down those steps. But she hasn't come back. Such a nice girl and so far from home, you know. Comes from Maine. She doesn't know this part of the world at all."

"Then what in hell was she doing as the guide?" asked John. "Aren't guides supposed to know more than the people they're guiding?"

"Well—she did worry about that, she said, but apparently the company thought she'd be fine. It was an emergency, you see. The regular guide didn't turn up and they called her in as a replacement. At the last minute. She had all these books and things she was supposed to read last

night to find out about where we were going." Mrs.
Green's voice hoarsened and she fell into a brief fit of
coughing.

"Can we get you some coffee?" asked Harriet. "Or tea?
I think there's tea, isn't there, John?" He nodded.

"Yes, please. I always find that—"

"Sugar? Milk?" asked John, and fled back to the galley.

In seconds John had the lukewarm drink in her hand.
"We're off to look around and catch a breath of air."

"And to get some warmer clothes," said Harriet. "But
we'll be back."

As soon as she stepped outside the bus, Harriet understood
why she had felt that they had driven into the absolute
darkness of hell the night before. The nose of the bus was
buried in the towering slope above them. The road looked
to have been carved into the side of the mountain at this
point, and rock, trees, and earth hung over them like a
roof. Only the darkest of evergreens and crawling plants
seemed able to find a foothold in that hostile environment,
and the result swallowed up light like a black velvet background cloth. On the other side of the road, the slope continued its precipitous descent, but another dark hill rose up
from the other side of the narrow valley at the bottom. The
effect was to enclose them in a black-sided box.

And they had indeed managed to park the van beside the
precipice, close enough to the edge to make backing out an
endeavor that would require steady hands and calmness of
spirit. Not that it mattered. Their second discovery made
the first one irrelevant for the time being. Someone had
paused long enough in his—or her—flight from the bus to
let the air out of all four of the tires on the van. Even the

front right one, the one that was lodged in a deepish pothole. John stared at it.

"Goddammit," said Harriet. "The bastards. Why did they do that? What was the point?"

"They didn't want us to get help in a hurry. I'm surprised they didn't just take your keys and leave in the van with all our stuff. That was what I was expecting."

"Maybe it was because I was clever and shoved the keys down between the seat and the back when they were searching," she said. "But, you know, I don't think that was the reason. They didn't seem interested in the van or my keys at all. They were looking for something smaller than the van and bigger than the keys."

"That narrows the field, doesn't it? Maybe they have a helicopter waiting for them somewhere near by," suggested John.

"A helicopter," said Harriet. "Those two bozos? Come on, Inspector, you're letting your imagination run away with you. They were having trouble driving a bus, much less piloting a helicopter—or whatever one does to it to make it work."

"Don't be so damned superior. They got the bus this far, didn't they? Over a pretty spectacularly bad road. And look where we are now. It was hard to see road last night, but I'd be surprised if you could find many spots to disable a bus that would be this difficult to get out of. Even on this road. I'm willing to bet he was planning to trap us by skidding into the hillside at this particular point. He certainly succeeded, anyway. And that means that he—they—have transport up ahead there. They assumed that we'd retrace our steps. And while poor old Wayne may not look very adept in life skills, his big brother impressed me as a man who knew what he was doing."

"I didn't like the way he was carrying that weapon," said Harriet, shivering.

"He looked to me to be about forty, wouldn't you say?" asked John. "Older than his brother."

"A lot older," said Harriet. "They could almost have been father and son. But at least ten to fifteen years."

"Cast your mind back twenty years. He would have been around twenty, right? And there must have been a hell of a lot of eighteen- to twenty-four-year-olds around here who learned how to fly helicopters and handle automatic weapons and all that sort of thing, Harriet. Did Gary look like a draft-avoiding college student to you? Just think."

"Okay," she said, "so flying a helicopter wasn't far-fetched, but for two guys like that to own one . . ." she added and shivered again.

"Are you scared?" he asked. "Or just cold?"

"Freezing. You did say you'd brought my heavy sweater, didn't you? There's a real wind blowing along this road." She licked her lips. "And it's gritty, too," she went on, as John opened the back and took out her sweater from his suitcase.

"What's in that dark blue thing with the spigot?" he asked.

"Spring water. Five gallons. I was thinking of shooting some things out in the desert if we had time. Rock formations. Maybe even cave dwellings and stuff like that. It's Kate's. She said I'd be stupid to try to kick around for whole days at a time in the desert on bad roads without carrying water. It's a sort of giant thermos."

"Five gallons?"

"I know," she said, answering the implied criticism. "But that's the size they come in. They hold one of those big car-boys of water. There didn't seem any point in not filling it.

The people at the store poured it for me," she added defensively and then stopped to look at him. "Why in hell am I apologizing to you for carrying water in the van?"

"Because you're tired," said John. "It was a wonderful idea. We may need that water before we're finished. What do you have in food?"

Harriet walked reluctantly back into the bus; she felt as if she had been trapped inside it for a month. It was a very unreasonable attitude, she supposed. But then she had never been a reasonable person. She paused at the second step and looked into the interior. It remained tranquil. The children slept on. Jennifer Nicholls was up and around in the back, quietly attending to the injured woman, the Kellehers were still out exploring, and Mrs. Rose Green was still in her seat, looking white-faced and tired. She couldn't bear to go in and sit down. Not yet. She felt consumed with a restless fury, helpless and enraged, and the last thing she wanted to do was to sit. Perhaps that was why all those others had crept away. Anything was better than sitting here.

"I'm climbing up there," she said to John, pointing to the section of the mountainside several yards back down the road where the slope was less precipitous than it was where the bus had come to rest. "Just to see what I can see. Are you coming?"

"Sure," said John. "It beats sitting in the bus doing nothing."

The first ten feet or so were both steep and slippery. Conquering it was not exactly a grand triumph, but it felt good, thought Harriet. Then the terrain leveled out slightly, and the trees grew thicker and more prosperously.

As they wandered toward a patch of light ahead that might indicate an opening from which they could get a view of the valley below, Harriet suddenly stopped. "That's what happened to at least one of them," she whispered. "He seems to have been after a good night's sleep."

"Who is it?" whispered John, drawing closer.

"Donovan, I think," said Harriet. "He's the right size anyway, and he's got a suit on. Don't you think we should wake him up?" He was lying on his stomach, apparently in profound slumber. "Mr. Donovan, are you all right?" she said. She gave Donovan's shoulder a shake. His body felt heavy under her hand, heavy and still and cold. "Oh, God," she said, pulling her hand away and looking at the dark, sticky red stain on her palm. "John. Oh, God. Look. John, he's covered with blood." She backed away, staring at her hand.

Sanders crouched beside him, lifting his shoulder and then dropping it again. "He sure as hell is," he said. "His throat's been cut."

CHAPTER 6

"I have to admit I didn't care for the man," said John thoughtfully, as he rocked back on his heels. "But someone else must have developed a truly intense dislike for him." He stood up and automatically brushed nonexistent dirt off his hands. "Wayne and Gary's farewell gesture, I suppose. Unless it was one of our fellow passengers. Come on, let's get back." He began to scramble down the slope in a direction that would take them a good hundred yards from the bus when they reached the road.

"Or someone who lives around here," said Harriet, moving cautiously from solid piece of ground to solid piece of ground, as she followed him. "And doesn't care for visitors." Glancing around automatically for a hostile local inhabitant, she forgot to watch where she was going, stepped on a flat rock, loosened it, and almost fell.

"Careful. This section isn't very stable," John said, turning and holding out his hand to steady her. "How about an old friend who invited him out for a refreshing stroll in the middle of the night to talk over what was going on and when he got him a convenient distance away, stepped behind him, and—gotcha!"

"You really think it was someone he knew? I mean, before last night? What makes you sure?"

"I'm not, of course. But it makes sense, doesn't it?"

"I suppose it does," said Harriet, in grudging tones. "Why would anyone wander off into the night with a knife-wielding maniac? And if he'd been dragged off the bus, wouldn't we have noticed?"

"I would have," said John. "He left under his own steam."

"Maybe he was going to meet someone," said Harriet. "But no one on the bus behaved as if they knew him," she added, moving onto a large piece of solid rock and stopping. "He did talk to those brothers as if he knew them, don't you think?"

"No. I don't." John stopped as well to look back at her. "He was baiting them, not chatting. Didn't you get that impression? As though he recognized them. Maybe he just recognized the type, though. One hood to a couple of small-time operators."

"You mean Donovan's crooked?"

Sanders looked at her and grinned. "We recognized each other, saluted, and passed on."

"And you don't think that Gary cut his throat?"

"Come on," said John, turning back in the direction of the road. "We really should be getting back."

"John—" Harriet was staring back at the terrain they had just covered with such difficulty, slipping and sliding, and starting minor landslides.

"Yes?" It was a "now what" sort of yes.

"Why in the name of God would any two people who could walk down a relatively flat road in order to have a conversation go for a stroll on *that*?" She pointed to the area they had just covered. "In fact, why would anyone come up here? Unless they're crazy, like us."

John stopped and studied the contours of the land. "Because it's the shortest route to that dip in the mountains up there," he said slowly. "That changes things, you know."

"How?" asked Harriet.

"It means that Donovan was heading for the hills, literally—"

"Trying to escape from someone—"

"Who pursued him up there very quietly and slaughtered him."

"My idea exactly," said Harriet triumphantly. "But why quietly?"

"No signs of struggle. Of course, Donovan was so damned big that you'd almost have to take him by surprise."

They walked back to the bus in silence. "Could you just slip in there and ask that nurse to come out here and have a look at him?" asked John, once they were within hailing distance of the vehicle.

"The nurse?" said Harriet, startled. "What do you expect her to do? Raise him from the dead?"

"Shut up, darling, will you? I know it's futile, but I prefer to get an expert to point out that death has occurred, and when, and why—and for the moment, she's the most expert we've got. Call it habit. Go get her, will you?"

"Sir."

Jennifer Morris had been happy enough to leave her sleeping patient, even on such a gruesome errand. She opened the supply cupboard at the back, took out another blanket, and followed Harriet up the gravelly slope. She stood leaning on a pine tree, and looked down at the man lying there. "Dead? God—I should say so. Look at the ground and everything around him. It's all soaked. He bled like a pig."

"He hasn't been dead long, has he?" asked John. "There's no sign of rigor yet."

She leaned over and wiggled one of Donovan's fingers, and then gave his jaw a small push. "That was a pretty comprehensive accounting course you took," she muttered. "You're right. He's barely cold, as they say. He can't have been dead more than two or three hours. It might be a good idea to turn him over and straighten him out before he stiffens up, though. Otherwise it's difficult for the emergency crew." She paused. "Wrap him in the blanket. We don't want the kids wandering by and seeing him."

They wrapped him in the blanket and laid him on his back in a dark, cool spot under the trees. The three of them stood around him, in a ragged circle, looking like a grim parody of a burial service.

"You're a cop, aren't you?" said Jennifer. "Night shift, rigor—you just don't talk like an accountant, somehow. And on the other hand, you don't sound quite arrogant enough to be a doctor."

"You need some acting lessons," said Harriet.

"After all those correspondence courses I took on how to talk like an accountant, too," said John. "Anyway, you're right. I got the feeling, though, that telling Wayne and Gary I was a cop might have unsettled them a bit." He shook his head. "And they were unsettled enough already."

"Probably a wise decision," said Jennifer. "In the circumstances."

"How did that woman get herself shot?" asked Sanders, curiously.

"It was his fault," said the nurse, looking down at the corpse. "He made a sort of lunge for the younger brother—at that point in our little drama Wayne was holding the rifle—and then the bastard ducked. The poor little tour guide was standing in the aisle right behind Donovan and should have taken at least ten rounds in the chest and abdomen. But Morris came tearing up the aisle and pulled her down, getting a couple of those bullets in her thigh. She has fast reflexes," she added. "And an odd set of automatic responses to a life-threatening situation. For a librarian. Also odd was that no one else was hit. I suppose the rest of the bullets are in the ceiling or buried in seat backs."

"Are you sure that's what happened?"

"We were sitting right beside the action. I'm positive."

"And she's a librarian," said Harriet.

"Right," said Jennifer. "Just like he's an accountant." She nodded in John's direction. "What is it with this trip?"

"I don't know," said John reflectively. "But maybe some of the people still on the bus do. It might be a good idea to ask."

"We can try, anyway," said Harriet. "How is Ms. Morris?"

"Not good," said Jennifer. "But she's scrappy—a real fighter. If I can get more liquid into her it would help, but I'm a trifle worried about supplies. What if it takes a day or so to get rescued? I don't know how much water is stored in the bus."

"We have spring water," said Harriet. "Locked in the van. Five gallons."

"Hang onto it," said Jennifer. "In case. We don't want

people using it to wash their hands and faces. But that means I can be a little more generous in the amounts I give my patient. If you've never lived in a dry area, you probably don't realize—" Her voice trailed off in sheer fatigue and she yawned.

"Where are you from?" asked Harriet, in a friendly attempt to keep the woman awake.

"Kansas. A farm in Kansas. We had water. But I've lived in the Southwest. I know about dry."

"What about food?" asked John, who was beginning to feel empty.

"There are snack trays in the refrigerator. I don't know how cold they are now that the bus systems have stopped functioning," said Jennifer, with a worried frown. "But the cheese and biscuits and raw vegetables will be fine. We might as well eat them now as later." She stretched and looked around her. "Foreboding, but beautiful, isn't it?" she said. "I have to get back to my patient. Come on—let's hand out the trays."

Kate Grosvenor awoke to a throbbing head and a ferocious thirst. After a brief and silent battle, thirst won. Keeping her head as motionless as possible, she eased herself slowly off the bed and transported herself with great care into the bathroom. She was still dressed in yesterday's jeans and T-shirt. At some time during the night, she had kicked off her running shoes and crawled under an edge of the quilt that formed a bright coverlet on the bed, but she hadn't managed to change and get under the sheets. How many times in the last two weeks had she crawled out of bed in the morning with her clothes on? Twice? Four times? A brand-new stage in the development of Kate. She felt inexpressibly grubby.

Five minutes in a hot shower helped. She dried herself off and examined her image in the bathroom mirror. A gaunt and haggard scarecrow looked back at her. She had spent so much time concentrating on the scarlet, dimpled, ugly disfigurement in her shoulder, avoiding bathing suits, cotton tank tops, all the good things of summer, that she had not noticed the whole woman until this morning. Compared to the rest of her, the wound was scarcely noticeable. She stepped back into the shower and shampooed her lank wet hair for the first time in weeks.

There was no doubt that clean hair and clothes helped. She even managed to control her gagging enough to brush her teeth. Maybe one day she would put on the makeup that she still carried around with her everyplace she went. She pushed open the door to her room, blinking painfully in the strong light and shivering in the cold morning air. Her physical misery—the cold, the brightness, the throbbing head—lent a reassuring sense of reality to the scene. Otherwise, it looked like the backdrop for a travel ad. The sun hadn't made it over the edge of the mountain yet, but the sky was clear and clean. The air smelled of pine, and was filled with the rustling of cottonwoods in the light wind. There was only one discordant note. The van that should have been sitting outside the next cabin was not there.

She drifted quietly over to the unit and peered furtively in the window. Nothing could look less occupied. The bright red curtains were still pulled back, and inside not so much as a glass or a towel had been disturbed. They had probably stopped for dinner and drinks, and in the end decided to stay the night in Santa Fe. Harriet could have called and let her know, Kate thought resentfully.

She needed coffee. And if she remembered correctly, that meant driving into town. It was likely that she also needed breakfast, but the thought of food this early in the morning made her gag. She turned back into her room, grabbed her handbag, and headed toward the car. "I can't get into that thing," she said to herself. "Not after yesterday. Not even to drive a block. Come on, Kate. The walk will do you good." And she set off for the Paseo and the plaza to look for breakfast.

Carl Deever had had a late night, and when the telephone shrilled in his ear at a quarter to seven in the morning, he did not react well. "This better be important," he said. Flat and loud and nasty. Fury was clearing the sleep out of his system and he was ready to fire or eradicate whoever was on the other end of the line.

"I dunno what happened, but Scotty hasn't been in contact. And the bus has disappeared. It's nowhere near the rendezvous point."

"What the hell?" he said. "Shit! Is that you, Ginger?"

"Yeah. Anyway, I dunno what's happened to her."

"I want to know where that fucking bus is. Now."

"I dunno. I've been driving up and down those roads all night. I didn't see nothing at all."

"Look—someone got that bus, didn't they? It isn't just off on its little tour route?"

"Yeah, someone got it all right. The cops are looking for it all over the state. Those cowboys Rocco hired probably got lost somewhere. Anyway, sorry to wake you up, but I thought you oughta know."

"The cops. Shit. Did the plane get off?"

"I think so. No one reported problems with it."

Carl Deever set down the receiver and stared out the window at the newborn day.

Chapter 7

When the sun finally crept over the mountaintops and touched the road, the thought of staying inside the bus became unbearable. The illusion of safety and comfort it had offered during the blackness of the night had disappeared, and the vehicle turned into a dark and hideous prison. The passengers fled into the sunshine, taking with them pieces of solid luggage to sit on. They sat hunched against the cold, dry wind that blew down between the hills, picking up sand and grit and tossing it into their faces. The scene had a two-dimensional, unreal look, reminding Harriet of those newspaper photographs that appear every news-hungry holiday weekend, showing exhausted passengers in jammed airports perched on their luggage, waiting endlessly for a flight to somewhere. But this airport was miles from anywhere, and someone had forgotten to order the plane. The passengers numbered only six now, not counting Diana Morris, still inside, still—as far as Harriet knew—struggling for her very existence. Harriet went back in to count trays in the refrigerator.

There were eight. "Do you think we should take one each and leave the rest in case the others come back?" she asked Jennifer, who had slipped in to check on her patient.

"Are they still cold?"

Harriet nodded. "Not bad."

"Then we might as well eat them, because they won't stay cold much longer. We'll each take one and split the extras. After all, you did say you had food as well."

There was plenty of lukewarm coffee and tea left in the thirty-cup urns to go along with Archway Tours special, gourmet-delight snack trays. The children had already classified the sandwiches in the same category as fried liver and boiled carrots, and went from tray to tray, exacting a sort of food tax, and stuffing their pockets with everyone else's peanuts, bits of cheese, and veggies. They collected as many cans of soft drinks as they could carry and declared their intention of going off to look around. Stuart intercepted Harriet's look of alarm and sighed. They were quite used to dealing with hysterical grown-ups, that long-suffering sigh indicated, and with infinite patience he launched into a well-rehearsed routine. "It's just past eight by my watch. We'll explore the road ahead for no more than thirty minutes, stop for ten minutes, and come back. So we'll be back in one hour and ten minutes or less. That's how we do things at home."

"That's right," said Caroline. "Then no one is allowed to worry about us until after then." They turned automatically to Harriet for permission.

Harriet glanced around at the rest of the group, trusting in some sort of consensus from the adults present. They were all studiously regarding other things. Even John, the snake. She looked at her watch and said, "Sure," feeling extremely annoyed that she had just been elected mother. If anything happened to them, she knew whose fault it would be. "But please watch yourselves, will you? Life will be a lot easier if we don't have to face any more disasters, even minor ones."

"We'll be careful," said Caroline. "If we see anything we

don't like, we'll come right back. And you're supposed to tell us not to go running into the woods, or getting lost." With that parting shot, the twins headed up the road, around the crippled bus.

As they rounded the corner out of sight, they were chattering and giggling, and poking at things they saw by the roadside. Now that the sun was shining, they seemed utterly confident that their adventure would be resolved happily. Sanders picked up his coffee and stared at it, wishing he trusted the judgment and crisis management skills of the crew sitting here—and that included himself and Harriet—as much as the children did, and wondering if he had ever in his life before felt so grateful for a cup of lukewarm coffee served in a poly cup. He looked around him. Except for Jennifer Nicholls bobbing back and forth, in and out, checking on her patient, everyone was quiet and relaxed. He nodded to Harriet and began to stroll along the road, very slowly, waiting for her to join him.

"What are you up to?" asked Harriet. "Why all these winks and nods? Conspiracy? Or are you just restless?"

"All of the above," he admitted. "But it seems to me that some decisions have to be made. And there isn't anyone here willing to take the responsibility."

"I'm not sure it's that," said Harriet. "If I were Mrs. Green, I'd be feeling a little helpless at the moment, wouldn't you?"

He paused and looked down. At this point in their stroll, the previous winter's snow and rain and wind had washed away a section of the road and he reflected that it had been a miracle that either clumsy vehicle had made it this far in the dark. The canyon bottom looked to be very far away. "I wish I knew where we were," he said, pulling a road map out of his back pocket. It had been folded to the area sur-

rounding Santa Fe. "First of all, I don't think we're anywhere near Taos. If anything, we're miles south of where
we started out. I'd guess we were on this road," he added,
pointing, "and then went off onto unmarked tracks somewhere between here and here."

"Maybe isn't much help, is it? Under the circumstances."

"No. The thing is, they won't be looking for us down
here, will they?"

"You mean, when they get around to noticing that a bus
has disappeared off the face of the earth?"

"They've noticed. Don't worry about that. This is a bus-
load of tourists with hotel reservations in Taos. We have
two kids whose parents expected them to jump off the bus
somewhere in the middle of nowhere into their waiting
arms. They'll be frantic. We're being searched for with
helicopters and dogs and Ouija boards and God knows
what else right now. Except I haven't seen or heard a single helicopter. Have you?"

"No, I haven't," said Harriet. "And I've been looking. So
we can't be anywhere near where they expected to find us.
And that means it could take them quite a while before
they spread out in this direction. What I was wondering
about though—" She paused.

"Yes? You were wondering?"

"All those people who left. Why did they go? And do you
think they know where we are? Or are they out there
alone, lost and starving? Have we been abandoned or are
we in the process of being rescued? That's the question,
isn't it? Why did they leave?"

"How about because they thought they were going to be
shot?" said Sanders lightly.

"Don't be stupid, John." Harriet was getting exasperated. "They ran after the goons had taken off. Otherwise

they would have tripped over them as they were charging out the door."

"Maybe one of them had a reason to leave," Sanders observed.

"Possibly," said Harriet. "Who wants to stick around with a fresh corpse you're responsible for? What about the others, though? If they went for help just as soon as they could—right after the goons left—and if they know where to go, then all we have to do is sit here and survive. If they were just fleeing a sinking ship for dirty motives of their own, we could be waiting a long time."

"Maybe one of the others knows something we don't," said John.

"Then let's go back and ask them."

"Of course we know that a bus has disappeared. The Archway Tours bus. The governor is very concerned. And we're on top of the situation, Mr. Deever." The governor's personal assistant—or one of them—was sweating visibly as he clutched the telephone hard against his ear, white-knuckled, listening to that cold, angry voice. "It just means we're on top of it. The investigation is going well and we expect a report any moment from the officers in charge. If you don't mind my asking, what's your particular interest in the case? In case the governor wants to know."

"My fucking wife is on that bus, that's my interest in the case," said Deever, clearly and precisely. "And I want her back, Frankel. Me, personally. And *we're* working on that. So listen to me, shitface. I don't want any interference. I don't want her talking to some stupid deputy sheriff who thinks he's Superman or something. I want to know what the cops have figured out so far, and I want to know exactly what they're doing, every minute of every day. Do you hear me, Frankel? You'll make sure of all this, won't you, Frankel? Unless you want to go back to that rattlesnake-infested patch of sand and rock your family calls a farm. In a little bag. For good."

A spasm caught Frankel around the throat. He tried to swallow, failed, and shook his head like a baffled horse. "I'm not sure," he started. His voice squeaked. "I'm not sure I can get that level of cooperation from the state troopers, Mr. Deever—not minute by minute."

"Then the governor can. And I expect him to."

Walt Frankel stared at the telephone in his hand in panic. The last time he had approached the governor on the subject of Carl Deever the reaction had been explosive. Sure, Carl Deever was rich. And money was important. But it seemed the governor had never cared for him much, and since the Santa Rosa hearings he had become pure electoral poison. And Deever didn't understand that. Just because he hadn't been indicted, he seemed to think he was clean. But one murmur in the press that the governor had done anything to ease Deever's path in life and they'd be collecting signatures for a recall.

The stupidest thing Walt Frankel had ever done in his short life had been to exchange a single word with Carl Deever. It had been at the first fancy party he'd been invited to as the governor's new personal assistant. Elated with expensive Scotch and drunk with the magic of his position, he had murmured vaingloriously in Deever's ear that he and the governor were close, that close, and he could deliver him, any time, any issue. And Deever was the kind of bastard who took you literally. The money started coming in.

He sat motionless at his beautiful desk with its telephone

and computer, in his office filled with well-tended, lush green plants. He reckoned that there was more growing here in his office than grew by nature over the entire acreage on his parents' miserable ranch. Frankel could feel the sun burning into his neck and taste the fine sand coating the inside of his mouth. The sand that blew in ceaselessly on the wind that never stopped rushing over their dry land. God—how he hated that wind and the sand. As soon as his bank balance was the right size, he was buying himself a chunk of Oregon, where the rain fell and the trees grew and there wasn't any sand. Not that he knew of, anyway. He stared at the blob of dark blue ink on his hand from the pen he'd been chewing. Shit—his mouth must be covered in ink. Ink. Ortiz. Ortiz owed him a big one. The governor's signature would never have landed on that piece of paper if it hadn't been for Walt Frankel. It seemed like a good time to collect.

Johnny Andreas hated trouble. He was willing to go miles out of his way to avoid trouble. That was why he always bought top-of-the-line equipment; that was why he paid top dollar to his permanent employees; that was why he always hired graduate students with top references to shepherd his tours. His buses and refrigerated equipment almost never broke down. His two drivers were always there, on time, cheerful and happy. Why shouldn't they be, as they built up bigger and bigger funds for their retirement? His graduate students were nice, polite, and well educated, and so desperate for money they were eternally grateful to him for their ten-day stints, no expense spared. Of course, that meant he had to run a top-of-the-line set of tours to pay all these exorbitant prices and salaries. But then, profits were good on top-end tours. People loved them and came back for more. He had people who'd taken at least one of his tours every year since he started running them. And now, after all this care and attention to detail, look what happens.

He was sitting in his tiled breakfast room/conservatory, overlooking the patio, at his beautiful tiled breakfast table, with a cup of excellent coffee by his hand, looking at a cop. Who was also sitting with a cup of coffee and had just finished explaining to him what they thought might have happened to his best, his newest state-of-the-art bus.

Johnny Andreas pulled himself together and started with the easiest question to deal with. "What's this 'relief driver' shit?" he asked. "I didn't call in a relief driver. Bert hasn't missed a tour since I hired him ten years ago. Bert's golden, absolutely golden. I had to call in a relief guide. Lesley Carruthers—she's my regular on the mysticism tour—booked off sick. But I always have a backup ready to call in."

"Just a minute, Mr. Andreas. You said that you never called in a relief driver on Friday? That Mr. Samson didn't call in sick?"

"Bert didn't call in at all. He just picked up the bus from the service area like always, cleaned and ready, loaded with everything—food, water, you know. And then as far as I know, he drove it over to get it filled and headed for the airport at Santa Fe. That's what he always did."

"Do you know it was Bert Samson who actually picked up the bus? Because it wasn't Bert Samson at the airport. Charlie Broca saw the driver, and he knows Bert."

"Sure he knows Bert. Everyone knows Bert. Just a minute." He grabbed a cordless telephone from the shelf behind him and punched the number two button. He drummed his fingers impatiently on the tiles in front of him while waiting for a response. "Joyce," he said. "Johnny here. Did Bert sign out number six on Friday?" There was a pause. "Personally? Like someone didn't come in and say he'd sign for him or any crap like that?" He nodded. "Thanks." He slid the phone back into its place. "Weekends are our busiest times. My staff gets off during the week, Monday to Thursday. To make up, everyone gets a month vacation. They like it," he added aggressively. "Okay. Bert came in and chatted with Joyce and signed the bus out himself. Wait a minute, though." He hit button seven. "Tim? Were you working Friday when number six went out?" There was a pause. "What do you mean it didn't go out? And you didn't report it?" He raised an eyebrow and shook his head in disgust. "Good point. We'll have to fix that." He clicked off the phone and looked over the table. "I can tell you one thing."

"What's that?"

"That bus isn't more 'n fifty or sixty miles away from the airport."

"Oh?"

"It never came in to get filled. Somewhere between the service bay and the pumps it just disappeared, and Bert with it. I'd guess it isn't too far away, sitting on empty. But I want to know where Bert is. Bert's my best driver, and I want to know what's happened to him."

So far John's attempts to turn the inhabitants of the bus into a functioning team had been singularly unsuccessful. Donovan's death had shaken them; and fear had melted any glue that might otherwise have held them together. No one had any idea why the rest had left, except that they were cowards, or stupid, or rats. Jennifer Nicholls had volunteered the rat theory. "Go off to get help?" she said, her voice shaking with rage—or perhaps amusement. "Brett? Risk his life for the good of the group? Are you kidding? He'd never get off his ass and do anything that strenuous unless he thought trekking through the fucking desert was his last chance for survival. Then it'd be worth the effort and the risk."

"Does that mean—?" Rose Green stopped and looked helplessly around.

"It doesn't mean a goddamn thing. He's too stupid to figure out the odds, and he knows piss-all about the desert. He panicked, that's all. They probably all panicked."

"Are you saying you think the Kellehers panicked?" asked Harriet. "They seemed to have their feet on the ground as far as I could tell. And what they were planning to do makes sense."

"What was that?" asked Jennifer.

"Climb up as high as they could get and see if they could tell where we are. They took my map."

"If you can believe that . . ." said Jennifer. "They just wanted to get your map out of your hands."

"You don't trust them?" asked John.

"No. But then I don't trust many people." She shook her head. "Look at Kelleher. He claims to be a software developer and he looks like a field worker. Unless he's been in prison, working on the roads or whatever they make people do around here, and they're on this trip to celebrate his release. And his wife. If Suellen—and I ask you, Suellen? That name is too good to be true—she grabbed it in desperation to try and sound Texan—if she's from Texas, I'm from Raleigh, South Carolina." Jennifer ended this homily on a flourish. "Hang on—I have to check my patient again."

"Did someone say they were from Raleigh?" called a sweetly affected voice from behind them. "That's where I was born, but I moved away when I was just a little girl. What are we doing? Telling life stories to pass the time?"

There was a scrambling of feet on the steep slope, and Suellen Kelleher came into view.

"We thought you'd gone," said Harriet.

"Not a chance." Rick Kelleher appeared and jumped down a steeper section onto the road. "Is there anything new? Where are the kids?"

"They went exploring up the road. Better than having them cooped up here, I thought," said Harriet defensively.

"You went off to see where we are," said John hastily. "Any luck?"

"Not much. Is that coffee?"

"It's cold, but there's lots," said Harriet. "I'll get you some."

"There's an interesting mesa formation up at the top of the hill," said Rick. "But it looked pretty deserted. There might be water down at the foot of this, if you could get down to it. I thought I saw the sun glint on something shiny down there at one point. But no sign of a stream or anything like that. No people, no cars, and this is the only road—if you can call it a road—that we found." He paused to finish his coffee. "There is one thing that disturbed me," he said cautiously after a while.

"Just one?" asked Harriet impatiently. "And what's that?"

"The bus is damn near invisible from up above. Your van can be seen, of course, but the bus just blends into the mountainside. And as far as I can see, that means we have to leave. There's water in the bus, of course, drinking water, and a reservoir for hand washing in the rest room. If we can organize containers for it—enough containers for it—we can trek out of here. If we have enough."

A new and powerful force had hit the group, and they all stirred uneasily. "Not everyone is going to be able to walk out of here," said Sanders. "We're talking more than five miles of rough downhill road, just getting down this mountain. Then maybe another five miles across the flat unless a car comes by. It could be pretty brutal."

"I couldn't, for one," said Mrs. Green. "My knees wouldn't take me one mile. And of course Diana Morris can't either, and I expect that means that Jennifer Nicholls won't."

"Then what do you suggest we do?" said Rick. "Sit here swapping yarns as we slowly die of hunger and thirst?"

"We weren't just swapping yarns, Mr. Kelleher," said Rose Green. "We were trying to come up with a plan. And I want to know who killed Mr. Donovan," she added.

"Donovan's dead?" said Rick. "When did that happen?"

"If Gary killed him," said Harriet, "it had to be before he left."

Rose Green shook her head. "No," she said. "Right after the lights went out, I fell asleep. When I woke up, Karen Johnson was gone, and so were the two drivers. They had been sitting on the step right beside our seat, whispering. And there was no one there. I even reached my hand out to see if I could touch them. Nothing but empty air. And then I heard Kevin Donovan tell Miss Suarez he had to get out, and would she let him by. And he went out of the bus and never came back. Then she left. And some of the others."

"My God, where was I while all this was going on?" asked Sanders.

"I think you were asleep, Inspector. You sort of jumped and woke up—I could feel it—when Donovan said something to Miss Suarez."

"How do you know it was Donovan? Maybe it was me, and I had to get out past Suellen," said Rick.

"In that case, why call her 'Teresa sweetheart'?" said Rose sharply.

"Maybe they came back and killed him," said Suellen.

"Why bother?" asked Sanders.

"Who elected you God and chief inquisitor combined while we were away?" asked Rick, with a glare at Sanders.

Excited chatter from up the road and around the corner interrupted the discussion before it could become irretrievably unpleasant. "There they are—there's the bus. Am I ever glad. You're heavy, you know." Caroline's voice carried through the clear air, preceding a sight more unexpected than the reappearance of the Kellehers. Stuart and Caroline came staggering around the corner, supporting between them the filthy, limping body of Karen Johnson, tour guide.

"Hi," said Stuart. "Look who we found. We gave her some of our soda, but I think she's still thirsty. She's been walking for miles in her bare feet."

Karen opened her mouth to say something. A small, hoarse sound issued from between her lips and she crumpled onto the ground.

CHAPTER 8

It was past nine o'clock when Kate arrived back at the motel. Still no cream-colored van sat parked in front of unit twelve. "Dammit," she muttered, and walked into the management unit. "Any messages?" she called from inside the empty office. And waited. She hit the bell on the counter. And waited.

The owner took his usual interminable time to poke his head around the door from his quarters. "Hi, Ms. Grosvenor," he said. "No calls and no sign of your friends. Now—about that room . . ." he began.

"Shit! Are you sure?" Of course he was sure. Everyone was sure about everything but her. "Look—I told you to hang onto the goddamn room for them, so hang on to it. You'll get paid." A wave of hot, painful fury slammed through Kate's already miserable body; for lack of a more cogent response she stormed out of the office and slammed the door. It didn't help. She stood wavering at the door to her room. What was inside? Her pills. Her Scotch. Nothing else. Not even a book or a magazine. And suddenly she was hideously thirsty again. She would walk back into town and get a bottle of spring water. Maybe she would have something to eat on this trip. She had ordered toast with her breakfast coffee and had been unable to bear even the smell of it.

She managed to fritter away an hour and a half before heading back to the motel, now supplied with some paperbacks, water, and a Danish. No sign of Harriet. She retreated to her room and stared for a long time at the two bottles beside her bed—one large, one tiny. No, Kate. Later. First of all she had to find out what in hell was going on, even if it meant calling every hotel in Santa Fe, and for that she had to be clear of head and of speech. She started to eat her Danish very slowly, and with great determination, like someone who has a gun to her head and is being forced to consume a revolting object. Yak dung, perhaps. Camel testicles. Unwise things to think about while eating. She managed three bites. She stuffed the rest of it back into its paper bag and threw it into the wastebasket. Still, for the first time in a long time, she had swallowed solid food before her first drink of the day.

Now what? She could call the airport. But even at small airports no one notices the people who arrive to pick up passengers. Or even the passengers pouring off flights. It occurred to her that she had no idea when he'd arrived or what airline he'd been on. Wonderful. Come on, Kate, think. What do you believe has happened that justifies raising a fuss? The answer sprang immediately into her mind. Harriet has been wiped out on the brief drive down to the city, and she is either dead or lying in a hospital near death. Otherwise she would have contacted you. Therefore whom do you call? The state troopers.

With that established, she looked up the number, pulled the telephone closer, and dialed.

It was already past twelve o'clock in the Eastern time zone. Those few government workers who were fated to toil away on Saturday were either finished for the day or out foraging for lunch in a dead, weekend city where most of the restaurants sat quietly filling up with dust. Two gloomy people who had been supervising various aspects of the Santa Rosa file looked at each other over a cluttered desk.

"Fill me in on what you've managed to get so far."

"It's still sketchy. New Mexico is trying to collect as much information as possible without alerting anyone at any level to our interest in the thing. It ain't easy, let me tell you," she added, her crisp, expensively acquired East Coast dialect falling into mock disrepair. "At the moment, we're doing our best to keep it looking like some psycho hijacking a bus filled with innocent tourists. Tragic, yes, but with implications? No."

"Is that possible?"

"Is what possible?" She sounded puzzled, her mind running miles ahead of her superior's at the moment.

"That it was some psycho hijacking a bus filled with innocent tourists, only it happened to be our bus?"

"Sure. And we could be hit by lightning as we sit here, too. Even though there isn't a cloud in the sky and we're trapped inside this building. Listen—I take two hours off on Friday morning to go the dentist and what happens? One of my most promising agents is sent into nowhere with zilch briefing, an agent who should have been on holiday right now. The agent *and* an essential witness are now both missing. I can't believe it," she added, in tones of anguish. "Only eight passengers on that goddamn bus and two of them are ours. An irreplaceable agent and a crucial witness. I don't believe in coincidence. Not beyond a certain point. With that witness we can wrap him up this time, and he knows it."

Her boss squirmed but ignored the criticism. "Who else was on the bus?"

"You think it was someone on the bus? Someone who knew what we knew?" She frowned. "I considered that. But we've been so damned careful. It just seemed too—"

"I don't think. I just want to know who else was on the bus."

"Well—the tour company is pretty well organized."

"With eight passengers to a trip, I should hope so."

"New Mexico faxed us the list and I have notes on a few of them. It's not easy to get information within seconds on a Saturday morning, you know." For the first time, she sounded a trifle querulous. "Anyway, you want me to give you what I got so far?" In the absence of a quick negative, she went on, almost without pausing. "Kevin Donovan. Gave an address in Chicago. Initially, he checks out, but I don't feel good about him. Could be I'm prejudiced, but you don't expect a guy traveling alone to be on a hokey trip like that." Her boss nodded sagely. Or maybe sleepily. "Rose Green. Got herself a senior's discount ticket. Lives in Worcester, Mass. There is a Mrs. Rose Green at her address in Worcester who has lived there for forty years and has no known involvement with organized crime or a record of violence."

"Now that's a refreshing change," said her boss. "A little old lady who's actually a little old lady."

The speaker reddened and darted a poisonous look at him. "We have nothing yet on the next couple, a Rick and Suellen Kelleher purported to be from Amarillo, Texas. A few communications problems there, I think. Diana Morris is listed as a librarian from Virginia, which checks. Brett and Jennifer Nicholls are from Minneapolis, but aside from apparently living in the house they say they live in, we have very slender information on them. Teresa Suarez lives in New York at her address and her neighbors say she works in an advertising agency. Which checks. It might take until tomorrow or Monday to get better information on all these people. Do we want one on Karen Johnson?"

"Who in hell is she?"

"The guide. Called in at the last minute."

"Yes. When I said everyone, that's what I meant. Call me here as soon as you have fresh information." He looked up. "Why was she called in at the last minute?"

"Haven't the faintest. I'll find out."

"And one of those is ours?"

She nodded her head. "Fred's the only one who knows which it is. Or who the witness is. There were so many leaks and screw-ups the last time, we agreed it was the only way to go. You authorized that, sir," she added grimly.

"So I did. It seemed to be a good idea at the time, didn't it? Who knows what levels the man has friends at?"

"So as long as one of them isn't Fred, we might still be able to rescue something out of this."

"If we can find them first."

Kate hadn't known quite what to expect from her inquiry, but it had not been a car screeching up in front of her room within five minutes of placing her call.

"Miss Grosvenor?" asked the man who filled her doorway. He had a dark, pleasant face, now composed into a grave expression. A bearer of lousy news expression. She felt sick.

"That's right," she said steadily, grateful that she had resisted the impulse to have that drink once she had made the call.

"Sergeant Rodriguez. You called us about a woman in a cream Chevy van with Missouri license plates who was supposed to meet you here in Taos." It was, and wasn't, a question. It was almost as if he wanted to give her a chance to say that it was all a mistake, that she had merely dreamed the van, and that she had no friend. There was something hostile and threatening in that voice.

Too tired and too sore to unscramble the message behind his tone and his words, she plowed on with the raw truth. "Yes, I did. She left Denver on Thursday; she was planning on spending Thursday night on the road somewhere between Denver and Santa Fe, then picking up a friend at the Santa Fe airport and driving him back here to Taos. She hasn't made it and I'm worried about her. We were going to spend a few days together. As a holiday. And before you think I'm just another hysterical female—" That sentence was going nowhere useful. She switched gears. "I know she's a grown-up, and it hasn't been that long but, believe me, please, she isn't someone who makes appointments and doesn't keep them. For one thing, she knew I'd called the motel and reserved two rooms."

"Lots of people reserve motel rooms and don't bother turning up. That doesn't mean a thing."

"You don't understand. She's one of those conscientious Canadians. She'd classify stiffing a motel owner right up there on the scale of things with robbing a bank." That drew a change of expression that almost qualified as a smile. "Anyway, when she hadn't turned up this morning, and hadn't called, I thought I should contact you people." Kate still felt as if she was talking into a large pillow. "Do you have any information on my friend?" she asked, exasperated, after a very long silence. "Are you even interested in the fact that she seems to have disappeared from the face of the earth?" Easy, Kate, easy. Calm down. She took a deep breath and then gasped as the pain bounced around her rib cage and shoulder.

"You okay?"

"Sorry," said Kate. She caught her breath with difficulty and went on. "Gunshot wound," she added automatically. "Souvenir of the Middle East."

"Military?"

"No—a photographer, news photographer. Just as hazardous at times," she added, with a wan smile. "But not as noble. Look, why don't you come in and we can sit down?" So far, this conversation had left her exhausted beyond all reason.

Sergeant Rodriguez walked in and looked around. "Nice rooms," he commented, and sat down at the table by the window.

"I'd offer you coffee if I had any—I'd offer myself coffee if I had any, in fact—but all I've got is spring water." She took a large bottle out of her canvas bag and set it on the table. "Help yourself," she added, pointing to the nest of glasses in the middle of the table.

"Just a minute," he said, went out to his car and came back with a large thermos jug.

Kate watched him move with fascination, temporarily forgetting her misery, her fingers itching to capture that fluid movement on film. He reminded her of the beautiful young men with rippling, controlled muscles whom she had photographed in hot, dry, bomb-scarred villages, scrambling over rocks and dropping out of second-story windows. Now dead, probably. Or at least most of them.

"Black with sugar," he said cheerfully, fortunately unaware what was in her head. "I hope that's okay. And that you don't object to drinking your coffee out of water glasses." He poured two glasses of coffee and two of spring water. "Now—let's talk about your friend. I'll start. We are interested in the fact that your friend seems to have disappeared from the face of the earth. Very interested. Particularly since according to you she was driving a cream Chevy van with Missouri plates. We think you might be in a position to tell us a whole lot, Miss Grosvenor. Let me explain the situation to you."

"It can't be true," said Kate, after she had heard him out. "No matter how sure people think they are. I'll admit that Harriet isn't one of my oldest childhood friends, but we spent a summer together, we've met at other times, we've done a lot of talking. She could not have kidnapped two children, for whatever reason. I'll tell you what's possible, though. If the kids appeared to be stranded at the airport, she is idiotic enough to offer to drive them home and then to get everyone lost in the process. She's very helpful and impulsive. She never seems to think about consequences— like being sued for driving away with someone else's children without authorization. She's also one of these people who believes that if she has a map she can find her way anywhere—and that means that she's always getting lost. But a kidnapper! That's just nowhere near possible."

"What about her boyfriend?"

"Ah—him." Kate looked intently into the lazy brown eyes flecked with gold that had been assessing her all this time. "Well, I'd be prepared to believe almost anything about him."

"Why is that, Ms. Grosvenor?" She had caught his attention at last. He leaned forward, and a lock of his glossy dark hair fell onto his forehead.

"Because he's a cop, that's why," she said, in a very con-spiratorial voice. "Harriet tried to tell me he was intelli-gent, and enlightened, and thoughtful, and all that crap, but you know what cops are like."

"Very funny," he said coldly, leaning back again.

"I'm sorry," she said, with a small grin. "It was a cheap shot. But I don't think a photographer is any more likely to kidnap two children than a police officer is. And she isn't crazy. If she wants kids, all she has to do is marry the guy and have some. He's willing, and she's thinking of it. We had a long talk about it."

"Did she bring up the topic of children?"

"No. I did. It's a subject that I've been considering very hard for the past few months—ever since I almost got killed. And so I forced it into the conversation."

"Is he a Canadian, too?"

"As far as I know. He's a cop in Toronto, where she lives."

"With the city police force?"

"Who knows? I think he's in the homicide division, or branch or whatever they call it there—but I'm not posi-tive—and his name is John. I'm sure of that."

"That's it? John? No last name?"

"Dammit," said Kate, "how am I supposed to know?" She pushed her hair off her face with an irritated gesture and turned to look out the window. "How do you put this gracefully? That I've been so sick and miserable lately, that I spent so much time while Harriet was staying with me moaning about my own problems," she said finally, "that I hardly noticed anything she said? The only reason I remember he's a cop is because we had a fight about it. It's awful, but it's true."

"But you know her name."

"Of course I know her name. I don't go around inviting strangers to stay with me. It's Harriet Jeffries. Here, I've even got her address somewhere, and her phone number." She reached into the canvas bag and pulled out a thick black book with a leather cover. "My life," she explained. "It used to have all my appointments in it, when I was working. And it has all my contacts—that way, no matter where I am, I can get onto people." As she spoke, she was flipping pages. "Here. Copy it down. And it's probably his address, too, since they seem to be living together."

"What was she doing in a van with Missouri plates?"

"She flew to Kansas City and rented the van. She was taking pictures there and in Kansas, for some project on industrial architecture, and needed a van because she carries a lot of equipment. When she got to the Colorado border she kept on going to visit me in Denver."

"I'd better call all this in," said Rodriguez.

"Be my guest," said Kate. "The phone's right there." As she pointed at it she could feel her hands trembling. She pulled them back, crossed her arms protectively over her chest, and tucked her hands under her arms. The headache, which should have been receding by now, was growing in intensity, to explosive proportions.

But instead of telephoning, Rodriguez continued to watch her with observant eyes. "Do you always sleep with a bottle of Scotch beside your bed?" he said at last.

"Yes," said Kate. "I find it comforting. All right? Or is there some law against it?"

"No—no law against it." He got up and walked over to the small cabinet beside the bed. He picked up the round plastic container and read the label. Slowly and carefully, as if he couldn't believe what it said. "How long have you been taking these things?"

"Since I got out of the hospital," said Kate.

"And when was that?"

"Not that long ago," she said. He was towering over her by now, the pills held accusingly in his hand. "All right. It was three—well, almost four months ago. And I think I'll take a couple now, if you don't mind. My shoulder hurts."

"I'll bet it does. And your head. Does that hurt, too?"

She didn't answer.

"And your stomach? And damn near everywhere else in your body? Except maybe for your big toe? Or does even that hurt?"

Tears of anger and self-pity welled up in her eyes. Furious, she turned her head away.

"You know what you are, lady? You're an addict. You are addicted to these goddamn things. Do you know what you're suffering from? Withdrawal. Not pain from a glamorous gunshot wound, but withdrawal. Just like any crack addict rolling around in the alley. And do you know where you're going to be very soon? Dead. Because I assume that when life gets a little too much for you, every few hours, you wash down a couple of these damn things with a large Scotch, don't you? And every day it's going to take less and less to bring you to that edge, and one day your hand will slip a little, and you'll pour too much Scotch into that glass and you'll be dead." His face had turned pale with fury as he talked. "Who in hell prescribed this many tablets for you?"

"My doctor," said Kate. The fight was draining out of her.

"Your doctor. Your own doctor. When did you last take any?"

"Last night," she said. "Before I went to bed."

"When did you last eat?"

"This morning. I had breakfast." She was beginning to hate this man. "What right do you—"

"I don't believe you. What did you have for breakfast?"

"Coffee and a cherry Danish," she said. Just thinking about it made her feel queasy.

He tucked her pills into his breast pocket, buttoned the flap, and reached down into the waste basket. He opened up the paper bag and inspected its contents. "Evidence," he said. "One Danish, slightly nibbled at. That's not eating. Unless you're a mouse. You eat yesterday?"

"Of course I ate yesterday," she said.

"When? What?"

There was a very long pause. "I don't feel very well," said Kate. "I'm cold." She pushed herself to her feet, and her head swam with dizziness.

"Of course you are," said Rodriguez. Without another word he picked her up and placed her carefully on the bed. He opened a cupboard on the other side of the room, pulled out a brightly patterned blanket, and tucked it around her. Then he disappeared into the bathroom with the Scotch bottle. With a combination of resignation and terror, Kate listened to the gurgle of one large bottle of Teacher's going down the drain. She closed her eyes, and in spite of the crashing inside her skull, drifted off into a light sleep. A voice reached her from far away. "I'll just call in."

Karen Johnson told her story in short gasps, seated on a chunky suitcase, drinking a plastic cup of water in small mouthfuls, as directed. Harriet knelt in front of her with Mrs. Green's first-aid kit, cleaning off her feet with wet-wipes, and applying Band-Aids over the cuts and broken blisters. "I have socks and sneakers in the bus," she said, when Harriet had finished. "I'll be fine if we have to walk."

The session was interrupted by another shout from the

road up the mountain. Striding along in chinos and long-sleeved shirt, with a hat tied on her head by a flowery scarf, and wearing running shoes, was Teresa Suarez. She had a small backpack and a sweatshirt tied around her waist.

"Where have you been?" asked Mrs. Green.

"Exploring," said Teresa. "I was hoping to find signs of civilization closer than twenty miles if I went that way."

"And did you?" asked John.

"There's nothing in that direction for better than ten miles, except mountain and mesa, and then the valley. I followed the road thinking it might curve back toward Santa Fe," she said, as soon as she settled down in the group. "I did run into people, by the way. During the night. I came by while they were getting a plane ready to take off from the mesa. Then just as I raised my arms to hail the pilot, reason intervened." She tapped her forehead. "I mean who has a little landing field out in the middle of nowhere? And why? I figured these people were not into rescuing stranded travelers. Maybe they were the good guys, but I didn't want to find out the hard way. If I did wrong, I'm sorry, but I've developed a powerful aversion to being shot at." She stopped in her narrative to swallow, and then take off her hat and mop the sweat from her face.

"We have water," said Harriet, handing her a cup. "Lots. Go ahead."

"Thanks. So do I," said Teresa, but drinking anyway. "That's why I thought I'd have a go at contacting the rest of the world. I had water and some dried fruit and nuts and a flashlight, so I figured I was as well equipped as anyone. As soon as the Brothers Karamazov crept away in the night, I gathered up my hiking gear and headed out."

"Did you see anything else?" asked John, persistently.

"Just what the bear saw. The other side of the mountain.

The road stops being a road at the point where it branches into the mesa. I would imagine that some enterprising soul has turned a logging or hunting or something trail into access for a tiny landing field—the purpose of a completely hidden landing field in the middle of nowhere is another question. Anyway, past the mesa, the trail gets too narrow for a vehicle. I followed it for another hour, but it didn't really go anywhere. At the rate I was walking, and considering how rough the terrain was, that hour probably represented an additional two and a half to three miles. I found a small stream, and so I drank the water I'd brought with me and filled my canteen. I have purifying tablets with me as well," she added. "I went on a bit, in case the stream was a harbinger of greater things to come—but no. I didn't see anything, and I didn't hear anything either. Except woodsy-type sounds—you know, birds and things. So I turned around and came back." She paused. "And that's my report. It's faster and easier to go back the way we came." She stood up and stretched. "I must get some stuff out of my travel bag."

"What's wrong with the van?" she said quietly, drifting over to John. "I expected everyone to be long gone by the time I got back."

"Tires are flat," said Sanders, turning to accompany her to the bus.

"Is that all?"

"I know. But if we cram everyone in it, the tires will disintegrate at once, I think. And that means we'd soon be without functioning brakes or steering. Also we have to back out of here for God knows how many miles before we can turn around, assuming we can get out of that pothole and on our way—backward—without tumbling into the canyon."

"Then don't take everyone."

"I thought of that, of course. But I'd assumed that someone would have stumbled across us by now, and I didn't
want to break up the group any more than it was already.
They have to be looking for us."

There was a thump at the steps of the bus and Jennifer
Nicholls appeared. "It's Diana," she said, apparently too
preoccupied to notice the return of Teresa Suarez. "She's
much worse. I don't think she's going to be able to last
many more hours without access to intravenous. Isn't there
something we can do?"

"Come over here," said John, nodding in the direction
of the rest of the passengers. Reluctantly, glancing back at
the bus, torn between conflicting imperatives, Jennifer
walked away from her responsibility and over to the group.
They had shifted their positions from the sun to the shade
as the day warmed up, and she shivered. The dry wind was
still blowing. It was too hot in the sun; too cold out of it.
Everyone looked red-eyed and weary and discouraged, as
if the promises of daylight had been broken, and hope was
drifting away.

"Explain your problem," said John.

Jennifer did, as briefly as she could. She looked desperately tired and acutely miserable.

"There is a solution," said John. "As many of you know,
the van is drivable after a fashion even though its tires are
gone. It'll kill the wheels and probably wreck the transmission, but not all at once. It would get us close to help, I
think, before going down on its knees."

"Backing out?" asked Rick Kelleher. "It was the first
thing that occurred to me, too, but it seemed a bit tricky,
especially for the first half-mile or so."

"I didn't even suggest it," said John, "because I honestly

believe that if we pile every one of us in it and try to drive away, no one could steer it down to a spot where we can turn it around."

"The worst problem is going to be getting it out of the pothole," said Kelleher.

"Without going over the side," added Harriet. "Look—if I can get positioned in a somewhat safer location before we try to load people on, then we can take some out, can't we?"

"You're not doing it," said John flatly.

"Why not? I weigh a lot less than you do, I'm not unreasonably nervous about heights, and I'm used to driving that cow."

"Not without tires, you aren't."

"So who else has taken lessons on vans without tires? Anyone else doing it is figuring out for the first time how loose the steering is on that damn thing. I know. I've driven it over a thousand miles."

"She has a point there," said Kelleher.

"Maybe we could winch it back—" John started.

"Sure we could. If we had a winch, and a tow truck—or maybe even just a rope. Anybody got a rope?" There was silence. "There you are. I'm driving it back." Harriet walked over to look at the situation more closely. The pothole that the front right tire sat in was just as deep as it had looked at first light, but its edges were considerably softer and less defined than she feared. The front left tire was entirely too close to the edge of the cliff; if she had stopped three inches farther on last night, they might have gone over. That was not something to think about. But no one could push them from the front of the van without the risk of losing his footing and going over. The only cheerful note was that both rear wheels seemed to be on relatively solid surfaces.

"Front- or rear-wheel drive?" said a voice beside her. She jumped. It was Rick Kelleher again.

"Basically rear, with automatic four-wheel drive on top," said Harriet. "It's worked pretty well so far, but I haven't really put it through any vicious tests yet."

"Then at least you have a chance of getting out of here."

"Of course I do. But first of all I think we should divide up the food and water," she said loudly. "In case it takes longer than we thought. How much is there in the bus?"

That, at least, had the effect of removing everyone's attention from her tires. Karen shouldered her way past the instant experts, and with a screwdriver in hand, undid a plate that revealed an upended two gallon jug, almost empty. "It's one of the few things they managed to teach me," she said. "How to change the water jugs." She swung out the jug and handed it to John. "Go fill it."

Harriet removed a box of crackers and six apples from the stores in the van, looked around for someplace to put them, and then impatiently stuffed them into the pockets of her many-pocketed photographic jacket, designed to hold four by five film holders, extra batteries, small cameras, spare lenses, and all the rest of the awkward and fragile tools of her trade. She hauled out the cooler and the bag of groceries and carried them back to the group by the bus.

John filled the jug from their container and handed it over to Rick Kelleher. "Now," he said, turning to Harriet, "what you should do is—"

"Listen to me, my love," said Harriet. "If you start giving me helpful advice and telling me to be careful, I will get nervous. And if I'm nervous, my hands will sweat and my arm muscles might jerk. Don't anyone say anything. Just go back to the bus and pretend nothing is happening." She touched her fingers to his lips and climbed up into the van, pulling her keys out of her pocket as she went.

Harriet carefully blanked everything out of her mind but the task ahead. It couldn't be simpler. The wheels were almost straight, turned very slightly to the right. She was going to have to get the engine going, the wheels straightened out, and then very gently reverse straight back. She wished the old cow had a standard transmission. She trusted her feet manipulating clutch and gas pedal to ease them delicately into reverse far more than she trusted the overeager engagement of the automatic transmission. But this is not a difficult situation, Harriet, she said to herself. You are merely backing your way out of a soft pothole, and your rear wheels are on firm ground. She started the engine; it had a solid, reliable feel, thank God, and so far had shown no signs of temperament. She straightened the wheels a hair, and had to force herself not to call John over to ask if they were straight. Don't be stupid, Harriet. Having John here would be a disaster. The wheels are straight. She moved the lever to reverse and, as she slid her right foot from brake to accelerator, gently set her left foot on the brake. The engine gave its usual roar and leap. A shrill voice screamed, "For God's sake, watch it," her arms jerked, and a chunk of earth pitched itself into the canyon.

McDowell waited until after lunch before tackling Charlie Broca again. Actually it was Mrs. Broca, with her talk of harassment and brutality as the day wore on, that he was building up the courage to tackle. But since Bert Samson had no relatives or friends they'd been able to trace—still no one knew about his pal Norbert from the Albuquerque detachment—Charlie Broca was the only local person he could think of to identify the body.

If anything, Charlie looked worse the second time they woke him up. His color and frame of mind weren't improved when he found out what they wanted him for. "Why don't you get one of his pals to do this?" he grumbled. He seemed to have forgotten his remorse of that morning.

"Okay. Who are they? Give the name and address of one close friend and we'll go get him."

Broca gave him a bleary-eyed look. "I don't know. He must have had some pals."

"Maybe he did, but we don't know who they are. We know who you are, though, Broca, and you owe us one."

"How come? What did you ever do for me?"

"We didn't book you last night, that's what. For generally screwing up an important investigation."

Charlie walked very carefully out to McDowell's car, like a man carrying a plate piled up with raw eggs on his head.

He walked even more carefully into the icy cold room and glanced quickly at the bloodless face in front of him. Then he raced outside, calling as he went, "Yeah, that's Bert all right. It's Bert."

"Thanks, Charlie," said McDowell, following him out. He felt a small surge of remorse for dragging him down, but it was quickly suppressed. "Go on home and sleep it off. You'll feel better tomorrow."

"Yeah? That's when my wife's going to go after me. Tomorrow."

Kate woke up, drenched in sweat, from a hideous nightmare in which Harriet was screaming at her for help, and she was too rubber-legged to move a step to protect her. "Hey there, just a minute, now," a strange male voice was saying. "You're okay. Bad dreams?"

She opened her eyes and focused on a man in uniform, sitting beside the bed. What in hell have I done? she wondered. And then memory flooded back in. "Sergeant Rodriguez."

"Got it."

"What are you doing here?"

"We're waiting for a telephone call from your friend. If she calls anyone, it's likely to be you, isn't it?"

"I don't know," said Kate, aware of little beyond her throbbing head, thick tongue, and terrible thirst. She closed her eyes again, and felt hands setting an icy cold cloth on her forehead. The cold burned into her flesh, but it slowed the beat and intensity of her headache. She heard footsteps move back and forth around the room.

"Okay, princess, sit up." She blinked and pulled away the cloth, before struggling to a sitting position. "Eat this."

Sergeant Rodriguez was holding a large bowl of something hot and savory-smelling almost under her nose. "What's that?" she asked suspiciously.

"Chili," he said. "Real chili, like the kind my mother makes. Not the crap you get in the tourist restaurants. It's soup, almost, and very hot."

"I can't eat that," she said, looking at the enormous bowl in front of her. "It would finish my stomach forever."

"No, it won't. It'll make you feel better. A lot better. Scientifically proven in cases like yours. And if you don't take this spoon and start eating right now, I'll feed you. Forcibly."

The first mouthful set her eyes watering and her nose dripping. Sergeant Rodriguez handed her a clean handkerchief. "Come on," he said, "keep going."

*   *   *

The screech of the warning blended into the sound of the engine, distracting and infuriating Harriet. The steering wheel jumped crazily in her hands for a second, but rage steadied her nerves and nothing affected the gentle increase in speed of the wheels turning in their flapping cases of rubber. The rear wheels caught, somehow, on something and pulled back, more or less steadily; the front end bounced up out of the hole, and the edge of the precipice they were sitting on broke off and fell into the canyon. Harriet moved the van back about three feet more, and straightened it until it sat parallel to the inside edge of the road. She stopped.

John was beside her in an instant. "Fabulous," he said. "I knew you could do it."

"The hell you did," she said, breathless with tension, and trying to smile. "Who was the bastard who yelled at me? I could have done without that."

"I don't know," said John, "except that it wasn't me. It wasn't the kids—they were not looking by staring into my belt buckle. I would have known if it had been one of them."

"Someone was trying to get rid of me," said Harriet.

"Or the van. Or both."

"Let's get a move on," she said. "Who are we taking?"

"Diana Morris and Jennifer, of course. The two of us, and when I pointed out to the twins that they would be more comfortable waiting at the bus for rescue they went a bit crazy. They're terrified of being left here—and I'm not sure why."

"Maybe they don't want to be separated from the only

people they know in the group," said Harriet. "Well—they can't weigh that much."

"As a percentage of the total weight of that thing, they're a negligible factor. Shall we take them?"

"Sure."

And once more John and Rick Kelleher were carrying the almost inert body of Diana Morris through the bus. It was a matter of less than a minute to stretch her out in the back of the van with a pillow behind her head and a blanket around her. Jennifer settled herself in back beside her, the twins buckled themselves into the backseat, and with an imperious gesture, Harriet waved John in and began the slow and painful business of backing her way down the hill.

Comfort was not one of the van's major design features, and on this track, riding on metal wheels, it was a horror. Harriet drove with her body twisted like a vine, staring through the windows in the rear doors. She concentrated on keeping the vehicle as steady as possible, trying to ignore her helpless passengers as much as she could. John craned his neck out his window, looking for a turning point. There weren't any. It seemed incredible that they— and the bus—had driven up this narrow, treacherous road in the pitch blackness of the night before. At last he brought his head in sharply. "There's a place. Start—turning—*now*."

And gently, very gently, she turned the vehicle in, stopped, and pulled it out onto the road facing down the hill at last. "Why don't we stop and get out for a minute," said Harriet. Her hands and feet were trembling with relief. "And I wouldn't mind changing drivers for a while, if you don't object," she added. "This is not my idea of fun."

The children were out of the van before she had finished

speaking, taking great gulps of air. Harriet walked around to the rear and opened the door. "How are you two doing back here?"

Jennifer looked up at her with tears running down her cheeks. "She's dead," she said flatly. "There was nothing I could do." She had pulled the blanket up over the woman's face, and wrapped it tightly around her.

"What? She can't be," said Harriet. "I can't believe it. Are you sure? Goddammit. It really isn't fair. You'd think someone was out to get us." She turned to beckon urgently to John. "She's dead," she whispered. "After all this."

"On a purely practical side," said Jennifer, much more composedly, "I think we should put her body out here by the side of the road. We can mark the place, and it can be picked up later. It will lighten the strain on the van and maybe it will get us all the way down to a major road. We don't want to have to walk any farther than necessary, do we? We need to get the others out, too."

"It seems heartless—but I suppose you're right. It won't matter to her now, will it?" said Harriet.

"Inspector," said Jennifer, "if you could just take her feet, I'll carry her head. Maybe you could go ahead and find us a flat place to lay her down on." As she spoke, she half-stood, grasping the upper part of Diana Morris's inert form in her thin but strong arms. John had no choice but to pick up the feet and begin to back away.

They laid her between two pine trees, a spot distinctive enough to mark and describe. "Should we cover her with stones?" asked Harriet, who suddenly had a vision of rapacious animals coming across the body.

Jennifer shuddered and went white. "That would take forever," she said. "And I'm not happy about Mrs. Green's condition. She's not up to stresses of this kind. Maybe you could make a little cairn here at the beginning of the trees, could you? I have to duck into the bushes—I've been so caught up in looking after her—"

"Go on. Duck," said Harriet, amused at this blunt woman's sudden embarrassment. "We'll find some rocks."

As soon as she was out of sight, Harriet clamped her hand over John's wrist. "What's that?" she said. And clearly, from the direction of the corpse, came a scrabbling sound. "My God," said Harriet, "it's something after her already."

But when they reached the place between the two pine trees, instead of an animal, they saw a very white hand reach up from the blanket and try to pull it away from her face. "Jesus," said John. "She's alive. Get that thing off her face."

As he was speaking, the familiar initial roar of an engine surged through the silence. He ran through the trees just in time to see the van wobbling off down the road.

CHAPTER 9

Whether it was because the chili itself had magical properties, or Rodriguez's glare had been sufficient to quell her rebellious stomach, Kate consumed it.

"How do you feel? Better?"

"That's overstating it a bit," she said. "Less awful, maybe. It would help if I had something for my headache," she said, trying very hard to sound dignified.

Rodriguez pulled a chair up to the bed, flipped it around, and straddled it, looking intensely at her as he leaned on the back rungs. "Do you know why you get those headaches?"

"Yes, dammit," said Kate. She set the bowl on the bedside table to lessen the temptation to smash it over his head. "I drink too much Scotch. Does that make you happy, you puritanical prig?"

"I'd be willing to bet it's from these things," he said, patting his breast pocket. "You get a hangover from the pills—or from the pills and the Scotch together—and then you take more pills to get rid of it, and on and on and on."

"You a doctor or something? Or just psychic?"

"No. It happened to my cousin. She damn near died from too many painkillers and booze and went through minor hell getting off them."

"Define minor hell," said Kate.

He shrugged. "You'd have to ask her. As I remember, it amounted to two-three weeks of misery."

"Sounds wonderful."

"For chrissake, anyone who can work in a war zone is capable of getting herself off these things. Do what my cousin did. Go for walks, do puzzles, take naps." Rodriguez's little pep talk was interrupted by the arrival of another car outside the motel unit. He pulled aside the curtains he had drawn while Kate was sleeping. The clear, bright light poured into the room. "Damn," he muttered. "It looks like someone for me. Excuse me a minute."

"You can tell him what he can do with his new assignment," said Rodriguez. "I've been off duty for hours now, if you want to get technical. If I feel like sitting in there and talking to someone—"

"Come on, Rodriguez. Word from on high. You're to get down to the drop-off point and coordinate the search for the two children."

"That is the stupidest thing I've ever heard. You know damned well those kids never got anywhere near that road. What are they talking about?"

"They're talking about grieving parents who are also taxpayers, and who expect a show of doing something to find their kids, that's what."

"And I'm supposed to work a double shift as a PR gesture? Who's going to keep an eye on her?"

"The locals are pitching in," he replied vaguely. "Don't worry."

*   *   *

"I'm off to hunt for the kids," said Rodriguez, looking down at Kate. He had an odd expression on his face. "Take care of yourself. Go out for dinner, and—"

"Yeah. Eat chili and stay off the sauce. I'll think about it."

It was a relief to have the motel room to herself at last, she thought, without her enormous watchdog in it, censoring every word and action. Except that it also felt very empty. Rodriguez had certainly irritated her; at the same time, he enlivened her tremendously. And made her think of something besides how sorry for herself she was. It was those eyes, she decided. Those brown and gold eyes. It was satisfactory to know that someone's brown and gold eyes could make her feel twitches and warm burning sensations somewhere below her arm and shoulder. Oh, Kate, you are too vulnerable to be left alone in a room with a man with soulful eyes.

Her relatively cheerful reflections were broken into by a heavy knock on the door. "Back already?" she called out, and forgetting all Rodriguez's injunctions to be careful, yanked the door wide open.

But no tall man in a trooper's uniform with brown and gold eyes lounged in the doorway. It was a large, unsmiling gorilla in a chauffeur's uniform who stood on the other side. "Ms. Kate Grosvenor?"

Kate's first impulse was to deny the charge, but that seemed foolish. He had obviously been told she was staying in this motel room. "I'm Ms. Grosvenor," she said, eyeing the man suspiciously, and wondering if her temporary landlord would hear her if she screamed.

"Mr. Carl Deever wants to see you, Miss Grosvenor," he said abruptly. "It's important. He said for me to tell you it was about your friend, Miss Jeffries."

"What about her?" asked Kate, narrowing the door opening as much as possible and backing away slightly.

"Mr. Deever said that he has some information that you might find helpful," he answered in a flat voice. "He didn't say what it was, only that he wanted me to drive you to the ranch. So if you'll just get in the car. It won't take long."

Just beyond him, she could see an enormous black limousine, purring quietly in the circular drive. "Right now?" asked Kate.

"As soon as possible. Mr. Deever's got to get back to the city soon. He told me I was supposed to bring you back here after." A slight smile creased his impassive countenance.

"Just a minute," said Kate. "I'll get my purse." She slammed the door shut in the chauffeur's face and looked around her. By the time she had walked the few feet into the room, he was staring in the window that Rodriguez had left open, watching her. She grabbed the four dirty glasses from the table, holding them from the top in one hand—a hangover from waitressing in cheap and noisy restaurants when she was a student—and with the other hand swept up the stub of a pencil sitting beside the phone. She whisked them all into the bathroom, locked the door, pulled out a paper tissue, and scribbled, "4:20. A large chauffeur belonging to Carl Deever has just arrived to take me to his (Deever's) ranch. He has news of Harriet, he says. I'm going. Kate."

"I may be rash," she muttered, "but I do like to leave myself covered." She knew about Carl Deever.

"She's gone," said Harriet, rather needlessly. She had followed John back to the edge of the wooded area in time to see the van lurch and wobble its way down the mountain road. "Jennifer. Of all people."

"We'd better get back to Ms. Morris," said John.

Diana Morris lay shivering, still wrapped in her cocoon of blanket, but now with her face uncovered. Her eyelids fluttered open, she made an enormous effort to focus and then they fluttered shut again.

"She doesn't look very comfortable there," said Harriet.

"I don't suppose she is," said John. "I hadn't realized before that it mattered. I just put her down where that bitch said she should go. Just a minute." He raised up her shoulders and freed her from between the two trees. Then he picked her up gently, carried her to the edge of the woods, and laid her on a fairly level and rock-free surface. He reached down and pushed up her eyelids. "Look at that, Harriet."

"Look at what?" said Harriet, who was scanning the area for the children.

"Her eyes."

"What about them?" Harriet yanked herself back to the scene and leaned over the unconscious woman. "I see what you mean," she said, looking at those fixed, unchanging tiny pupils. "Drugged?" Another thought bounced into her head. "But that's impossible. There wasn't anything on that bus to drug someone with," Harriet added. "That was one of the problems—she was in terrible pain. Remember?"

"Only at the very beginning," said John. "When did we last hear a sound out of her?"

"Where did the drugs come from?"

"How about our handy, well-equipped nurse, who has left us all to die of thirst and exposure in order to save her own little hide?"

"What do we do? Is it safe to let her just sleep it off?"

Harriet suddenly remembered old movies, where drugged heroines were walked up and down, mumbling and protesting, being fed gallons of hot coffee, until they smiled and came back to life. "Or does that mean she's going into a coma?"

"For chrissake, Harriet, I have no idea," said John. "She looks pretty far under to me, but I'd hate to make a guess, even. I'm not an expert on overdoses. All they taught me was when to yell for help. What we really need is—"

"Hot coffee," said Harriet. "You saw the same movies I did."

"We don't have any hot coffee," said John irritably. "But weren't the kids drinking Coke?"

"Of course," said Harriet. "I had some in the cooler and there was some on the bus. I think they grabbed all they could carry."

"Where are they?" asked John, looking around. "Stuart? Caroline?" he called. Their names echoed across the valley and bounced back and back and back.

"Hey," cried a high-pitched voice from above their heads. "Up here."

Two heads and waving arms appeared from behind a rock far above them. "Come down," called Harriet.

The heads and arms disappeared. There was a considerable pause, marked by occasional thumps as bits of the landscape disintegrated, and then the children appeared around another outcrop of rock.

"Do you have any Coke left?" asked Harriet. "Ms. Morris was given more painkillers than she was supposed to take and it's really important to give her something to wake her up."

"Just a sec." And from places on their persons, the children produced four cans. "You can have them all," said Caroline. "There's other stuff to drink."

"Where have you kids been?" asked Harriet.

"Following the road from the rocks up there. It's a lot harder, but not nearly as far to go. We were watching up there," said the girl, pointing to an outcrop of rock to their left, "when Jennifer got in the van and drove away."

"By the time we realized what she was doing, it was too late to say anything," said Stuart. "We would have stopped her if we could." He slid away behind the rock again before anyone could stop him.

"Don't worry. We'll be all right, even without the van," said John, as much to himself as to the others. "Once we get Ms. Morris on her feet, so to speak, we'll be fine. Sugar and caffeine are what we need, and that's what we've got."

"But we can't walk her up and down the road. Not in her state," objected Harriet.

"No—but we can try to wake her up."

"Did you know," said Stuart, who appeared again, silent and ghostlike from between two trees, "that a man has been following us?"

"Following us? Don't be silly. How could there be?" said Harriet. "We're miles from anywhere. And if there were someone trying to follow us he'd have to have a car or a motorcycle—something with an engine—and we would have heard it. Have you heard anything?"

"No," said Stuart. "But I've seen him, twice, so far. He's been on foot. And he hides whenever he notices someone."

"Is he someone from the bus?"

Stuart shook his head. "I don't know. He could be. Maybe."

The ride to Mr. Deever's ranch was uneventful and silent. The chauffeur reacted to Kate's attempts at conversation by closing the window between them. She settled back to memorize the route.

The ranch screamed obscene amounts of money to Kate. It had been built in fake pueblo style, with touches of someone's idea of how the rich ought to live. Three sleek horses cropped the grass that lay on either side of the long drive up to the house; Kate shuddered to think how much irrigation water must have gone into developing and maintaining the deep green of their pasturage. The house was adobe, and sprawled low over the ground, except for a high tower to the left of the entrance. As they approached, Kate realized that its lack of height was an illusion springing from its size; it was actually U-shaped and two stories high. Thick adobe walls, pierced by wide, heavy iron gates, joined its two wings to form a central courtyard. Ornate wrought-iron grilles covered every window on the first and second floors. Only the narrow slits that formed the attic windows in the tower had been left unprotected. To Kate, it looked uncomfortably like a prison with a guard's tower in one corner, overlooking the exercise yard. The chauffeur pulled up in front of the gates, stalked around the car, and opened the door for her. "We're here," he said.

Unlocking the gates was a major production, accompanied by much screeching and grinding of metal parts and, no doubt, silent curses on the part of the chauffeur. No unheralded visitors for Mr. Deever, reflected Kate. She slipped through the small opening he created for her and waited while he went through the business of locking them again. The courtyard, she admitted grudgingly to herself, indicated that Mr. Deever either had some taste or a good designer. There was no intrusive grillework on these windows. There were none of the major horrors that a pleasant enclosed space outdoors seems to evoke in people who can afford to own them. A simple fountain made up of three concentric bronze dishes played water very delicately into a lily pond on one side of the walk; on the other side, several orange trees and some shrubs Kate didn't recognize took advantage of the sheltered location. Local gravel covered the ground; an arbor provided shade near the fountain. In the lily pond, a fish surfaced and snapped at some edible morsel. Kate shivered, in spite of her warm sweatshirt and jeans. The sun was getting low in the sky and cold air tumbled down from the mountains in the near distance. The key clanged in the gate and she followed the chauffeur to the massive, dark-stained, beautifully carved door. It was not new. Either her host had pillaged a monastery for it to give his fake adobe hacienda an air of authenticity, or the adobe hacienda was genuine. It was a sobering thought.

The door was opened by a dark-haired, slightly overweight man in his forties, dressed in jeans, boots, and a plaid shirt. Whatever effect he had been trying for when he put his clothes on, what he achieved was more stockbroker than stock handler. Shifty stockbroker. "Miss Grosvenor?" he said. His lips pulled tight in a smile and his eyes narrowed unpleasantly as he spoke. "I'm Carl Deever. Forgive me for dragging you out like this. Do come in." The floors were tiled and beautiful, and his boots clattered unbearably sharply in the enormous hall. It rose to the full height of the building, and contained almost nothing beyond a broad staircase that split halfway up and led to rooms off a gallery. High windows directly opposite her let in the angry red of the setting sun; it bounced off the white walls and was consumed by the dark woodwork. He led her sharply to the left and through a low and narrow door into a smallish room. He motioned her to sit. She must be at the bottom of the tower, she decided. On the desk in the corner a monitor flickered silently as data scrolled by. Market results. A prop or had he turned himself into a captain of finance? "Ginger will drive you back to your motel as soon as we've had a chance to talk. In time for any plans you may have had for the evening."

Plans, thought Kate. Sure, and then with a slight jolt of recognition realized that he knew perfectly well that she had had no plans. "What news do you have of my friend?" she said abruptly.

"May I get you a drink?" he asked, and once more his eyes narrowed.

"No, thank you," she said. "I—" No explanations, Kate, she told herself. Every extra word lays your weaknesses open wider. And he knows them already. The unfinished sentence sat between them. She crossed her legs and smiled.

"Are you sure?" he said. "It must have been a long and dusty drive out here." With great deliberation, he opened a small cabinet in the wall, took out a bottle of Teacher's, and poured a couple of fingers from it into a heavy crystal glass. He opened the refrigerated cabinet below and took out ice and a jug of water, added both, and set the glass down beside her.

"Hardly," said Kate. "That limousine of yours is more climate and pressure controlled than a space shuttle. The drive couldn't have been more comfortable." Her mouth was dry, her lips were cracking, and her throat constricted from thirst. One mouthful—no. Not a mouthful. "Now—about Miss Jeffries. I came out here because I understood that you had some information about her. If you do, I would appreciate hearing it. I'm very concerned about her.

And of course," she added primly, "the police are also very interested in finding out where she is." Kate's first shot, over his head and to the right.

"Well, isn't that the strangest thing," said Deever, his voice sweet as poisoned candy. "I believe there's been a misunderstanding. I'm the one who's looking for information, Miss Grosvenor." He smiled. "You're the one who's going to supply it." Counter shot.

Instead of flinching, Kate settled back and gave him her best casual, disengaged look. The confident look that had once succeeded in slipping her out of the hands of an enthusiastic little group of youthful terrorists in the Middle East. "Information?" she said. "But that's the whole point. I don't have any information. That's why I'm here. Otherwise, I have other things to do. Lots of them."

Mr. Deever was not impressed. There was anger behind the dull slits of his eyes. Genuine anger. "You have lots of information, Miss Grosvenor. Why—you know the color, make, and model of your friend's vehicle. You told all these things to the police, and they found them particularly interesting. So interesting that they told me. You just might want to remember that. I have some very good friends among those gentlemen in the local and state police forces. And more good friends all the way up to various governors' mansions. But we won't worry about things like that right now. You see, you know where she was going and why. You let the police know some of this when you were talking to them and so I guess you must know why she was interested in a tour group that I also happen to be interested in."

"A tour group? I can't imagine what interest Harriet would have in a tour group. She's not a tour group kind of person at all. She hates organized vacations." Kate's hand automatically reached over to the low table beside her chair for the glass. She snatched it away again.

"Don't waste my time, Miss Grosvenor." His voice was becoming harder, and more clipped. A telephone rang with a sharp, nasty sound. Deever swore, scooped it up from the desk, and barked into it. "I'll be with you in a moment, Miss Grosvenor," he said. "Make yourself at home." And Carl Deever left, slamming the little door behind him. Kate heard the faint and unmistakable sound of a key turning in a lock.

She walked quietly over to the door and tried it. "Damn," she murmured to herself, and began to pace carefully around the small room. There was another door on the opposite side of the room; from its configuration it probably led into a closet, or perhaps a tiny bathroom. It, too, was locked. She pulled aside one set of heavy draperies and looked out at the lush green paddock and an evening sky through barred windows. One of the horses paused in the serious business of grazing, raised his head, and gave her a pitying look in her tiny prison. She shivered and began muttering to herself, "I am perfectly calm," over and over again. Each time she passed her chair, she looked at the drink waiting there for her. He's done this on purpose, she thought. The slimy bastard. And one of them is probably watching through a peephole or with a hidden camera to see how I react. Whether true or not, the thought steadied her more than a dozen drinks would have. She ambled over to the other window and pulled back those draperies.

This gave her a view through unbarred windows that overlooked the courtyard. The fountain splashing reminded her of how thirsty she was; the trees and shrubs, protected as they were by enclosing walls, still shivered in the evening breeze, and reminded her how cold and miserable she felt. But her eye soon picked out her host, half-hidden by the fountain. He was facing her, talking to a man who towered over him. With a very delicate touch, she turned the catch of the casement window and pushed it open an imperceptible amount. The soft indistinguishable murmur turned into a clear, well-differentiated conversation between two very angry men.

"I don't give a fuck whether she's safe or not. She could be hanging by her hair out a tenth-story window for all I care. I—want—to—know—where—she—is." He spoke the words very slowly, very carefully, and with equal emphasis on each one. "Right now. Where in hell is the fucking bitch, Rocco?"

"Don't call me that."

"Listen, Rocco, the money I pay you, I'll call you Mary or Daisy if I feel like it, understand? Where is my wife, Rocco?"

"Where's my money, Carlos?"

"You'll get your money when I find out where my wife is. Listen, shithead, you can't keep this up forever. The state isn't that big, and I'll find her sooner or later. Probably sooner. And when we do, you know what's going to happen, don't you?"

"Listen to me, Carlos. You offered me one million to execute the commission without any repercussions. That was the deal. I cover my own expenses. I accepted it and I'm not bitching about the terms. But I've had expenses. I hired people and they wanted cash up front. I spent my own money, Carlos. To do you a favor. All I want is a down payment on what you owe me, or I don't play any longer. Like, maybe, seven-fifty. And don't start thinking you can get rid of me and finish it off on your own. You know you can't do that. Just give me my money and let me run this my own way."

"Look, Rocco—"

Suddenly Kate sneezed. By the time they had located the direction of the sound, the window was closed and the curtains were back in their accustomed place. When the key turned in the lock and Deever stormed in, she was standing on the other side of the room, staring with fascination at Deever's book collection. He paid no attention to her. He had left the door open, but his companion was standing in it, blocking any exit. She gave him a quick glance, but he was just a black blob against the darkness of the hall. She turned her attention back to Deever, who went around the desk, opened a section of wood paneling—a relief after all those safes behind pictures, thought Kate—and behind the cover of his crouching frame, ran through the combination.

Once the door was open, he took out a battered briefcase, opened it, and removed several bundles of cash. These he returned to the safe. Then he closed the briefcase and walked over to the door. "Seven-fifty. You get the rest when I get her, you fucking son of a bitch."

"Sounds good to me, Carlos." And he turned on his heel and disappeared into the darkness.

"I'm terribly sorry to have neglected you for all this time, Miss Grosvenor," said Deever, turning to her again with a cold smile. "A most important business transaction. Can I get you another drink? Ah—you haven't finished that one. Let me freshen it up for you." He grabbed the glass and poured in more Scotch and two more ice cubes.

"Now—what were we talking about? I remember. It was your friend's interest in a tour group. You were about to tell me what it was."

"I'd be surprised if I was about to do that," said Kate. "Since I haven't the faintest idea what it could possibly have been." And then, without thinking, she reached out for the drink on the table. She converted the movement into a grab for her purse, and in so doing, sent the glass flying onto the floor. It hit the tiles and smashed. "So sorry," she said. "I really am a klutz. It's not safe to leave anything breakable within range of me. Waterford, was it?"

"Think nothing of it," said Deever. As he said the words, his mouth formed itself into a hard line in his white face.

She smiled, located a tissue in her purse, and blew her nose. "What is *your* interest in the tour group? Or do you own it?"

"Certainly not," he said. "My wife's on that tour, and she's disappeared. I want to know where she is. And I want the name of the person she's with. And, Miss Grosvenor, as you probably know, I usually get what I want."

"Do you now," said Kate. "That makes things difficult, doesn't it? Because how do you imagine that I could have any idea where your wife is? I don't even know where my friend is, and she's more important to me than your wife. I assume my friend is lost, and will call me when she finds a telephone. Perhaps your wife will do the same. Otherwise, I don't see the connection between my friend and your wife and a tour bus."

"It won't do, Miss Grosvenor. That might have worked with the dumb cops you've been talking to, but I know who you are and who you know, and I just don't believe you." Now his crisp educated tones faded into the harsh nasal drawl of some other and more menacing dialect. "I'm not a very patient person," he said. "And I haven't got a hell of a lot of time to waste playing games with you. What agency is your friend with?"

"Agency?" said Kate, for once completely puzzled. "You dragged me out here to find out who her agent is?" Then with a click she realized what he meant by agency, and was even more puzzled.

"Very funny," said Deever coldly. "I got no more time for you, Miss Grosvenor. Not now, and let me tell you, that means, as far as you go, never. Because either you know piss-all, and you're no use to me, or dragging it out of you is going to take more time and effort than I got. You had your chance, and that's it. Unless you want to start talking right now." His eyes had almost disappeared by this point.

Kate looked at him in silence. Her brain was rapidly assimilating what he was telling her, and it didn't sound good. It failed to suggest a useful response beyond whimpering in terror, which probably would be worse than useless, and so she continued to fix her eyes on him.

"Very well. Ginger," he called sharply. The small door opened and the chauffeur walked in. "Take Miss Grosvenor upstairs. And get her another drink. Scotch. You might as well drink this one, Miss Grosvenor. You won't have a chance to drink another."

Kate looked up at the chauffeur with the improbable name from the disadvantage of the armchair she was sitting in. A multitude of instant calculations flooded her brain. Over six foot four. Over two hundred pounds. And probably psychopathic. Fight? Probably not. Scream? Out here in the middle of nowhere? Not much use. She relaxed as much as possible and smiled.

He grabbed her by the arms and pulled her out of the chair as if she were a large soft sculpture. The pain from her injury battled with terror for control of her impulses and in the confusion, reason won. Show no weakness, Kate. Just remain calm and unperturbed. Ginger took her by one arm—the injured one—and piloted her toward the other door in the room. With his left hand, he drew a heavy key out of his pocket and unlocked the door. He pulled it open and revealed a circular staircase. Grabbing her injured arm one more time, he forced her onto the first step. He knows which arm to take, she thought, surprised that she hadn't realized that before. The idea steadied her enormously as she walked slowly up the narrow stairs.

After an eternity of steps, she came face to face with another doorway. Ginger gave her another push and she understood that they were not pausing at this one. It must lead out onto the second floor. She moved on, propelled by those heavy feet and hands behind her. Several more steps and her head touched a wooden roof. She could move no farther. Ginger reached around her with his fat hands—she had never seen a man with such fleshy hands—and pushed open the trapdoor. Without a word he propelled her up and in and closed and locked the trap behind her.

She prowled around her new cage. The only door in the room led into a small bathroom, complete with clean towels. Each of the four walls had two tall, very narrow casement windows, unequipped, as she had noticed before, with the pervasive iron grillework that Deever seemed so fond of. The south windows were covered with heavy curtains against the sun; the rest offered no privacy. There was a single bed with a bright red cover, a couch with large pillows in a rough fabric, a dark wood table and two chairs, and under the south windows, a bookcase. A carved wooden chest stood at the foot of the bed. Kate remained in the middle of the room and looked around her, slowly and carefully. There was something very peculiar about the entire setup.

Before she could figure out what it was, the trapdoor opened again, and someone slid a tray with a bottle, a glass, ice, and water onto the floor. It shut and she could hear the sound of the lock. She picked up the tray and set it on the table.

From the south windows she had a view of high plains and mountains. Down below was a smooth drop directly to the ground. A long way. The east windows were above the paddock. Now if she could convince a horse to stand directly under the window— No, Kate. Don't even think about it. The north windows overlooked the courtyard. Shinny down the wall and end up behind iron bars. Wonderful. Walking carefully over to the west wall, avoiding the trapdoor, she eased her head out the window and looked down onto the roof. Because the tower didn't connect to the rest of the house, the roof was six feet down, but that didn't matter. The question was, could she get out of these windows? And having done so, could she get off the flat roof below without killing herself?

The sound of voices floated up from somewhere below. Kate pulled her head delicately in from the window and drifted silently over to the opposite side. The limousine was pulled up in front of the gates again, and Ginger had them opened.

"What about her? You want me to leave her there?" Ginger's voice was unpleasantly like Deever's, only higher-pitched and worried sounding.

"Wait till I'm in Albuquerque, and then get rid of her. Otherwise she's going to keep right on raising hell and screwing things up. I remember that bitch from the hearings— she works for *Time* or something. Wait till she's passed out and then dump her at the motel. That way, nobody'll ask questions. Key's in her purse. If you want to get fancy, leave her on a park bench with an empty bottle and a small bag."

"Yeah, well I said I'd take her back, didn't I?" And he laughed.

And Kate could see Rodriguez looking down at her body, sodden with Scotch and filled with coke, dead, ugly on a bench somewhere in Taos. Ending up just as he said she would, dead of booze and drugs, not brave enough to face the simple process of getting off them. And Deever was right. Nobody would question what had happened to her. She had set the whole thing up. She hated fulfilling other people's prophecies. Hated it.

Suddenly it came to her. This room could not be as difficult of access as it appeared, or it would not contain any furniture larger than a pillow. No one could have wrestled that bed, the couch, the table, any of these things up here through that stupid Edgar Allan Poe staircase. Come on, Kate. Start looking.

She started with the windows. The fit between the adobe structure and the spanking new casement windows was her first concern. She ran her fingers up and around the framing. Solid. Then she looked at the window itself. It had hinges, of course. She tried dismantling the bottom one. It stuck. The memory of skills learned at college tweaked at her; her dorm had had windows exactly like this. She grasped the handle that worked the closing mechanism, twisted it backward, and unscrewed it neatly and quietly. The ultimate irritation weapon, disabling your neighbor's windows. The handle was not quite as useful as a screwdriver would have been, but it did help start the bolt. One thwack and it was on its way. A little yanking with her fingers and shoving with the handle and she had it out. The second hinge was a breeze, now that she had a system. With

the window loosened, she could twist it in its track until
she parted it from its closing arm. Sweating with triumph,
she dragged her prize into the room.

The resulting space was almost wide enough for a
human body. Maybe it was actually wide enough for someone who didn't fear getting caught in tight places more
than anything else in the world. She looked down at the
roof below, waiting for inspiration to come.

They didn't drag beds up through an opening this wide.
She examined the two windows and the space between
them with more care. No ideas jumped into her brain. No
little rosette that you press and the whole wall comes away,
not as far as she could tell. She walked over to the south
wall and pulled back the curtains. Night was closing in.
The bottom of the windows was covered by the bookcase;
with a gasp of effort she pulled it aside enough to see what
was there. And discovered that the windowsill connected
two complete windows and the space in between. That was
all a fake structure, no doubt fairly easy to remove. And
when gone, it would allow for good-sized pieces of furniture to be dragged up from the ground. Her elation
drained away. Even if she could create room for ten women
by removing those windows, she would undoubtedly break
her neck getting to the ground.

Maybe there was a rope. A ladder in case of fire. She
yanked out all the drawers, threw open the bathroom cabinets, almost wrenched off the lid of the chest. Nothing but
a few dust curls, more towels, and a duvet. She started to
calculate how far down they would get her if she managed
to tie them together, looked at the intractability of the
materials, and gave up in despair.

*　　　*　　　*

"It's getting late," said John.

The injured woman was lying on the ground, with her head in Harriet's lap. They were taking turns keeping her awake enough to pour a little liquid down her throat. Her eyelids fluttered and opened more frequently now, but except for that, progress was dishearteningly slow.

"How are the kids doing?" asked Harriet.

"They're being very quiet and stoical. Stuart is off on another of his scouting missions. It keeps his mind off things. Are there any more crackers in that box? I imagine they must be hungry."

Harriet shook her head. "Not many. I still have apples. And no water."

"Harriet?" A voice called from the rocks above them. A child's voice, filled with interest but no panic.

"That you, Stuart? You'd better come down while you can still see well enough not to fall."

"I am." The voice was accompanied by a rattle of dirt and gravel, and running footsteps. "I saw the van," he said. "It's not that far down the road. We could walk it easy following the road. Honest. And then we could sleep in it."

The fear of sleeping out in the open, at the mercy of all the things that prowl the night, informed his voice.

"It's an idea," said John. "I can carry her for a while, anyway. She'd be more comfortable in the van. And a little warmer."

"I wonder where Jennifer is," said Harriet. "Did you see her?"

Stuart shook his head. "She must have gone."

"I can walk, I think. At least for a little while. It would be good for me." The voice, when it came, was so hoarse and faint and unexpected that everyone jumped.

"Diana?" asked Harriet. "You think you can walk?"

"Sure. I'm groggy, that's all. She's been giving me something pretty strong. But if you'll hang onto me, I can walk."

It was an odd procession that started down the mountain road. Caroline held the flashlight that had been in Harriet's jacket, Stuart walked beside her for support, then John and Harriet and, propped up between them, a woman who staggered and stumbled and apologized in a thick voice about an equal amount of the time. "I'm sorry," she said at last. "I have to rest for a while. Leave me here. I'll be all right."

"It's not far from here," said Stuart confidently. "Right around that next curve there's another and then a long straight stretch, and then another curve with a funny-looking black rock. Just beyond there."

"Why don't you rest here," said John, "while I go have a look. Do you mind? The children can stay with you—and Harriet."

Harriet looked over at him, startled, caught the expression on his face in the fading light and smiled. "Certainly. Just check to make sure that it's our van, eh? Who knows how many cream Chevy vans might be littering the roads around here."

John took the flashlight from Caroline and headed off, but as soon as he was around the curve he killed the light. Stuart's remark about someone following them had disturbed him considerably more than he had admitted, and he had no desire to advertise their presence. Once he'd rounded the curve out of earshot of the children's voices, the only sound he could hear was that of his footfalls, light on the dust and gravel. But his body was convinced that he was not alone. His back twitched, feeling the eyes measuring it, and his scalp tingled with the sense of a hostile presence. But no matter how often he paused to listen and watch, the mountain appeared empty and deserted.

The chunk of black rock loomed up to his right. One last corner and there it was, the van sitting on its pathetically misused wheels. As he approached it, a richly unpleasant and too familiar smell wafted over to him on the night breeze. He walked to the window, switched on his flashlight, and shone it on the gaping wound in the neck of the blood-drenched corpse of Jennifer Nicholls. One more throat had gone.

CHAPTER 10

"You can't climb out that window and let yourself down to the roof, Kate Grosvenor. Your arm is too weak; it won't support you. It'll give way and you'll fall." For the first time in more than an hour Kate was dragging her physical condition into her considerations. "It'll be fine, you stupid jerk," she continued, having one of those Kate to Kate conversations she'd used since childhood to solve most of life's overwhelming problems. "Look at what you've just done with it. And besides, even if you fall, it's not that far. What do you think you are, a piece of irreplaceable china?"

She had been sitting in the dark on one of the hard-backed chairs, staring at the narrow space in front of her, earnestly talking to herself. Anything to keep from thinking of the word *stuck*. Time was passing. A dangerous amount of time. "Okay, then how do I get off that roof? I'm still two stories above the ground." The answer popped back at once. "There'll be something out there to climb onto. You'll see."

She paused in her arguments and dropped her head into her hands for a moment. "Right. I'm going," she said, and stood up. And just as she was about to climb onto the windowsill, a happy farewell thought hit her. She picked up the bottle, carried it over to the trapdoor, unscrewed the cap, and poured the fifth of Scotch down the crack. Then she set the water jug and the ice bucket artistically on the edge opposite the hinges where, with a little luck, they would spill on the head of the next person coming up. As a final touch, she picked up the window she had detached from its hinges and perched it delicately on top of everything else. "There you go," she said. "A nice little surprise."

The search for the children had turned into a purely neighborhood affair, efficiently organized by the wife of a local landowner, and assisted by tracking dogs brought in from headquarters. "Hi, Rodriguez," said the man lounging behind the wheel of his car at the central point, working on a crossword puzzle while he coordinated negative results as they trickled in. "What in hell are you doing here? Haven't you heard?"

Rodriguez leaned his elbows on the car door and looked in. "You mean that's it's all a waste of time?" he said. "Sure. But I was sent down to coordinate."

"The hell you were," he said cheerfully. "I'm coordinating this thing and we're on until nightfall. The day you outrank me and then some, I'll give over sitting in here in comfort to go busting my ass poking around under bushes. I never got orders to turn anything over to you."

"Christ," muttered Rodriguez. "What in hell is going on?"

Rodriguez stalked back to his car and snarled something at his radio. "What in hell do you mean, a mistake?" floated through the evening air over to the trooper in the other car. "You sent me out to the middle of nowhere by mistake? You know how many people there are out here already? We're tripping over each other." A pause. "Oh. Yeah. Thanks."

"Some anonymous bastard screwed up," he said. "And now that it's all straightened out they tell me I can drive all the way back to town. Enjoy yourself."

"Sure, Rodriguez."

It was almost nine o'clock when Rodriguez walked into the café on Bent Street and looked around for his brother. One of his brothers. That was what the message had said. "Meet your brother at the café when you get off." Neglecting to mention which brother. Or, in fact, which café.

It didn't matter. They were both there, nursing beers. "What's up?" he said. Out here in the world of work and tourists, they generally communicated in English. As a policy. Especially in a crowded restaurant.

"Not much. Nobody's seen you lately, that's all," said Guillermo, the oldest of the three. "We called at work because it's easier to find you there than in that miserable hovel you call home. You know, if you want, I can get you—"

"You look like hell, both of you," said Rodriguez. "What's wrong? Is everything okay at home?"

"Nothing's wrong. For chrissake, stop worrying. There was a party last night and I tied one on. Got to bed at five and had to be up at seven. Worked all day." Guillermo yawned and grinned; he drained his glass and waved for another.

"What are you working on?" asked Rodriguez, pouring his beer and ordering the chicken with rice.

"Same thing," he said. "Big contract with lots of money. I'm almost finished."

"You smell like a horse," said Roberto.

"So? I came home early and went riding. Trying to get the kinks out and clear my head."

"Why don't you try showering? Clear your head and the air."

"Shut up, Roberto. You're no rose yourself," said Guillermo expansively and leaned back.

"What are you doing in town this weekend?" asked Rodriguez, turning to the middle brother.

"Her cousin's getting married," said Roberto curtly.

"And they didn't invite you?" Rodriguez was filled with genuine astonishment. Roberto's girlfriend's family had been angling for him to marry her since she'd been seventeen. He couldn't imagine them bypassing an opportunity to work on him like that.

"Yeah, they invited me. I just didn't feel like going. I'm getting sick of Isabel's mother and all her maneuvering. Isabel wants to graduate and maybe even get a job, before she starts in on the fourteen grandchildren it would take to keep the witch happy."

So this turned out to be old news. "What are you working on?" Guillermo asked, turning to Rodriguez.

"A tour company lost a bus," he said laconically. "We're trying to find it."

"What do you mean, lost a bus?"

"Just what I say. There was a bus, and then there was no bus. We came into it because we were told there were a couple of kids on the bus and when they didn't turn up their parents began raising hell," said Rodriguez. "Naturally. Their parents, of course, are in our jurisdiction. But there weren't any kids on that goddamn bus. They were in a van, maybe, being kidnapped by some other people. But we can't find the van either, so it doesn't matter, does it? In short, no one knows what the hell is going on, and if it's a hijacking or a kidnapping, they're taking their own sweet time to contact us and tell us what they want." He yawned. "I haven't had a lot of sleep either." Then he looked at the beer in his hand, at the crowd in the restaurant, and pulled a twenty from his pocket. "Look, cancel my order if you can, or eat it yourselves. I can't stay. It was really nice seeing you guys, but won't you be home tomorrow?"

"Sure," said Guillermo, vaguely, his mind on other things already. He was pointing at the two empty chairs. "Linda, Sam," he called. "Over here. Lots of room." Two women who were standing at the entrance waved cheerfully and pushed their way past the crowd waiting for tables. The waitress frowned and decided not to make an issue of it.

"We'll talk then," said Rodriguez.

Roberto pushed back his chair at the same time. "I'll walk down with you. I got to drive over and pick up Isabel."

"So you're going after all. You just don't want to miss the party," said his brother.

"There's some of that," Roberto admitted.

They walked through the narrow, twisting streets and alleyways between closed shops and little galleries, avoiding the noise and traffic only a block away. The dim lights from shop windows made the warm bricks and stones of the pavement glow; the night was warm for May but cool on exposed flesh. Rodriguez thrust his hands in his pockets and stared at his feet as he moved. When they came to the corner, he turned right, further into the maze of small stores and restaurants, instead of back toward work. "What's wrong?" he asked.

"Nothing."

"The hell it isn't. You were damn near throwing beer in Guillermo's face."

"Ah, shit," he said. "I was bored. So would you have

been, listening to him going on and on about how wonderful his life is."

"Is everything okay with you and Isabel?" he asked. "I don't know when I last saw you alone on a Saturday."

"With Isabel? And me?" He laughed. "She worked out this whole scheme. I'm picking her up at the hall and we're off."

"So I guess you're using the cabin tonight."

"Hell no. We are spending the night in a hotel close to where the reception is. A luxury hotel with room service and monster beds. What's the point in being employed if you don't spend it? Tomorrow, Isabel will arrive home, all demure, having spent the night with another cousin. You know, we're running out of excuses for Isabel to spend Saturday night somewhere else. Getting around her mother is turning into a real drag."

"You shouldn't have fallen for someone who's half your age, then."

"She's only nine years younger than I am," he said defensively. "That's nothing. Our father was—"

"Now, there's a hell of an example to follow. You know, if you can't spend a day on your own without turning into a snarling bastard, you'd better marry her. Or get a hobby."

"Oh—I had lots to do today. It wasn't that."

Rodriguez glanced over at his brother, who was staring gloomily in the window of a bookstore. "I might use it myself tonight," he said. "The cabin, I mean. It's about the only place I know of where I can sleep and they can't find me."

Rodriguez knocked on the door of the motel room, hard. For the second time. Come on, come on. Answer the god-

damn door, he screamed at her silently. Or are you too
drunk? He walked over to the windows and shook his head
in fury and exasperation. The stupid, stupid bitch had left
one of them open. With the curtains pulled back. Anyone
could have walked in. He heaved the sash up as far as it
would go and climbed in himself to prove his point.

But she was not in the bed asleep. Drunk or sober. In
fact, since he had last seen it, the bed had been tidied, the
blanket folded, and the cover straightened out. The bathroom door was open; the lights were out. The place was
empty. He turned on a light, closed the window, and pulled
the curtains shut. "Okay," he muttered, "she's gone to get
something to eat. What's wrong with that? It's legal, even
in the middle of an investigation." But a little voice nagged
at him that it was not the speed and the thoroughness of his
investigation that he was concerned about. I probably
drove right past her without even noticing, he said to himself. Like hell, Rodriguez. You were searching for her on
every street you drove down. He noted that she had left the
dish he had brought the chili in beside the bed, but had
cleared away the glasses from the table. What did that
mean? Nothing, Rodriguez, you blundering fool. Nothing
at all. Except that maybe she was interrupted in the middle
of cleaning up. By whom? Or what? He flipped on the light
in the bathroom and looked around.

There were the four glasses, lined up in a row. On the
mirror, right above them, Kate had drawn a scowling
happy face in lipstick. What in hell did that mean? Face?
Lips? I'm sad and have gone out to get drunk? He looked
around for inspiration. She had left a small overnight bag
on the counter, open. He peered inside, pulling out various
zippered plastic-lined bags containing makeup and toi-
letries. He started to do a rapid check. Shampoo and hair

things. Deodorant, skin lotion, and pricey-looking soap. Makeup. Lipstick. Why leave it here? The women he knew carted their lipstick around with them. Lipstick. He groaned. A clue. One so obvious that even he would get it. More like a bad pun. He took out the tube and tried pulling it apart. It resisted for a moment, and then gave suddenly with a pop. A tightly folded tissue was wrapped around the inside tube.

He spread it out on the counter and read the brief message. "Kate Grosvenor," he muttered. "At Carl Deever's. Shit. How could anyone be that dumb? So stupid, ignorant, idiotic—" He ran out of words. Not to mention that little clue. The first person who walked in here would go directly to that lipstick tube.

He wiped the lipsticked face off the mirror, pocketed the tissue, and headed out to his car.

Kate stared down at the roof for a measurable length of time; it was still only five or six feet below her. She climbed up onto the sill and began to study the situation carefully. The window opening looked to be nine or ten inches wide, she thought, maybe less, and the adobe wall it was set in was more than a foot thick. Thin as she was right now, it was still going to be a tight fit for her hips. The sweat of pure terror poured off her face and trickled down between her breasts as she tried to distract herself with these basic and not very useful calculations. There was nothing for it. Turning her body suddenly sideways, she stepped off the ledge, one foot at a time, through the long narrow opening. Using both hands, one outside, one in, to clutch the fat section of wall between the two windows, she rapidly eased herself down and out. Just at the point where her feet were dangling helplessly, the sharp edges of the wood framing caught her hipbones and held her fast. She wrapped her arms as tightly as she could around the center post for support and breathed out with as much force as she could muster. She wriggled from side to side within the frame, using an up and down pelvic motion. And almost laughed hysterically as she realized that she must look like someone performing an obscene dance with a house. Except for putting a nice polish on the inside of the window frame, though, she was accomplishing nothing. And she was never going to be able to work her way back up through the window. She was caught there, trapped, unable to move. Panic burned through her system, screaming at her that she was choking, that she must breathe.

Then suddenly her thighs and buttocks freed themselves and her sharp hipbones smashed against some other obstruction in there. It hurt. She wrenched her frame about once more, forcing her hips past the narrowest part of the opening. She felt herself sliding down and out until her rib cage caught on the wood framing and stopped her once more.

She knew that she was compressible enough to get through. She also knew that the wood frame was going to squeeze all the air out of her chest and that she was going to go mad if she didn't make it out in one fast movement. Her head had room if she faced straight out, and her thin shoulders shouldn't have any trouble if she kept them at the correct angle. She exhaled forcefully, loosened her grip on the frame, and threw herself toward the roof.

She landed with an enormous thud and collapsed. For a while she lay there, panting, acutely aware of pain for the first time in what seemed like hours. Her arms throbbed, her scraped chest burned, her bruised knees hurt where she had landed on them. She glanced back up at that horrible little window and shuddered, her heart pounding with terror.

It took forever for the fear to recede and for Kate to regain control of her body. She lurched unsteadily to her feet to see where she could go from here. To her left was the south face of the building, perfectly smooth; to the right there were a few projections that might help her get down, but she would land right in the courtyard. Behind bars, in full view of the world. Straight ahead was the only possibility. She walked as lightly as she could over to the edge and peered down. The drop directly ahead of her seemed unpropitious, and even in the darkness, she could see that she would land on a stone terrace in a walled garden. Stupid and painful. But if she followed the central section of the building around, there was a one-story structure attached to the back of the house. It might offer the possibility of climbing down in two stages. She padded over quietly and looked down. Ten feet? Onto a slightly pitched roof. If she could count on her arms to lower her that meant an easy drop of four and a half. Repeat that and she would be fine. That is, all she needed to do was to rely on the strength of an arm she had been babying like a sick calf for three or four months, and abusing so strenuously for three or four hours that now it trembled with weakness. She sat down on the edge of the roof and cried for the first time in years.

Rodriguez made it to the posts that marked the Deever ranch in no time at all. He screeched to a halt a hundred yards or so back from the entrance, killed his headlights, and coasted slowly up the drive, stopping some distance from the wrought-iron gates. The house was dimly and partially lit, as if a ghostly skeleton staff wandered from room to room each night, checking out the possibilities for fun and games. But Deever's study and bedroom were both dark, and that wasn't very promising. He considered whether walking around the building and peeking in all the windows would be worth the risk and time it would take, and decided that he would prefer to confront the man himself—or his lieutenant—whoever was home.

With practiced ease, his hand found the bell push in its ornate metal flower and pressed it hard. A loud peal sounded through the almost empty residence, reverberating in the courtyard. As it died down, the fountain splashing once again became the only sound in the still night. Suddenly, lights sprang up in the courtyard, illuminating fountain, trees, and gate. The front door heaved open and a large figure was silhouetted against the brightness of the great hall. Ginger. The chauffeur stalked down the pathway and stood on the inside of the gate, making no effort to open it.

"Rodriguez," he said. The voice was not welcoming. "What in hell do you want?"

"To see Carlos," he said. "On official business."

"He don't have official business with you. Ever. He told me."

"Maybe not, Ginger, but he has my witness and I want her back."

"What witness?" said Ginger lazily. "We don't have a witness here. Nobody here but Maria and Pedro. You want to ask them something?"

Rodriguez hung onto his temper. "I want to come inside and talk to my witness. Open that fucking gate."

"You got a warrant, you can come inside. Otherwise

nobody allowed in. Mr. Deever's instructions. You want me to lose my job?" He smiled as if smiling were a new accomplishment, not yet practiced enough to be convincing. Then something caught his attention, wiping the insincere grin from his face, and making him turn his head to look over Rodriguez's left shoulder. "What's that? Who you brought with you?"

"Who in hell am I going to bring with me?" he said. "Look, Ginger—I don't think you understand what you've got here. Miss Grosvenor isn't one of your cheap hookers you can buy off with a few threats and fifty bucks, you know. She's famous. She works for *Time* or one of those magazines. Not someone you can just grab and rough up a bit because Carlos wants her to talk—"

"Oh—is that who you want? Miss Grosvenor? You should've said. She ain't here," said Ginger quickly, still troubled by whatever he saw over Rodriguez's shoulder. "I took her back to town hours ago. She was here. Yeah. She and Mr. Deever, they had a drink, talked some, and off she went. Nice lady. Famous, like you said. Then I come back and get Mr. Deever to Albuquerque. He has a party to go to. I just got back." He peered into the darkness again.

Rodriguez turned and followed the direction of his look. A black face with a white blaze looked back at him and whinnied. A bored and lonesome horse. Ginger must be getting edgy. "Some drive. Albuquerque and back and it's nowhere near ten yet," he observed. "You must have been really flying. How come he didn't want you in Albuquerque with him?"

"Don't be so goddamn stupid. I took him to the airport. And I never asked him why he wants me to stay. Mr. Deever wants me here, I stay here. That's how it works."

"How come he didn't fly himself down?"

"He don't like flying at night. Now you got any other questions? It's late and I'm going to bed."

Rodriguez considered the situation in front of him. Trying to move Ginger with arguments was a futile exercise and always had been. Trying to break into this place without a tank was just as futile. Ginger was no legal scholar, but he knew a search warrant when he saw one—kidding him on that score was also impossible. Shooting him through the gate would help relieve his irritation, but it wouldn't get Rodriguez into the house. The gate opened with a key, and Ginger was standing too far back to allow him to grab it. It would also get him into a certain amount of hot water.

"Listen, Ginger. I'm leaving but I'll be coming back. And then it'll be with two cars and a search warrant, and we're going to tear this whole goddamn place apart. You won't even recognize it."

Ginger looked pretty terrified, cowering there behind his gate. "Yeah? Sure. You wanna know where to find a judge to give you a warrant? It's easy. You know where they all are? At that party with Mr. Deever." He laughed and turned his back. Ginger was a real humorist.

Just as Rodriguez was about to try one more assault with reason, someone leaned on his horn and blasted away the peace of the night. He paused for a millisecond, startled. "Jesus, it's my partner," he said smoothly. "No more time to waste. You tell Carlos I wanted to see him. No—don't bother. I may go to Albuquerque and tell him myself."

Kate's tears had been instantly halted by the sound of a vehicle pausing in its headlong rush along the road. She glanced over in time to see its headlights go out and the ghostly outline of a car creep slowly up the drive. It was either Deever come back to kill her, or Rodriguez come to rescue her. No matter which one it was, she had to get off this goddamn roof fast. She grasped the nearest wooden roof beam and lowered herself down as far as she could. Her strength gave out halfway, she plunged the remaining distance, lost her grip, and fell. She landed unsteadily on her feet, took a step, sat down, and almost immediately began to slide down the slope. Then right below her, a male voice exclaimed loudly in Spanish, and she froze. It was answered by a softer voice, the conversation ended in a burst of music, and she realized that she was listening to a television set, nothing more. With any luck, whoever was down there had been so enraptured by the program he was watching that he hadn't heard her clumping about over his head.

Without more delay, she crawled on her hands and knees to the edge of the roof. No exposed heavy beams here. She grabbed onto the metal gutter and lowered herself in the same efficient but graceless manner. This time she was aware of the pain, but only as a hindrance, a nuisance, something that might keep her from what she ought to be doing. She let go carelessly, almost defiantly, daring her body to betray her now, and landed hard, on her feet.

As she started toward the corner, a lamp was turned on in the addition, catching her in its revealing light. She rolled onto the ground and in toward the house, out of the line of sight of the window. Someone pushed it open right above her; Kate held her breath. After an eternity of heart-stopping time a deep voice said, "*Nadie.*" No one. The light went out again and she rolled back to her feet. She started to run, impelled by leftover panic, until she was past the addition. There, a solid adobe wall blocked the light and windows behind it. She slowed to a walk. If she tried to run all the way around the house, she was going to trip and fall on the uneven ground, or maybe even collapse. Either would be counterproductive. And so, stumbling and tripping but staying on her feet, she walked past more windows, all barred, and finally past the curtained fastness of Mr. Deever's study. Where was that car, and whose was it?

As soon as she rounded the corner and climbed the fence into Deever's combination front yard and horse paddock, that question was answered. She could hear his voice, harsh, scolding, censorious, and she was ready to cry again from gratitude and relief. And a certain manic joy that she hadn't yet defined. In the faint glimmer from the stars and the light that was thrown up from Deever's courtyard, the car stood out clearly. And so did Rodriguez, standing in front of the gate, arguing with Ginger. Beautiful Rodriguez, angel-eyed, big and strong and right there on the spot when you needed him. Distracted by these cheerful reflections, she hit something with her foot and knocked it over. Ginger's head whipped in her direction, and she froze. Then in the silence, someone laid a warm hand on her shoulder and she knew it was all over.

But the hand made a peculiar soft grabbing motion on the fabric of her sweatshirt, and breathed warm but powerful breath onto her neck at the same time. She turned her head and looked straight into the dark eyes and white face of one of Carl Deever's horses. "Hi, gorgeous," she whispered, and got an appreciative nicker in return. "Stop eating my shirt and let's go." She positioned herself at the animal's far shoulder and took hold of its halter. Together, in perfect friendship, they ambled very slowly toward Rodriguez's car.

*　　　*　　　*

When Rodriguez opened his car door, flooding the interior with light, he snarled, "For chrissake, Joe, what in hell's wrong with you?" and shut the door again before Ginger could establish who it was sitting there in the passenger's seat. He started the engine, reversed, and turned in a squeal of rubber and was off down the drive, headlights blazing. "I was worried," he said, as he made a left onto the road. "I guess that's an understatement. I was— Are you okay?" His voice dropped.

"The funny thing is, I think I am. I shouldn't be, but I am. I feel exhausted and exhilarated and all sorts of things starting with ex. Except dead. Like ex in expired. He was going to kill me, you know," she said, speaking faster and faster as she went on. "He was. With booze and drugs and leave me on a park bench for you to find." She began to shiver so hard that her voice was shaking. "And you would have thought that I hadn't the guts to go through with it and you would have despised me."

"Despised you? Me? Jesus," said Rodriguez. "I have to think about this one." He slowed, his brow furrowed in concentration. "How did you get out of there? He's damned near turned the place into a fortress."

"Out one of the tower windows," said Kate. "It's a tight fit, but I made it. Just. I was sure I'd get stuck. I'm a bit claustrophobic." Her knee jumped; she had started to shake all over again.

"You must be even thinner than I realized," he said, and made no other comment. Then he braked, flicked on his turn signal, and turned the car up a narrow road.

"Where are we going?"

"Somewhere peaceful and quiet."

"With chili?"

"With chili."

"Because I'm famished. I haven't been hungry in months, and I'm famished." She leaned her head back on the seat and fell instantly asleep.

John stood on the road, contemplating the van. There was no question of anyone sleeping in it tonight. Even if he moved the body out of the front seat and stashed it by the side of the road, the stench from the blood-soaked upholstery would persist and grow; it would probably give the children nightmares for the rest of their lives. What had the murderer taken, beside the life of the little nurse? He went around to the back and opened the doors. Not much. Their luggage was still there, and Harriet's cameras, and the emergency water supplies. A crumpled blanket lay tossed on the floor, along with a piece of old canvas that Harriet used for some obscure purpose from time to time.

He took out two knapsacks, each one half-filled, and jammed the blanket and the canvas in on top of Harriet's fragile equipment. He slung one over each shoulder. The water container had a handle on top; he could carry it with one hand. There remained Harriet's duffle bag, his suitcase, her camera case and tripod, and her film cooler. The one with the real film in it, as opposed to the one that carried extra film, beer, and food. He transferred a few things from his suitcase to the duffle bag, and made a silent promise to the rest of the camera equipment to return for it later.

Harriet had found a flat piece of ground hidden by an outcrop of rock, where she stashed Diana and the twins. She sat above them on the rock, screened by a bit of juniper, guarding her charges and watching the road. Silence, and the brooding mountain, and the endless night sky exacted its toll. Panic tightened her chest muscles. Surely the van wasn't that far away. Where was John? He'd been gone a hell of a long time. And then the idea that they were being followed by an unseen person flitting about from tree to tree like the villainous beast in some fantasy film crowded into her brain and made her feet and hands go cold.

Out of the dark came the sound of footsteps. She crept silently back to the others. "Stay back here," she whispered. "I'll just be a minute. Don't move."

She scrambled up and over the rock toward the road as quietly as she could and crouched once more behind some shrubbery. A huge, bearlike creature came shuffling up, stopped and looked around, and then called out softly, "Harriet?"

"John?" she said tentatively, stepping out from her hiding place. "What are you covered with? You look like a hunchbacked grizzly."

"Everything I could carry. I haven't got your camera case or film cooler or my suitcase, but I do have water and some stuff to sleep on."

He was whispering, and she automatically lowered her voice to match his. "My God. What's happened?"

"I found the van all right. Jennifer's in it. Dead."

"Dead?" The whispered word echoed in the still night air. "What happened?"

"Her throat's been cut. There is someone out there. Some crazy. The van is—we couldn't spend the night in it. So I came back," he concluded lamely.

"Good," said Harriet softly. "Let me take some of this stuff."

"Where have you stashed everyone?" he asked, peering into the dark and empty landscape.

"I found a sort of niche behind there with lots of dead leaves and stuff in it. It's protected in its own way and not too uncomfortable." She paused. "With the kids talking about seeing someone, I thought maybe we should lie low. I guess I was right."

"We should go back for the rest of the stuff. Get everything out of there that we can."

"For God's sake, John, you're not going to leave them here with a maniac who wanders around slashing people's throats?"

"We don't know that it's a maniac," said John. "It may be someone who had a reason to get rid of Donovan and Jennifer."

"And the two guys who hijacked the bus? That's four people, John. I think we should stick together as much as possible, don't you?"

"Nervous?"

"No—terrified," said Harriet.

"You could be right. Well—let's get the party settled for the night, then."

The canvas and two blankets made a sufficient bed for one invalid and two children, with the duffle bag underneath their heads as pillow. "We don't like sleeping outside," said Caroline in a panicky voice when it became clear that they were staying where they were.

"Sorry about that," said Harriet briskly. "But John had a look at the van and it's not safe to sleep in it. You're better off here. We'll be just up there," she said, pointing to a spot slightly above them. "And we're taking turns keeping watch."

After the previous night's horrors and the hardships of the day, the children were too exhausted to protest. Harriet gave them a reassuring pat on the shoulder and climbed up on the rock to join John. "Poor kids," she murmured. "It's scary at night to be deprived of family, room, and bed all at once. But they'll sleep. It's a pity we can't."

"Wake up, Kate. We're here."

"Where?" Kate's eyes fluttered open reluctantly and saw almost nothing but velvety black.

"At my brother's place. No one will look for you here. I don't think even Deever knows about it. Tomorrow I'm going to stash you with my mother, but it's too far to drive tonight. I have to go on duty pretty soon." He got out of the car and walked around to help her out. She stumbled after him along a rocky path and up a couple of steps she couldn't see, feeling like someone in a strange dream.

Once inside, he struck a match and lit an oil lamp. Kate looked around the cabin astonished; she felt as if she had just awakened from a deep sleep and found herself on another planet. This was so distant from Deever's ranch, so safe and clean and honest, that it seemed a small, enclosed paradise, even if it was very like hundreds of other mountain cabins. He carried the lamp into the corner of the room that functioned as the kitchen, and she limped after him. Every time she sat down, her bruised body stiffened further and she felt worse.

Primitive stopped at the kitchen. Rodriguez pulled a container from the freezer and popped it into a microwave. He took a package of frozen tortillas, turned on a gas range, and set one in a frying pan. "In spite of the oil lamps, you see we do have power out here," he said. "For essentials, like freezers and microwaves. But I hate it. It's much too bright unless you have to do something that needs light."

"Frozen tortillas?" said Kate.

"That's what happens when you have a place owned by two bachelors. Of course there are a couple of stones out there in back and a bushel of dried corn if you want to start grinding your own."

There was a slight edge to his voice as he spoke and Kate searched her weary brain for something more gracious to say. "Thank you for coming out to Deever's to get me," she said at last into the silence and the cooking noises. "I'm really very grateful."

"It was a pretty stupid place to go," said Rodriguez. "Don't you know who he is?"

"Actually, I do," she admitted. "I realize he's not exactly St. Francis of Assisi."

"And you went out there anyway?" He hooked a stool out from under a counter that divided the kitchen from the rest of the room and pushed it over to her.

"I thought I had no choice."

The simplicity of her response shook him. "Couldn't you have screamed for help?"

She sat down. "No, no. It wasn't that. I figured the risk was worth taking—the calculated risk that I could find something out and get away again. Just in case he did have information on Harriet that he wasn't going to hand over to the police. Of course, I should have asked myself why he would want to give it to me. Since giving things away never was his style. I miscalculated," she said ruefully.

"You sure as hell did. I thought you got in that car with

Ginger because you didn't know who Deever was. You know—big-time journalist, too wrapped up in her glamorous overseas career to know about home-grown viciousness."

"Oh no," said Kate. "I knew. Overconfidence—or if you prefer, stupidity—took me out there, not ignorance. I was part of a team covering the whole Santa Rosa story. The girls he had kidnapped and brought in from Mexico. Right up to the hearings. Remember that one?"

Rodriguez nodded grimly.

"I still can't figure out how he got off. You'd think they had enough evidence—"

"There's never enough evidence to get someone like Deever," he said. There was bitterness in his voice. "It's not just that he has lots of money, but he knows exactly where to put it. Where it will do the most good."

"Is he still going in for things like that?" asked Kate. "Selling children, I mean."

"No," he said, setting the last tortilla in the frying pan. "Even Deever began to feel the heat on that one. He likes to maintain an air of respectability. He's slid over into other enterprises, just as profitable."

"You know, I really didn't think he'd recognize me," said Kate. "But he did. That was another miscalculation. People don't, usually. You shove a camera in their faces day after day and they don't notice you. You stop being a person. You're just a lens."

He opened the microwave and removed the container of sweet and hot-smelling chili. He ladled a generous amount into their wide flat bowls, handed her the basket filled with warm soft tortillas, and set the plates on the counter. "Simple, fast, and ought to be good," he said.

"What's in it?"

"Pork, I imagine. And chilies. My mother makes it, usually. She's a better cook than I am. Now—let's not talk about Deever while we eat. The man gives me indigestion."

They sat on the stools, leaning on the kitchen counter, and chatted in a desultory and disorganized fashion about everything but the events of the previous twenty-four hours. Kate told him about her Denver grandmother who had brought her out to Colorado every summer to stay with her in the mountains, since any intelligent person knew that the East was an unhealthy place. Rodriguez told her about his uncle's farm, and working on it whenever he could, and learning how to cook and ride and everything else important in life.

"Do you know," said Kate groggily, as sleep began to overcome her again, "what *la noche oscura del alma* is?"

"The dark night of the soul," he said. "Of course. Something we all have to fight through at some point—like death and taxes. Why?"

"I knew I'd meet someone someday who understood," she murmured, her eyelids drooping. She began to tip sideways in the direction of his shoulder.

"I can't stay," said Rodriguez suddenly. "You're going to sleep up in the loft. If you'll give me the key, I'll collect the stuff from your motel room. Take the oil lamp with you—there are matches up there and a flashlight." He put a hand on her arm and then took it away. "When you're up there, raise the ladder. It's not difficult."

"You'd better show me," she said, yawning and blinking herself awake again. "I'm too sleepy to figure much out for myself."

"It's simple. Come over here," he said, nodding at the back wall of the kitchen. "See—open this box and yank on that handle."

As she did, she heard a loud snap. Above her, a trapdoor

dropped open and a ladder slowly lowered itself to the ground, revealing a square opening at its top.

"That's your bedroom up there. The system works with counterweights and springs and God knows what else. My brother Roberto is a mad inventor—it's his creation. Go on up."

Kate took the lamp he handed her and climbed awkwardly up the steps. The loft was finished and considerable in size. A double bed, two small chests, a desk, and two comfortable chairs were swimming in all that space. She sat down on the bed.

"Don't fall asleep. Not yet. This is the important part. You see this rope? Pull it down until you get to the loop— see?—and then hook the loop over this cleat. It draws the ladder up and seals the opening behind it and keeps anyone from opening it down below."

"What a security-conscious brother you have," said Kate, yawning. His eyes looked even more golden in the warm light of the lamp, and his skin glowed. He crouched down in front of her to answer, and to Kate he smelled headily of sunshine and cut grass.

Rodriguez laughed. "No—I walked in on him once with a woman—I mean he had the woman, not me, and he spent the rest of the year coming up with a foolproof system for keeping unwanted visitors out of the bedroom. To get out again, you just remove the rope from the cleat and unsnap the hook that holds the trapdoor in place. As soon as it's released the counterweight will let the ladder down. If you need to exit in a hurry, as in an emergency, there's a rope ladder fastened to that window over there, beside the bed. You can open it if you like. Once you've doused all the lights. It's not far to the ground. There's a little bathroom behind that door." He took one of her hands in his. "Please don't show any lights, and don't come down, no matter what, until I get back here, myself. In person. And before you open the trapdoor, be sure it's me."

"How?" she asked. His hands were cool and strong, gripping hers without hurting.

"I'll give my name. My actual name. If some guy turns up and says it's Rodriguez, or claims to be one of my brothers, or a friend of mine, don't move. Or if someone says he works with me," he added. "That's an old trick of Deever's. Remember that. Just lie low if anyone knocks on the door—or even breaks in. They won't find you up here."

"But I don't know what your name is," she protested. "I can't go on calling you Rodriguez all the time anyway. You don't call me Grosvenor."

He shrugged. "Everyone calls me Rodriguez." He seemed to realize that he had been gripping her hand for some time and let go suddenly, laying his own square, strong palms on her knees and continuing to scrutinize her face.

"What is your name?"

"Fernando," he said slowly. "After my grandfather. Fernando Cristobal Jaime Rodriguez. Not one name in there an Anglo wouldn't butcher. My brothers, now, are lucky. They can just call themselves Bob and Bill, except when they're at home. I've got nothing left but my last name, and so I use it."

"Fernando," said Kate. "It's beautiful. I suppose you could call yourself Andy. For us—uh—Anglos and our notorious inability to deal with any names but our own." She grinned, and the classical purity of her face broke into sparkling life.

"Andy," he said, sounding horror-struck. "It doesn't go

with Rodriguez. Doesn't sound right." He looked at her laughing face and turned red. "All right. You win. My mother would kill me. She'd rather they all called me Rodriguez. Just don't call me—"

"Rod. Yeah. I know. Everyone called me Grover when I was a kid. Hell, isn't it?" She leaned back on her arms and let her hair fall down over her back, swinging and heavy and sensual. It was a long time since she'd been aware of it and the feeling was intensely satisfying. "Does your mother do anything in the work-for-profit world when she isn't making chili? Or is she a genuine housewife?"

He shook his head, amused. "She's a teacher. Very fierce but lovable. I think you'll like her."

It was an unanswerable remark. A heavy silence fell between them, and they stayed where they were, frozen in their positions, looking at each other. "Thank you for doing all this," said Kate finally, sitting up and trying to look brisk and friendly. "It's a miserable little thing to say, but I really mean it."

"You're welcome. It's been my pleasure, Miss Grosvenor."

"For God's sake, call me Kate. Miss Grosvenor sounds as if you're about to give me another lecture."

His face turned blank for a moment and he leaned forward to touch her face gently. "You're very beautiful, you know. Kate. As well as very brave. I must go. Don't forget to pull up the ladder after me." He lowered it rapidly and almost jumped to the ground floor.

Rodriguez hadn't been off the Deever property for more than a minute when Ginger decided that it was time to check on things. The house for one—he didn't trust Pedro to look after it—and his prisoner, who in spite of being a scrawny bitch and a lush, had a certain classy appeal. He started with Pedro and Maria. They simply looked annoyed at the interruption. They had had seen nothing, heard nothing. No telephone calls, no visitors, except for the person who rang at the gate for Ginger a few minutes ago. A very quiet night, and with the help of God it would stay that way. Mr. Deever paid them handsomely not to notice anything and that's exactly what they did.

He retreated in defeat, as he always did after trying to confront them, and headed for the study. The door to the circular staircase was still safely locked, he noted with relief. Vague fears that the door would be wide open and his bird flown had been troubling him ever since he had first seen Rodriguez. He flipped on the lights and headed up.

The pervasive odor of Scotch whiskey—growing stronger and stronger the higher he climbed—filled his nostrils. She must have passed out and spilled the rest of the bottle on the floor. Or maybe she broke the bottle to slash her wrists. That might be awkward.

He unbolted the trapdoor and pushed cautiously upward. Kate's little farewell joke turned out to be an unqualified success. The water spilled sideways onto the floor, instead of onto his head, but quickly rushed to the opening and poured onto his shoulders. The ice bucket, however, fell through, turning as it went, and scattering cubes and freezing water in every direction, including all over him. He swore, gave the trap a violent push, and the window that had been sitting on top flew against the wall and shattered into a thousand tiny pieces. One of them landed in his cheek, piercing it slightly, and causing him to bleed. "What in hell is going on?" he said, emerging into the room and turning on the lights. But he was speaking to himself. The bird had indeed flown. Through the bars in its cage and as far as he could tell into the sky. "She's a witch," he muttered and crossed himself before he realized what he was doing. "No one could get out of here. No one."

It wasn't a happy phone call. "I'm going to get Rodriguez," said Deever. "Rodriguez! Where did that sanctimonious little prick get the nerve to mess around in my business? Find that woman, Ginger. Find her right away and get rid of her. Before she was just a potential danger. Now she's a menace. She can testify. Against both of us."

From which terrible words Ginger derived that Carl Deever was really serious this time when he said he wanted her out of the way. If Rodriguez had taken her, then she was probably still with him. He thought for a while, searching his brain for the most efficient way to track down Rodriguez if he didn't want to be tracked down. There were too many possibilities; that was the problem. This was going to be work. He sighed and went round to the back to get the Jeep. The limousine was entirely too visible.

CHAPTER 11

"Why don't you get some sleep?" said John quietly. "It's going to be a long night."

"I'm too edgy to sleep. If this is going to be our last night on earth, I'd rather stay up and enjoy it."

"Don't be so pessimistic," he said comfortably. "Look at all these rocks. Great weapons. Not as efficient as a knife, but he'll have to take us by surprise, and that won't be so easy. Not from here." They had settled themselves at the head of the small crevice where their sleeping band was lying; John leaning on the outcrop of rock, Harriet on him.

"Why do you say 'him'?" asked Harriet.

"No reason. Anyone can cut a throat, but women don't, usually. It just seems more statistically probable that it's a male. If you prefer, we can call our unseen villain 'her.'"

"That's okay. I'm not that insistent on the forms of equality. Are you comfortable?" she whispered.

"Mmm," he murmured. "Amazing how quiet it is, after living downtown." He stared into the enclosing darkness, silent except for the small rustles of the night, punctuated by a clear sharp bark in the distance. "Would you like to live somewhere like this? Or do you need the city?"

"I'm not sure," said Harriet. "I've always had to live where my clients were, and that's in the city. I try not to dwell on things that can't be changed. It just makes me miserable."

"Don't you? That's where some of my best dreams come from—changing the unchangeable. One or two of them have even come true."

"Like what?"

"You," he said simply. "There was a point in my life before I met you when I believed that any kind of happiness—I mean, personal happiness, love or whatever you want to call it—was an impossibility, a dream created by poets and songwriters who knew it wasn't achievable. And that the only way to make your life worth living was to get somewhere in your job. But I'm not the type to make chief and I knew that, too."

"What type is that?"

In the distance a twig cracked to remind them that they shared the mountain with other living entities. They both listened with painful intensity to the ensuing silence before he considered her question. "A manipulator," he said at last. "And that's not a criticism. You can't function in that job without being able to manipulate the board and the politicians and all the people who work under you. They all have different theories on why you have a police force, and what it ought to do, and if you listen to all of them they cancel each other out." He stopped to listen again. "And nothing gets done. If you make one segment the most important, the others get sore and nothing gets done. I haven't the patience or the sly cunning to make each group work with the others and still believe that it's running the show."

Harriet smiled into the darkness. "And how old were you when you worked that out?"

"I don't know. I must have figured it out a hell of a long time ago. I have to admit I never put it into coherent words until right now."

"It's all this clean air," said Harriet. "It stimulates the brain cells. Or maybe it's the prospect of being butchered before dawn. That concentrates the mind, too, they say."

"I keep forgetting that women are much more gruesome and bloody-minded than men. Not to say realistic. And pessimistic." He squeezed her shoulder affectionately. "I've been sitting here pretending there isn't anyone out in the woods slaughtering innocent civilians because I didn't want to upset you."

"Upset me? Ignoring danger upsets me." She reached up and brushed her lips against his cheek. "I'd rather be looking so I can see it coming. Then I know when to hide. Women are more practical, that's all."

"You wanted to see me?" The words were polite and softly spoken; the stance was militarily correct.

Nonetheless, the man on the other side of the desk felt a twinge of recognition as he looked into those brown eyes. Behind them lived a mutinous, insubordinate, and arrogant bastard, and one of the best younger officers he had. But the code of conduct said nothing about eyes as far as he knew, and he yawned. There had been a time when his own eyes must have been pretty insubordinate as well. "Yes, Rodriguez, I wanted to see you. Actually, I wanted to stay in bed, but someone senior to me wanted me to see you. So here we are. Just one question. What in hell were you doing at the Deever ranch tonight? I was dragged out of bed in the middle of the night to listen to a report that you tried to break into Carl Deever's place, that you threatened one of Deever's subordinates, and that you accused both Deever and the subordinate—we talking about Ginger here?"

"Yeah. We're talking about Ginger."

"—of various and unspecified crimes and said that you were going to get them. Deever found himself a judge, the judge got on to one of the governor's assistants, and everyone is shitting their pants in case poor Deever gets annoyed. Except the governor, of course. He's on your side. He loathes Deever."

"It beats me," said Rodriguez. "Where the man gets his clout, I mean. One of these days we're going to yank one key card out of his operation, one positive and solid thing, and the whole house of cards will come down around his ears. Then it won't matter how goddamn rich he is. Anyway—you already know that. You want to know about tonight. Okay—here goes. I received information that a major witness in the disappearance of those two children— Caroline and Stuart Rogers—had been picked up by a car owned by Mr. Carl Deever and that she—the witness—had been driven out to the Deever ranch. Needing further information from her, I went out to the ranch and rang at the gate. The bell was answered by Mr. Deever's chauffeur, Ginger. I asked if I could come in and speak to my witness, Ms. Kate Grosvenor. He refused me admittance in the absence of a warrant, as was his right. Then he informed me that he himself had driven Ms. Grosvenor back to Taos earlier in the evening. He volunteered the information that she had an appointment for dinner. At that point I left. I wasn't actually on duty at the time."

"Clearly you were on overtime," said his boss, yawning again.

"Thank you, sir."

"Give me a copy of your report and I'll take care of it. And I'll get those bastards for dragging me out of bed. I thought you'd taken a tank to his gate this time."

"Never touched his property except to ring the bell," said Rodriguez, all innocence.

"And the witness?"

"I'll see her tomorrow morning. No problem."

Rodriguez brooded over Deever's instantaneous overreaction. Something about Kate upset Deever, and he was a dangerous man when upset. If he interpreted his assignment and his recently completed interview literally, he now had some breathing room. He turned the car back in the direction of Kate's motel to pick up her belongings.

He was a little late. The room was already a disaster. Someone had been in there searching for something he hadn't found, and had taken his fury out on the physical surroundings. Rodriguez looked around thoughtfully, picked up Kate's suitcase, and began putting everything in it that didn't look as if it belonged to the motel. He gathered up the makeup, soap, and shampoo from the counters, from inside the bathtub, from the tiled floor, and anywhere else he found it and dumped it into the overnight bag; she could sort it out better than he could. Last of all, he picked up the pieces of her camera with great care and set them, as they were, very gently into her camera case.

Kate lay in bed and stared at the ceiling. She had slept for a couple of hours, very heavily, until she had been awakened by a dream of getting stuck between two walls, unable to move, with pursuers behind her and no escape. By the time her heart had stopped pounding, sleep had fled. She went to the bathroom. She drank a glass of water. She stared out the window—the one with the rope ladder, so convenient and easy to use—into the blackness of the woods behind the cabin. She needed a book to distract herself from herself and there were no books up here that she could see. Really she should go downstairs and find a book, some juice, and a comfortable reading chair with a light. Then she could read until she felt sleepy again. And stop thinking.

The flashlight was beside her bed. She would use that instead of trying to light the lamp and carry it downstairs with her on the ladder. She went over to inspect the opening mechanism of the ladder–trap door system. It was a simple catch that looked as if it could be easily snicked back with a thumb. She gave it a tentative pull, discovered it was too stiff to budge, and just as she was switching to her left hand—stronger basically than her right, and almost as deft—she heard a car outside and froze in panic. Scarcely daring to breathe, she slipped back into bed and pulled the covers over her.

"Wait there," she heard someone say. "I'll be right back."

The footsteps took forever to reach the front porch. The car must have been parked some distance away to avoid alerting her. Someone banged loudly on the door. "Ms. Grosvenor. Are you in there? It's Bob Rodriguez, Ms. Grosvenor. My brother sent me to pick you up."

Rodriguez's warning rang in her ears and she pulled the covers more tightly over her head.

"Is she there?" This was a second voice.

"She's supposed to be. Get that door for me, will you?"

There was a screech of metal and a scream of wood

being torn apart. Then footsteps clumped about just beneath her. "Shit," said the first voice. "Are you sure Rocco said she was here?"

"He said, 'probably.' He never said he knew she was here. I told you that."

"Well, she isn't. Let's get the hell out before someone turns up." And the two sets of footsteps crashed away into the night.

It was a long time before Kate even rustled the covers that covered her.

"You know what?"

"What?" asked Harriet sleepily, since some response seemed to be expected of her.

"How can there possibly be someone out there? Unless we're a hell of a lot closer to civilization than we realize. Who could have followed us all the way out here without having some kind of vehicle? And if there'd been another car, truck, anything, we'd have heard it."

"Unless he lives out here all the time. And only wants to protect his mountain from strangers. Like those wild men living in the woods in Oregon and Washington. Survivors from Vietnam, screwed up with shock and paranoia, hiding from the world."

"Okay. But if he'd been doing this for a while—slaughtering everyone who turned up, cutting their throats and all that—wouldn't someone have noticed that everyone who camped here disappeared? And what about all those corpse-filled cars littering the mountainside?"

Harriet began to giggle. "John, stop it. You're trying to make me laugh, and it's not fair. Or right and proper."

He rubbed her shoulder appreciatively. "Not really. I'm puzzled, that's all."

"Well—maybe whoever it is came off the bus with us. Maybe it's one of the guys who took off in the night."

"Like Brett Nicholls?"

"Killing his own wife like that?"

"You were ready enough to believe that the husband in my last case had killed his wife and daughters until we couldn't find any evidence to prove it, remember?"

Harriet nodded. "Okay. But it seems bizarre to wait for a trip like this for an opportunity to do in your wife."

"What could be better? Then you wouldn't be the obvious suspect."

"So who killed the sunshine boys? And Kevin Donovan? Did Brett kill them, too? Just to establish the idea that there was a serial killer wandering around the mountainside?" She shivered. "I can't believe anyone would be that cold-blooded."

"Or crazy." He paused. "At least if it was Brett, then he won't be killing anyone else."

"Why not? Oh. I see. His objective has been accomplished. But what if it was one of the others? Rick—"

"Kelleher."

"Or one of the women," added Harriet. "Teresa Suarez. Or the guide. Karen Johnson."

"Or Mrs. Green, who turns out to be a karate expert? Really, Harriet," said John in exasperation. "Stay within the bounds of reason."

Even though Kate had been convinced that fear would keep her awake and trembling until dawn, the next time a car pulled up and footsteps sounded on the porch steps she was deep under. The pounding on the door came to her from a very great distance away. Then directly under her head a familiar voice called her name with urgency. "Kate! Wake up! We have to get out of here. It's Fernando," he said, and she smiled.

"Hi, Fernando," she said. Nice to know he was who he said he was.

She rolled out of bed, so stiff that she could hardly move. And bruised. And sore, especially around the rib cage. No wonder she'd been having such awful dreams. She grabbed the flashlight once more and followed it to the latch for the door and the ladder. She removed the loop of rope, flicked the latch with her thumb, and the beautiful mechanism began to open slowly, allowing the ladder to slide down to its appointed place. For a second she wondered why she had not been able to work it the night before, and then Rodriguez was up the ladder. "Are you okay?" he asked.

"Sort of," Kate said. "People came looking for me. Two men. I hate to admit it but I was terrified. I stayed up here and practiced my survival-without-breathing techniques." She laughed in a shaky voice.

"I can see that," said Rodriguez. "They did in Roberto's door. We really ought to get out as quickly as we can."

"Just let me go to the bathroom and put on my shoes," said Kate. "Do I have time to brush my teeth? Is there a toothbrush?"

"Put your shoes on in the car. No, you don't, and I don't know. You can clean up at the nearest truck stop."

"Where are we going?" said Kate, carefully removing the top from a cup of coffee and taking a sip before handing it to Rodriguez. She had found a comb, her toothbrush, and toothpaste in the mess in her overnight bag, as well as a tube of madly expensive moisturizer that she had bought before her Middle East assignment and never used. Now, with her hair pulled back neatly, her teeth clean, her face washed and smelling pampered, and coffee and a dubious-looking muffin to keep them going, the terrors of the night had begun to recede.

"To Albuquerque."

"Isn't that where Deever lives?" One more second and she was going to get the shakes again, she knew it.

"Deever? In Albuquerque? Good God, no. He lives in Dallas when he's not at the ranch. Or near Dallas. He's been trying to turn himself into a Texas man, although I guess your average Texan wouldn't be that proud to claim him." He accepted another mouthful of coffee from their joint cup and handed it back to her. "Actually, no one seems to know where he comes from. I've heard people say that he's really a Cuban and that his family came over when he was just a kid because of Castro. But he doesn't speak any Spanish—not more than a few words."

"Then why are we going to Albuquerque?"

"That's where my mother is." He sounded surprised at the question. "It's the safest place in the world for you at the moment. And I think you'll get along with her all right. She's—well—she's an interesting woman. And so are you. In different ways."

"Does she live alone?"

"No. She lives with my little sister, Consuelo. And, of course, the dogs," he added, as an afterthought.

"What do you mean, 'and, of course, the dogs'?"

"Well—when I left home, my mother decided to get a dog. Reasonable enough. Two women living alone, concerned about companionship and protection. But she isn't a reasonable woman. Interesting, wonderful in many ways, but not reasonable. She went into the whole matter of breeds and temperaments and all that sort of thing and decided to breed her own dogs. She has five or six at the moment. Maybe seven. Along with various puppies. We don't count puppies. She's built them a huge yard with one of those professional-type mesh fences all around the house—you know, like a scrap yard—to keep them safe. She doesn't want anyone trying to steal them. So you'll be fine there."

"What kind of dogs?" said Kate, with a mental vision of a crowd of Yorkies snarling behind a great mesh fence as a dognapper swooped down on them with a big net.

"Rottweilers."

"What?" said Kate. "Somehow I can't imagine someone crawling into a yard full of adult Rottweilers, intent on robbery. Are you kidding me?"

"Certainly not. But you're right. I can't imagine anyone trying to steal them. Especially since some of them are bitches with puppies," he added. "Protective. Very protective. But theft is what my mother says she worries about."

"Where does she find the time to look after all those dogs and hold down a teaching job?"

"She's very organized. And Consuelo helps. She's just finishing high school. And she has someone come in several days a week."

"Look—you can't just dump me on her like that," said Kate, sounding very worried. "Won't I drive her crazy? An extra person around all the time, getting in the way, creating more work? Besides, teachers are always on their knees with exhaustion. What grade does she teach?"

"Grade." He paused, slowing down to let a very impatient little car get in front of him. "She doesn't exactly teach a grade. She has a couple of undergraduate and one graduate course she teaches. Usually. Spanish literature. She's a fifteenth- and sixteenth-century specialist."

"Who breeds Rottweilers. Your mother is a professor of Spanish literature at the University of New Mexico."

"Yes."

"And she probably writes books and articles and gives abstruse talks at important conferences and all that kind of thing."

"That's right."

"Then where in hell did you pick up that pathetic little peasant boy disguise? You do everything but shuffle your feet and pull your forelock and call me ma'am. Working in the fields. Your mama's very own chili indeed. You practically had me in tears over that chili."

"Antonia did make that chili," he protested. "She makes terrific chili. Just because you teach Spanish literature doesn't mean you can't cook."

"Antonia?"

"My mama, as you say. We always call her Antonia. She's hardly older than we are."

"So tell me about her. I need to know if I'm going to stay there."

"No—she'll tell you herself. She likes talking about herself. I will tell you that she's a widow, and that my father died fifteen years ago, and that we gather that she doesn't exactly miss him, so you don't have to be careful."

"By the way, who's Rocco?"

"I don't know," said Rodriguez. "Or maybe I should say, I'm not sure." He glanced over at her. "Where did you hear about Rocco?"

"At Deever's. He came to collect his money. Something to do with Deever's wife, who is missing. And then one of the guys who broke into the cabin said that Rocco had told them that I was there. Or that I was probably there. I just wondered who he was."

"So do I, Kate. So do I."

"Are you cold?" asked John.

"A little. But not cold enough to wake the kids so I can drag more clothes out of the duffle bag. I'll be okay." Harriet yawned and moved closer against John's chest. "I could use some bacon and eggs and hot coffee right now, though. And toast. Piles of toast."

"There's the end of a box of crackers."

"Ssh. That's for the kids. For when they wake up. Children don't stand up to hardship very well." Harriet tucked her hands under her arms to warm them. "Or so I seem to remember from my own childhood. I'll survive with my fantasies. My love keeps me warm, as someone said once. And fed, you might say as well. How are you doing?"

"Fine," said John. "A few days without food or sleep ain't gonna hurt me none, see? Real men are like snakes— they only have to eat every couple of weeks or so, and then they sit down and finish off a five-pound steak and a heap of fries."

"And a pile of hot rolls," said Harriet, starting to laugh. "With butter."

"With a plate of spaghetti and meatballs on the side."

"And apple pie. With cheese." She held her hand over her mouth to cut the noise down.

"Don't forget the ice cream, too. With whipped cream and a maraschino cherry."

"Ugh. That's going too far. Do you remember that song about Nellie? Eating oysters and beer and johnnycake and ham and jam and I don't know what else? I loved that song when I was a kid, and I always wanted to know what johnnycake was. It didn't figure as an item in our family diet."

"Nor in ours. I haven't the faintest idea what it is."

"I wish we could sing songs," said Harriet. "And laugh out loud and tell jokes."

"We'll wake the children if we do. And Diana."

"It's amazing that she can sleep."

"Her system's still full of drugs, I suppose. A good thing, too. That slab of rock she's sleeping on doesn't look very comfortable. Would you like to have children, Harriet?" he added without any change of tone.

"Why do you ask?" she said cautiously.

"No particular reason. You seem to be fiercely protective of the twins, that's all. And very good at dealing with them."

"Anyone would be good at dealing with them," she answered evasively. "They're bright and absolutely angelic in behavior."

"That's not an answer."

"No, it isn't. Do you mean, if I—if we survive this experience, this night, would I like to have children?"

"Or a child."

"I might. It's another of those things I never let myself think about, because it never seemed possible." She paused. "Think of the seething cauldron of suppressed desires I must be—all for things I refuse to let into my conscious mind." She tried to laugh, and it was a sad, shaky sound. "It hadn't occurred to me before."

"I don't understand why you should think so many things are closed off for you," said John. "My God—you're beautiful and talented and so damned competent to boot. You'd think the world would be opening at your feet wherever you went."

"Maybe it did, and I didn't like the size of the hole in front of me," she said. "But no—I might be all those things, but you've forgotten that one little phrase."

"What's that?"

"For a woman. So talented for a woman. So competent for a woman. And you're the only man I've met who never adds it, except for the architects who hire me, of course. In that world, my work is as good as anyone else's. Or better. But you don't get rich and famous doing architectural photography. Not usually, anyway. And I've had to work hard to make a living, and I've had to live where the work is. Not much room for dreams there."

"I hadn't realized how bitter you felt."

"Not bitter, John. Really, I'm not bitter. I love what I do. It's tremendously exciting and satisfying and everything like that. But I am realistic. I know you can't have it all."

"But you can have some of it, Harriet. You don't have to look things right in the face and then run and hide from them."

"Oh yes you do. It's a great way to survive that jungle out there."

He didn't reply, except to wrap his arm more tightly around her shoulders and drop his cheek down on top of her head. They sat like that until Harriet began to feel her chilled feet and legs going to sleep. "Surviving the jungle out there," said John. "It's an interesting idea."

"What do you mean? It seems pretty simple to me. I would have thought you'd find it even simpler."

"No. One of the reasons I joined the police force when I did—just one of them, and there were other, better reasons, like needing to earn a living, fast—was that it was a potentially dangerous job, with high pensions, relatively, for the widows and children of men killed on duty. Life was a jungle, I guess, but I wasn't all that interested in whether I survived or not. But I did feel I had family responsibilities."

"To your ex-wife."

"To Marie. Yes."

"I don't think I quite understand what you're trying to tell me," said Harriet. "Or if I do, I don't like it much."

"I got in and out of some situations because I wasn't scared. And I wasn't scared because I didn't care what happened to me. That's how I got my promotions, I think. And a few citations for bravery and stuff like that. And I dragged Ed up after me," he said, thinking about his partner. "He's a better officer than I am, in many ways, but his life has always meant something to him."

"Because of Sally."

"I suppose so. He met Sally when they were fifteen and seventeen, and fell in love with her, and hasn't looked at another woman since. He doesn't want to get shot. Even a minor wound would have taken him away from her for a while. So he's careful. And that keeps him from taking stupid risks, and makes him use his head instead of wading into things the way I always did." He stopped again and looked up at the starry sky as if seeking confirmation of all he had to say. "And now here we are, and I don't know what the hell is going on, and for the first time in my life it matters what happens to me. I don't want to miss all that time with you, Harriet." He stopped again. "And don't tell me I haven't been spending much time with you lately," he added quickly. "You have a genius for destroying delicate and sentimental moments."

"I wouldn't dream of it. But if you keep going on like that I'm going to cry and that will spoil everything. If we had kids, do you think they'd be sentimental like you?"

"Only the boys. The girls will probably be hard-boiled and mean like their mother." He took a deep breath and threw his head back. "The stars are fading a little, don't you think?"

"Either that or I'm going blind from the stress and difficulties of the last day or so. Do you think it's dawn? And we've survived?"

"I wouldn't want to speak prematurely," said John.

"Then don't," said Harriet, in sudden terror. "Don't say anything until we know we're safe."

"We're almost there," said Rodriguez. He reached his hand out in the direction of Kate's knee to wake her and then withdrew it.

"At Albuquerque?" said Kate, yawning. "You see—I'm awake. I know where we're going. I even know who you are."

"Good for you. We'll be at my mother's house fairly soon. She lives at this end of the city, more or less."

"Look at the sky," said Kate, with another yawn.

"What about it?"

"The stars are all gone and it's beginning to turn gray. What time is it?"

"That's just the effect of big city lights," said Rodriguez. "It's still night."

"You're lying to me, aren't you? It's dawn, isn't it?"

"Yes. It's dawn."

CHAPTER 12

They drove through the broad, still streets of Albuquerque in silence. Every topic of conversation that leaped into Kate's head seemed meaningless under the circumstances, and her words died on her lips before they were spoken. She wasn't sure what was keeping Rodriguez quiet. Shyness, perhaps. Or exasperation.

He had exaggerated the security arrangements at his mother's house. There was chain-link fencing, but it started flush with the front of the house and encircled a large garden behind and to each side. The front was sculpted in rock, gravel, trees, and shrubs, reminding Kate of an understated version of the courtyard at Deever's ranch. Rodriguez pulled up into the driveway and handed Kate out of the car with all the gravity of a chauffeur. "Since when did I turn into royalty?" she whispered fiercely. "I know how to get out of a car."

"You look to me as if you could use a hand. Stiff?"

"That's like asking someone with a concussion if he has a headache," said Kate. "Yes, I'm stiff. I was using muscles last night I haven't used since I was in my crib. There wasn't that much climbing in and out of windows in my last job. But give me time—by next week I'll be first rate at it."

As Kate hobbled up the flagstone path to the broad porch, the door flew wide open. In the darkness of the hall beyond, she could just make out the outline of a slender woman. "Fernando," the woman called warmly. "Wonderful to see you." Consuelo, the little sister, Kate decided.

"Kate," said Fernando, "come and meet my mother. Antonia, this is Kate. She needs a little sheltering and food for the next few days."

Antonia Rodriguez stepped closer and Kate realized that this elegant and beautiful woman was indeed not a teenager. There was too much experience written across her face, too much acuteness in her eyes for youth. Even so, it seemed impossible that the woman standing in front of her could be the mother of the man who was urging her forward to be introduced. Antonia's dark hair was pulled back from her wide forehead and hung casually in a plait over her shoulder. Her loose robe, dark red in color and rather oriental in cut, moved with the voluptuous slither of silk, and made her warmly olive skin glow with the same seductive aura as Fernando's. She grasped Kate's hand firmly, and drew her into the house. They stepped over the first of many Rottweilers, this one stretched out in the front hall, guardian to the entryway. It opened an eye, moved its tail in acknowledgment, and resumed its interrupted sleep. Two broad rooms filled the space on either side of the central hall, both painted white and hung with rugs and tapestries. Antonia, still towing Kate along like a shy child, led her through the one to the right, a dining room containing a large, dark-stained table, and into a kitchen with tiled floors and a wall of glass. Outside she could see a patio, a patch of grass, and—clearly in the strengthening light of dawn—the kennels and a couple of fenced-off runs. They were a generous size. There were apparently a lot of dogs.

"Now," said Antonia, "you must be famished and exhausted. Fernando can go days without food or sleep and forgets that the rest of the world is not like him." Her English was flawless, except for the slight hesitant sibilance of the native speaker of Spanish when faced with certain English consonants. "Sit down, and I will get you some breakfast. Fernando, pour us some juice and coffee." The juice came from a pitcher and had been freshly squeezed; the coffee was rich and continental in flavor. It was served with a pitcher of hot milk, and Kate felt wrapped in luxury and European cosmopolitanism. Except for the wonderfully homey odor of frying bacon. "Fernando tells me that you are a photographer and that you need someplace quiet and peaceful to stay for a few days. And safe. And having said that, that I am to forget it." She smiled, and Kate saw where her son had acquired his shyly melting expression. "That is not a problem in this house. I am very forgetful," she said, with a vague wave of her hand. "And we are certainly quiet and peaceful here. Except for the dogs, sometimes. People who need to perfect their Spanish often stay here for a while. Government people on trade missions, for example. It is something I started when we were short of money—we survived some bad times in that way—and I continue to do it for special people. I think that is what you will be. I shall call you Lola and make you a specialist in textiles."

"But I don't know anything about textiles," said Kate, in a panic.

"Neither does anyone else you're likely to meet here." All her vagueness disappeared; she concentrated her alarmingly intelligent eyes on Kate. "Do you speak any Spanish?"

"Some. I studied it in college."

"Perfect. You're probably convincingly bad." Antonia slipped eggs, bacon, chili, and toast onto Kate's plate and put it in front of her, and then did the same for herself and Fernando. "You will keep this story up in front of Consuelo—although she is very discreet—and my other two sons, who are likely to visit because it is Sunday. Roberto and Guillermo. They are good boys but not necessarily discreet. But you must sleep as soon as you have eaten some breakfast. Before you go to bed I will introduce you to the dogs and then they will look after you, too. You will be safe here."

"He has seen her," said Fernando. "He knows what she looks like."

"Then she will not look the same. Shall we cut her hair?" Her eyes danced with the excitement of the game.

"No," said Rodriguez. "It's too beautiful to cut. How about one of those strange colors you put on yours?"

Antonia shook her head, looking at Kate judiciously, as if she were a room that needed redecorating. "Curls, I think. Lots and lots of curls. Blond ones. It will change her completely." She laughed. "I have a wig that will do. We won't touch her hair."

"Can I say something?" asked Kate, bristling slightly at this conversation that was taking place around her. "Cutting it makes more sense. When they saw me, my hair was loose and wavy and very windblown. It hid my face. I look very different when it's cut short. And it grows quickly, so that doesn't matter. It was short three or four months ago."

"Good. We'll do that right after breakfast, shall we? Fernando will show you your room. You will probably want to shower and change—I have put out a robe for you. I have about thirty minutes' work to do right now, if you will excuse me."

And Kate realized that no one put Antonia out of her routine.

"She is an awe-inspiring woman, your mother," said Kate after Antonia had swept her way out a door on the other side of the kitchen that must lead into another room in the back of the house, overlooking the kennels. "Is that her study?"

He nodded. "Forbidden territory. No one disturbs her if that door is closed. She often works all night and then naps in there for a few hours before dashing off to teach. She doesn't seem to need sleep like the rest of humanity. But she never stops other people from indulging in normal weaknesses, like sleep and food and—" He stopped suddenly.

"And—" said Kate, widening her eyes.

"And I'll show you where your room is." He walked back through the dining room to the hall. "Upstairs," he said. "Can you make it? Or are you too stiff?"

"Of course I can," said Kate, and winced as her leg went through the first set of complicated motions involved in climbing a stair. "Ouch," she said. "It's embarrassing to admit that in the space of four months you have let yourself turn into some kind of limp vegetable."

"Here," he said, lifting her in one easy motion. "You're much too light," he added, frowning, when they reached the top of the stairs and he set her down. "I hope you're not pleased with yourself."

Not at all pleased, thought Kate. And certainly not pleased with being put down again. "Uh uh," she said, shaking her head. "I look like a skeleton. It's awful and I have no muscles left. I wouldn't survive half a day on an assignment." She looked around the hall in curiosity. To the front of the house was a large window, with a window seat, broad sills, and plants. Near it, there was a desk pushed up to the wall and a couple of chairs. Otherwise she faced five closed doors.

"Antonia's," said Fernando, pointing to the southwest. "Consuelo's is next to it, and I get the one across from Antonia if I sleep here." He opened the door in front of them. "This is yours. It's the official guest room, reserved for official guests. Sons not numbered in that group."

It was a large room, with windows facing east and north. The sun had just started to warm the horizon when Kate pulled back the heavy curtains to look. Down below, the dogs that slept in the kennel were waking up and trotting out into the yard, stretching and shaking themselves free of sleep and looking around curiously to see what new things might have dropped into their territory overnight. "It's terrific," said Kate. "Real luxury."

"This is your bathroom. Plenty of towels. Antonia is obsessive about towels and stockpiles them everywhere," he said huskily. His eyes never left her as he spoke. "And the bed." And he stopped again.

The head of the bed occupied the wall space between the entrance and the bathroom door; it was big enough for the tallest and weightiest trade official and covered in a bright blue homespun cotton that made Kate's eyes look luminous and full of promise. "That bed looks enormously tempting," said Kate, and suddenly realizing what she had said, and wondering what devil in her subconscious made her say it, turned scarlet. "I mean—" She looked up at him, and laughed ruefully. "I probably mean exactly what I said, but I didn't mean to say it. I'm sorry if I embarrassed you.

And in your mother's house. I can be impossibly tactless." God, Kate, shut up, she said to herself, and felt her cheeks burning even brighter.

He was gazing thoughtfully at her, as though her embarrassment had wiped out his own. "You're beautiful with color in your cheeks," he said. "It makes your eyes shine, like—dammit—I don't know what they are in English, and, anyway, it doesn't matter." He pulled her to him and kissed her, running his hands through her hair and over her body, and then drawing her closer and closer to him. "Am I hurting you?" he murmured at last.

She raised both arms and held him around the neck before letting her head fall back a little. "No," she said, looking up. "And it doesn't matter, anyway. It doesn't matter at all. It feels good."

"Jesus," he said. "A little masochist. And I forgot my whips and chains."

"No, never," she said, laughing. "But my body feels alive. My God, it's wonderful. I'd rather hurt than be numb. And they're sapphires."

"What are?"

"The things my eyes shine as brightly as." She pressed herself against him once more, hungrily. "How much time do we have?"

"Right now? None. In the long term—forever, if we're lucky. Forever, Kate. Forever. But from now on, I have to call you Lola." He grinned and then suddenly broke into laughter. "Trust Antonia to pick that name. I always hated it. There was an awful little girl in my class named Lola who used to make fun of the way I pronounced things." He looked down at her and shook his head. "I can't believe it. Antonia must have smelled something over the telephone.

Watch her, *querida*. Lolita *mía*. She's a lot fiercer than she looks. And very, very sly." And he laughed again. "Go take your shower. And I guess you're supposed to wear this." He picked up a bright blue silk robe that was lying on the foot of the bed and threw it at her. It floated through the space between them and landed on her shoulder, as soft as a leaf falling.

"It's day," said John, in Harriet's ear. "I think I'll head down to see what we can rescue from the van. Want to come along? It's not far. The kids are sound asleep. And even if they wake up they shouldn't be too scared. It's bright out. The sun's almost up."

Harriet yawned. At some point—at several points—in the night, she seemed to remember snatching a little sleep, but it had not been enough. Not nearly enough. "Oh, goody," she said. "Just what I need. A nice brisk walk." She ran her hands through her hair and then looked at them. She felt inexpressibly grubby. "Sorry, love," she added. "You're right. After all, it's mostly my stuff. Let's sneak out of here as quietly as possible."

"It really is just around that next curve," said John. "You can tell by that odd-shaped black rock."

"It wasn't that far," said Harriet, trying to sound upbeat and optimistic, as befitted someone in charge of a pair of twins and a wounded librarian. And, to some extent, a worried police inspector.

"I'd stay away from the front of the van, Harriet," said John as she moved ahead of him around the curve. "It's pretty gruesome." He had lowered his voice to a whisper almost involuntarily as soon as they drew close to the identifying rock.

"Are you sure?" Harriet whispered back.

"Of what?" He laid his hand gently on her shoulder and looked past her. There was nothing there. No van, no body, nothing. "I'm positive," he said. "It was just past that rock." He stared down at the loose, gravelly surface. Here and there were the grooves that might have been made by a van running along on dead tires and metal rims. "It's gone."

"Look over here," said Harriet. She had walked over to the canyon rim and was examining the dirt at the edge of the road. Her voice sounded ominously hard.

He walked over beside her, and looked closely at the soil. There were gouges and skid and slide marks all heading for the precipice. "Oh no," he muttered and peered over the edge. Somewhere, way down there, he thought he could see the muted sheen of a cream Chevy van with four-wheel drive, filled with a hideous corpse and Harriet's camera case. Camera case, hell. Her film. "Oh, shit," he said. "The Kansas project. It's all down there, isn't it? All your exposed film. Harriet, I'm sorry."

"What are you sorry for?" she said. "You didn't do it."

"No—I didn't do it. But I could have brought your film with me. It wouldn't have been that much more to carry."

"Oh, John," she said, halfway been laughter and tears, "you couldn't have brought that and the water. And without the water who knows what would happen to us?" She buried her face in his chest for a moment and then straightened up. "The children. For God's sake, let's get back to those children."

*   *   *

But the twins were safely asleep when they returned, panting and out of breath. The rising sun glinting on the mountain peaks across the canyon promised an end to the cold of the night. Diana Morris cried out, woke herself, sat up, and looked around.

"Who are you?" she said, looking directly at John and Harriet.

"I'm John Sanders. This is Harriet Jeffries."

"What's happened?" she asked abruptly. "What are we doing here?"

"You've been injured," said John. "Shot in the leg."

"You weren't part of the tour group," she said, looking suspiciously at them.

"No, we weren't," said Harriet soothingly. "We were at the airport. You may have seen us."

Diana looked thoughtfully at the children. "The light-colored van," she said, searching through her memory. "The kids were on the plane from Dallas."

"That's right. How are you feeling?"

She stopped, as if to inventory the situation. "My leg hurts, but not excessively so. It seems to be healing. I am very thirsty, somewhat hungry, and in need of a ladies' room, that is, a convenient bush, I suppose," she added, looking around her. "My head is clear for the first time in a while."

Harriet scrambled to her feet. "Let me take you behind those rocks," she said. "You may find you have some trouble walking."

When they returned John filled their sole plastic mug with water and handed it to Diana Morris. She drank cautiously. "What is the water situation?" she asked.

"We had three gallons yesterday, and have used a bit since then. You're the one who needs it most, given your physical condition."

"Where are we, exactly? And how did we end up here, just the five of us?" she asked. "What's happened to the others?"

"We're not sure where we are. We've been trying to get the van out. Some of the others are with the bus. Some disappeared the first night."

"The first night? How many nights has it been?"

"Only two," said John. "It's Sunday."

"Oh," said Diana. "Why bring me out, and no one else?" she asked. Suspicion seemed to be her major emotion.

John took a deep breath and started to explain.

"And for some reason," said Harriet, as he wound up his account of the last forty-eight hours, "it looked as if you were being systematically drugged."

"I wouldn't be surprised," said Diana, and with a click you could almost hear, changed the topic. "What food do we have?"

"Three apples, and the remnants from one box of crackers," said Harriet. "That's it, I'm afraid. We of course had expected to reach civilization by last evening."

"Then we'd better make a run for it, I'd say. We could stay here for a hell of a long time waiting to be rescued if they don't want us rescued."

"A run for it," said Harriet. "But you're—"

"It's not that bad. I could use a heavy stick to lean on, if anyone can find one, and maybe I won't be able to carry my share, but I can make it to a point where we can flag down a car. I suggest we drink lots now, eat a little, and carry what we can."

"Maybe we should wake the kids up first, before we go," said Harriet, who was beginning to find this woman irritating.

"Of course. Look, I'm sorry to be pushy, but I have reason to believe—as they say—that it would be a good idea to start moving."

Lesley Carruthers had been in bed for three and a half hours when someone leaned on her doorbell. Its high-pitched, irritating buzz filled the bedroom, penetrated her dream, and at last dragged her awake. She blinked. The sun was shining. Then the doorbell was joined by the strident whirring ring of her alarm clock. She slammed her hand down on it. It stopped; the doorbell didn't. Her mouth still tasted of a surfeit of beer and taco chips; her head pounded in resentment at this untimely summons. "For Christ's sake, hang on a minute, will you?" she muttered.

She had thrown the window open before she realized she had nothing on. She picked up a shirt from the floor and, holding it to her chest, leaned out to see who her early visitor was. "Would you get your finger off that fucking buzzer?" she yelled. The noise stopped. Behind her, in the sweaty bed, something male snorted, rolled over, and began to snore. The smell of stale booze polluted the morning air. "What do you want?" she went on.

"Lesley Carruthers? Miss Lesley Carruthers?"

"That's me. What do you want Lesley Carruthers for?"

A hand held a leather folder containing a picture and identification up as high as it would go. "Federal Bureau of Investigation, miss," the voice intoned. "We have a few questions we'd like to ask you."

"We?" she said, and realized that someone else, equally large and menacing-looking, but not as loud, was lurking around the bushes. "Just a minute and I'll let you in. I have to put some clothes on first."

Five minutes later, after a rapid shower, Lesley

Carruthers looked very carefully at the ID being presented to her through the crack in the door, undid the chain, and let in the two agents. She had been told that FBI men looked like accountants with badges. They didn't. These looked like mean cops in pin-striped suits. A glance into the living room of the house she shared with three other graduate students told her that the party lingered on. Some unlovely creature was asleep on the couch, and another dozed uneasily in the easy chair. "Come into the kitchen and I'll make coffee," she said. "You guys sure as hell get up early on Sundays."

"We like to get to people's houses before they've left for the day," said the doorbell man. "It's more efficient that way."

"Not to say tackling them when they're at their lowest ebb as well. Sound military tactics. Right?" As she talked she put on the coffee, stacked beer bottles in boxes near the back door, cleared off the kitchen table, pulled up three chairs, and sat down.

The two agents sat down as well.

She got to her feet again and opened the refrigerator. "With luck," she muttered. "Aha. Some angelic person brought o.j. last night and didn't drink it. What luxury. Want some juice?" She pulled out a cardboard container and poured herself a glass. The two men shook their heads. "Okay," said Lesley. "Shoot. What do you want from me?"

"Miss Carruthers, did you hear anything about a bus hijacking on Friday—"

"Hear anything? My God, of course I did. Did you know that should have been me? If I hadn't quit my job. I was scheduled to take that tour—I used to work for Archway as a guide, part-time. But I guess you knew that or you wouldn't be here."

They nodded, in unison.

"Want some coffee?" she said, getting up and pulling the pot out from under the filter. "Don't worry," she added, seeing their looks. "The dishes are all really very clean. It's just our friends who are slobs." She took out three mugs, showed them to the agents very solemnly, and put them on the table. She got out a quart of milk and some brown sugar cubes and poured coffee in a very civilized manner. "Anyway," she went on, "why the feds? And not the local police?"

"Kidnapping," said the door man. "Federal offense."

"Of course. Basic civics. Well—what do you want to know?"

"You called in sick on Thursday evening."

"That's right. The very latest possible time to do it, really, if they're to find a replacement and get her up there."

"Were you actually— You said something about quitting. Was there anything—"

"Weird about my not being on that tour? Is that what you want to know? Because the answer is yes. And I was planning on having a fast talk with the police today about it. I only found out about the hijacking yesterday afternoon and we had this party last night so—"

"What was weird, Miss Carruthers?"

"Well—some guy comes to see me two weeks ago, on Sunday—no, Monday. Here, at the house, which is weird because my official address—the one everyone has—is my department at the university. Only a few close friends knew about this house until last night. Anyway, he comes here and says he has a little proposition for me. His niece, he says, is on the waiting list for a tour job with Archway. She needs the experience, he says, because she hasn't had many jobs, and he is willing to pay me a thousand bucks to call in sick at the last possible moment. Well—I get five hundred plus room and board a pop from old man Andreas, so if I accept this crazy offer, I am up five hundred *and* I don't have to work. Then on Wednesday I found out that I'd won a research fellowship, and that I could get a last-minute ticket on a charter flight. I decide that I'd better quit. It's a nice job, and I like Andreas and the work isn't hard but it's really time-consuming—one week out of four, usually, and my professors are getting really pissed off at me. Anyway, if I take this guy's offer, and quit on Thursday evening, I get the extra thousand. And that means I can take that money and go on my dig this summer, and next fall when the grant comes in I have lots of money to live on. So that's what I did. I felt sorry for Andreas, because he had to scramble to fill the hole, but not a thousand bucks sorry." She looked over at them, her eyes bright and clever again, all their morning fogginess dispelled. "And when I heard about the hijacking, I realized that they wanted to get me out of the way so they could put their own person in to facilitate things. I felt terrible. Until it occurred to me that they could also have arranged to have me mugged a little too energetically instead of just asking me. In this neighborhood, who would question it?"

"Can you describe the man who came to see you?"

"Of course. In fact, if you don't mind waiting just a second, I can do better than that." And she jumped up and ran out of the room. They heard her bare feet on the stairs going up, at least two at time, and then bouncing down. "Here," she said, waving a large pad of paper. "I tried to get him on paper as best I could as soon as I realized it was important. It's not too bad a likeness, if I say so myself."

They stared, mesmerized, at the pencil sketch in front of

them. "You draw well, Miss Carruthers," said the second agent in respectful tones.

"I came to archaeology because I bombed out of fine arts. All I could do was the painting and drawing component, and the pots. I hated all the other stuff—confusing, boring, or worse. I'm not good enough to make a living at painting, so I headed for the pots." She craned her neck to look again. "Yeah—that's what he looks like. Mean-looking bastard underneath, isn't he? Basically. Pleasant exterior, plausible, smooth, and educated-sounding. Now—he did mention something about me losing a few fingers and maybe an ear or two if I didn't keep this whole transaction to myself, but I figure once they break the law all bets are off."

"I wouldn't take these particular men lightly, Miss Carruthers. You might be in more personal danger than you think once they realize—"

"Don't worry about me," said Miss Carruthers. "I'm long gone by nightfall. The thousand bucks has already turned into a plane ticket, and my dig starts on Wednesday. This was a bye-bye party. I'll be out of here before those guys in the living room wake up."

"But—"

"Don't worry. You can reach me through the university. And, at the rate you guys work, I'll be back in time to testify. Look—I hate to run, but my cab is coming in an hour or so, and I have to finish packing."

It was a tattered little band that began the long march into civilization, carrying all that they could and leaving the rest. Some of the remaining water had gone to soaking the bandages off Diana Morris's leg. She'd insisted with almost insane vehemence on looking at the bullet wounds. "I really think we should leave it as it is until we can get to a doctor," said Harriet. "After all, we're not—"

"I'll tell you what I know. That woman who bandaged me would just as soon have slipped a knife between my ribs. God knows what she was doing trying—or pretending to try—to save my life. I don't trust her not to have rubbed road dirt into the wound while she was at it. Besides, she's tied it too tight. I won't be able to walk. It's a wonder I haven't developed gangrene."

"You know that," said John. "That she was out to get you."

"I know it."

"Just the way she knew you were a trained and professional law officer," John observed.

"I see. She said that, did she? It would go a long way toward explaining her attitude."

"It had something to do with the way you reacted to the presence of armed men and to gunfire. You definitely didn't behave like your average librarian. Several people remarked on it."

Diana frowned in annoyance. "Doesn't follow. I could have been in the army before I became a librarian."

"Perhaps you were," said John. "It doesn't matter to me, but Mrs. Nicholls did mention it."

"It's irrelevant now," said Diana. She pulled up her split pant leg and looked coldly, almost indifferently, at the mess underneath it.

Once the matted and blood-soaked bandages had been removed, the wound itself was an anticlimax. "There's only one," said Harriet, surprised.

"One?"

"Karen told me you had been shot twice in the leg. I was expecting something much worse. After all, it did bleed a lot," said Harriet.

"Everything bleeds a lot. Try cutting your finger. People always overestimate the amount of blood loss because it looks so gruesomely large and makes such a nasty stain." As she spoke, she was pouring alcohol from John's shaving kit over the wound, and then carefully wrapping strips of one of Harriet's clean shirts around her leg.

"Doesn't that hurt?"

"Mmm," she said. "A bit. I have a high pain threshold— or is it the other way around? It hurts, but not as much as it might hurt someone else. It's handy, but dangerous."

"I can see that," said Harriet, who didn't believe a word of it.

And they set out, Diana clutching a piece of wood to support herself as she limped along. Her face was gray and taut with pain and the effort of walking, but when she spoke, she sounded almost angrily cheerful. "I wish you'd let us help you," said Harriet.

"I'm fine," said Diana. "You worry about yourselves and the children. I can manage."

"You could put your other arm around my shoulder and lean on me." She raised a hand to stop her objections and turned on her in a fury of anger and frustration. "You're not going to be much good to anyone if you pass out. You'll be a hell of a lot more difficult to carry, but we'll try, you know. We'll have to try. Because by now you've convinced us you're in danger, and that means John will never leave you behind. He's trained as well. And I'm going to be furious if either one of us gets killed because you're too goddamn stupid and stubborn to accept help."

"You really make a girl feel good, don't you, Harriet," said Diana. "Okay, lend me your shoulder and we'll see."

*   *   *

"What are you trying to say to me, slimeball? Are you saying you can't find someone when you already know where she's stashed? And you know who put her there? And you know how to find him?"

"But, Carlos, we're not sure he was the one who stashed her." Ginger leaned against the study door, not deigning to answer, but his companion was sweating globs of ice as he tried to find something to say.

"Whaddya mean?"

"Well—we just figured he was the one who had her. Seeing as how he turned up at your place looking for her. And she disappeared right after. Who else would it be? But then you know he drove off and went back to Taos. Checked in on his shift, had coffee, all relaxed and everything. No girl, nothing. Then he booked off for the twenty-four hours he had owing and took off. By himself."

"Where is he?"

"Home for Sunday dinner, probably." He shuffled. "Or off with a girl somewhere. Not the one you're looking for—just some girl. That's all I know."

"So find him. It can't be that hard." Deever turned his chair around and stared out the window at the fountain. "And where's Scotty?" he asked. "He was supposed to get in touch yesterday morning. What in hell is going on around here?"

The other man looked around and decided that he had been dismissed. Ginger watched him leave and shut the door before answering. "Scotty wasn't supposed to contact us until everything was cleaned up and it was safe to move. He wasn't carrying any communications equipment, just in case, so he can't call in. If Scotty hasn't shown up it's because he hasn't finished. He told me he was going to stay behind and make sure that all the details were taken care of and then leave the bus where it was and get picked up. I don't worry none about Scotty," said Ginger, with a delicate amount of emphasis on the name.

Deever swiveled around again. "Then who do you worry about?"

"Where's Rocco? And what does he do when he sees Scotty on that bus? And when he figures out why he's there? Which is about five seconds later."

"Rocco doesn't know Scotty. You're the only one around here who knows Scotty. He's never been close to this place before."

"Rocco gets around," said Ginger. "He gets around."

"Shit! Why hasn't he been in touch? You'd think he'd want the rest of his money."

"I don't know. Maybe he doesn't figure it's worth picking up. He could have just taken off, leaving us here. Not even knowing where the fucking bus is."

"Yeah. But they don't either, do they? Not yet, anyway." He paused to run through his mental checklist. Things weren't adding up. A lot of things. "The bus has to be on the mesa road. Where else could they take it and hope to get away?"

"A lot of places," said Ginger.

"Well—I don't think they did. They're not smart enough, none of them. Has anyone driven along the road to check if the bus is hidden? Like under some trees or something?"

"You can't hide a bus along that road. You couldn't even hide a donkey on that road. We flew over it. There's no bus down there."

"How could you tell from a plane if the bus was there or not if the goddamn thing is hidden? Drive along the road. Take the Jeep. Go alone. And if you see it, for God's sake, just back off and leave it to me. Don't let them see you."

"How do I do that? By the time I see them they'll have seen me."

"Then stop the Jeep around every curve and get out and check. It's not far."

"It's ten fucking miles," muttered Ginger. "I won't get back until late this afternoon."

"So—I'll live till then. Get going."

Kate woke up from a deep, deep sleep, groggy and stiff and in pain here and there, but happy. Deeply happy for the moment, anyway. She climbed out of the trade-official size bed and went into the bathroom. Antonia had done a remarkably professional job on her hair—the result, she claimed, of those years of poverty when she had been forced to learn how to cut her children's hair—and Kate admitted it really didn't look bad. The deep, wonderful bathtub called out to her and she turned on the taps. There was a container of bath oil bubbles on the counter; she took an orange one and threw it into the hot water. Almost instantly the room was filled with the scent of orange blossom sharpened by a light underlay of orange. She climbed into the tub while the taps were still on and waited for the water to crawl up to a proper level.

She turned the taps off and slid down with a luxurious sigh into the smooth, scented water. The only intimation she had of his presence was the puff of cool air that he brought in with him. "Hi, Kate," he said, kneeling by the tub. "How does it feel?"

"Wonderful." She turned her head lazily in his direction.

"I am rediscovering the pleasures of the flesh. First food, then sleep, and now bathing."

He dropped a kiss on her forehead and then ran his hand delicately over her scar. "Someday you must tell me about it. When you're feeling stronger, much stronger. Not now."

"It's ugly," she said, turning her face away from him.

"Nothing about you could be ugly. It's sad, but not ugly. I'll even get used to your hair in time."

"By then it'll be long again and you won't have to." She turned to look at him again. "And maybe by then I won't be so thin."

"I hope not."

"What's going on out there?" Kate asked, waving her injured arm carelessly in the direction of the rest of the house and scarcely noticing the resulting jab of pain.

"My sister, Consuelo, is finally out of bed. She has had breakfast and has gone to visit a friend. My brothers arrived, and Antonia developed a passionate desire for a family visit to Uncle Jaime, who's sick. They won't be back before five, Consuelo tells me."

"Do you think that was on purpose?"

"Probably. To keep the house quiet enough for you to sleep was what she told Consuelo, who may or may not have believed her. And so we're alone." He caught Kate by the wet hands and began to pull her toward him. Her hands slid out from his grasp and she fell back, laughing. "You're too slippery," he said. "If you don't get out of that bath soon, I'm coming in after you. Boots and all." He stood up, grabbed a huge towel from the stack on the counter, and held it out to her. As she stepped out of the bath, he enveloped her in the towel and began, very slowly, to pat her dry.

Long before she was half dry, she had pressed her damp body against his and wrapped her arms around his neck. All during the years she had been working around the world she had been pushing men away in self-preservation, telling herself she was being professional. She had seen enough messy liaisons between journalists and idealistic guerrilla fighters in areas that were minefields of political intrigue, and the weary frustrations of those who formed lasting bonds with colleagues who always seemed to be instantly transferred to God knows where. Slowly she discovered that men no longer tempted her enough to break her self-imposed rules, and she began to doubt her own sexuality. But now endless years of contained desire exploded and burned right down to the soles of her feet and she clung to him like a starving creature.

"Just a minute," he murmured, and went into the bedroom. She leaned dizzily against the counter, trying to catch her breath. She could hear the rattle of curtain rings and the clump of boots hitting the floor and then almost at once he was back, as naked as she was. He picked her up and carried her to the bed; he dropped her gently down but she held onto him tenaciously, pulling him with her, preventing him from drawing away. "Don't be so anxious," he said, laughing, as he awkwardly maneuvered himself into the bed beside her. "We have all afternoon."

"Ssh," she said, and pulled him on top of her, wrapping her long legs around him. "Don't tease me," she murmured, "not this time. For once when you put me down on a bed I want you to stay right here. I can't wait any longer."

When they finally fell apart, sated for the moment, Fernando tickled her belly. "Are you hungry?"

"Famished," she said. "Whimpering with hunger."

"Just a second." He got up and walked over to the work table in the corner and came back with a cold shrimp on a toothpick, covered with hot sauce.

"Food," she said, and demolished it. "Where did you find that? And is there any more?"

"There's lunch," he said. "Antonia put together some lunch for us. It's sitting there on a thing of ice, keeping cold, but we'd better eat it now, I think."

On the table were the shrimps, some olives and tomatoes, a dish of guacamole, a basket with bread and rolls, a cold lentil salad, a plate of cut fruit, and a pitcher of lemonade, its ice cubes rapidly disappearing. "My God," she said, awestruck. "This is unbelievable. Not only are you fabulous in bed, but you produce a banquet to go along with it."

"I like the way you put that, but I'm afraid Antonia is responsible for the banquet. She sent it up as a test," said Fernando. "To see if you meet her standards in eating. I told you you'd have to watch her."

CHAPTER 13

Their progress was hideously slow. Diana Morris leaned more and more heavily on Harriet's shoulders; her legs ached under the strain of holding up both of them. Then the injured woman lapsed into semiconsciousness, dragging one foot after the other, her head drooping, until she buckled at the knees. Harriet caught her around the waist. "She's passed out," she said. "Give me a hand, John. Quick."

He set down the water and grabbed her from the other side; together they eased her down by the side of the road. "Jesus—now what do we do?" whispered Harriet.

"Try water. Hold her head up a bit." He poured a little water into his cupped hand and splashed it on her face. She opened her eyes groggily and he held a cup to her lips. "Drink that. Goddammit—don't pass out on me. Drink."

"Five minutes," she gasped, "and then I'll be fine." Her eyes closed and she was out once more.

They waited ten, splashed more water on her forehead and pulled her to her feet again. "Can you manage her?" asked John.

"Better than I could manage that cumbersome thing of water and those knapsacks." And they set out one more time. The wind blew fine dirt and sand into their mouths and eyes, and the sun, almost tropically high, beat through

to their brains. They tied bits of clothing over their heads
and kept going. The children had treated the exodus as an
adventure in the beginning, but now they trudged wearily
as well, too tired or perhaps too stubborn to complain.
Diana's knees buckled again; Harriet let her down to a sitting position and they poured more water down her throat.
They gave some to the children, and forebore themselves.

"Listen," said Stuart. "Do you hear that?"

"No—what?" said Harriet.

"It's an engine. A car engine," said Caroline, her voice
rising in excitement. "Someone's come to rescue us." She
ran ahead, demonically energized. John took off after her
like a greyhound after the rabbit.

"Caroline, no," yelled Harriet. "Wait."

The child stopped and turned. "What's the matter?"

"Get back," said John. "Let me look first." And he loped
off with his economical, long-legged stride, running easily
up to a rock formation that blocked their view of the next
stretch of road. He began to climb, moving quickly until he
disappeared from view.

"We don't know who it is," said Harriet quickly. "It
might not be someone who wants to rescue us at all." And
clutching Diana tightly around the waist, she hustled
everyone into the thin shelter of the forested slope beside
them.

They waited silently. The engine noise grew louder and
then died abruptly. The ignition had been switched off. An
ominous quiet was restored to the mountain. A rustle
behind them heralded John, moving like a ghost from tree
to tree until he was crouched by their sides. "Don't budge.
I don't know who it is, but he isn't from the bus and he
doesn't look like a rescue patrol. He's carrying a rifle and
trying very hard not to make any noise. He was about to

climb those rocks when I made my tactical retreat into the woods."

At that point, the driver pulled himself silently into view, and checked out the half-mile or so of road that could be seen from his vantage point. It was impossible to read in that impassive face whether he had found what he was looking for. Then he disappeared as abruptly as he had appeared. They heard the sound of the engine starting, the whir of wheels against dirt and gravel, and a dusty Jeep came around the bend and drove past them without slowing down. As it reached the next curve, the driver stopped and began the whole process again.

They stayed where they were until the vehicle had gone again. The children, rested and impatient, raced off as the adults pulled themselves up to continue on. Diana Morris waited until they'd left before commenting. "It's not a good sign," she whispered. "He's looking for me, and if he finds me on his way back, he won't leave much of any of us."

"You know who he is?" asked John.

"He works for a man named Carl Deever. His name is Ginger," she said laconically. "Shall we carry on?"

At the next curve, the road plunged down alarmingly. With any luck this was the steep slope they had driven up when Harriet first turned into this road, a lifetime ago, it seemed.

"We're almost at the intersection," she said, trying to sound cheerful as she wondered how in hell they were going to get Diana Morris down anything that steep. "I remember this stretch. It's not very long. And we're bound to find a car on the other road."

"Sure," said Diana, "there'll be a car," and collapsed again.

This time they let her rest for a while, and walked to the

brow of the hill to consider their next move. "How do we get her down there?" asked Harriet. "She can barely walk on relatively level ground."

"We can carry her," said John. She wasn't tall or heavy, but the thought of carrying her down that hill made him realize how tired he was. "After all, it's downhill. That's better than up."

"Not much," said Harriet. "As you ought to know. Not on a hill that steep. And who carries the water and all the rest of the stuff? The kids?" She sat down and studied the road. At this point it left the edge of the canyon, and twisted and turned through an ancient dry streambed, offering little in the way of resting places, or, in fact, hiding places. Certainly not ones that were easily accessible to someone carrying a half-conscious woman. "We could do it in stages," said Harriet at last.

"What kind of stages?"

"Short ones. We stash her and the kids up here, carry the water and equipment down until we find someplace to hide them, come back, and the two of us carry her down. Stash her there and do it again."

"What if we don't find that someplace?"

"So be it. We improvise. It's that or leave her here, John."

He stared down at the road for so long that Harriet decided he had fallen asleep. "No," he said suddenly. "We can't do that. She's too helpless to fend for herself if anything unexpected happens. We improvise. Can you hear anything?"

"No," she said. "But we'd be better off asking the kids. They have ears like bats. Caroline? Stuart? Can you hear the Jeep?"

They stopped their conversation and listened, with great

concentration. Caroline turned to her brother and shook her head. "We can't," said Stuart. "But if you want us to listen for it, it'll be easier if we stay up on the rocks. You can hear everything up there."

"Can you follow us from up there?" asked John.

"I think so. Most of the time. We're quite good at climbing," said Caroline. "Sometimes we may have to come down to the road, but then we can go up again. So as long as you're not going too fast—"

"We won't be," said John. "Now—this is what we're going to do."

Ginger stopped the Jeep at the path to the cabin. Because if they had brought the bus up the mesa road, and if they hadn't made it to the plane, then they had to be at the cabin. It wouldn't have hurt Scotty to call from there and let people know what the hell was going on, but maybe he felt he couldn't risk it. Scotty had always been a very cautious sort. Ginger took the rocky path with the long and powerful strides of someone who has lived in mountains most of his life, and has been forced to walk more than he ever drove. It was less than a mile to the top at this point, and in comparative terms, a gentle climb. He crested the hill and stopped to observe the situation. There was, as Rick and Suellen had discovered, very little to see.

Then he let himself half-run, half-fall down the path on the other side, until he came to an almost invisible fork. The right-hand side would take him, after a long and thirsty walk, back to the main road. He took the left.

It wasn't more than a hundred yards to the cabin from the fork in the trail. Carl Deever's really hidden hideaway. One could get to it by knowing the trail and walking, either from the mesa road or the highway; or one could fly in and walk a much shorter distance. That was how all the supplies and equipment came in. But no matter which side you approached it from, it blended with the mountainside and the trees, invisible.

He knocked on the door, not expecting a response, but knocking all the same. No one answered. He drew a fistful of keys from his pocket and unlocked the door.

Someone had been here. Scotty, of course. He had detailed contour maps of the entire region with him—and the keys. Ginger turned the handle on the tap and water came out. Someone had been here long enough to bother turning on the water system. An empty beer can stood on the counter; there was a dirty plate in the sink, along with a fork and a cup. The coffee on the stove was cold, and so were the beans still in the pot. He sniffed the beans. They hadn't been there all that long. And Scotty must be coming back. He knew Carl hated a mess.

He washed the dust off his face, drank a couple of glasses of water, washed the dirty dishes in the sink and the pot on the stove, and headed back to see if he could find the bus. Or Scotty.

He whistled cheerfully as he climbed back up the mountain and headed down the other side. His legs always felt cramped walking on flat ground, and his feet hurt walking on pavement. Someday, maybe, he'd have money, and he'd go back home and buy a little place— Out of the corner of his eye he glimpsed something that shouldn't be there over to his right. He stopped to listen. Satisfied, he turned his head to see.

Something multicolored—white, brown, blue, rust-colored—lay in a heap under a tree. He stepped cautiously in its direction to have a look. The blue blanket that had been decently shrouding Kevin Donovan's remains had been pulled aside by inquisitive teeth and paws during the night. "Jesus," said Ginger, looking down at the mangled face. No point in looking for Scotty anymore. Mr. Deever wasn't going to be pleased.

Instead of continuing on to the Jeep, Ginger moved quietly across the wooded slope until he heard the sound of voices coming up from the road below. He slipped closer and then gently crouched down. Directly below him, largely hidden under a jutting piece of ground, he could see the edge of a dark blue bus. He had been wrong. There was a place to hide a bus, and by God, those local boys had found it. He rolled quietly onto his belly and crawled as close to the edge as he could. He lay there in silence as people walked back and forth, chatting, lying stretched out in the sun, and even reading. A tall woman, wearing a hat tied on by a scarf, came around the curve of the road and walked up to the bus, where she disappeared from his view. Ginger nodded in satisfaction and began to crawl backward until it was safe to stand.

The first two stages in climbing down the hill had proceeded successfully enough. Finding a place to stow their goods that would also hide Diana proved more difficult than carrying her down. Although that was hard enough. Every footstep on the uneven, gravelly surface of the track was potentially treacherous. Coordinating their movements sufficiently to carry such an awkward burden was almost impossible. And so sometimes they both carried her; sometimes John did. Sometimes she tried to walk, but that was the least efficient of all, never lasting more than a few steps. The children drifted above their heads, scrambling silently over the rocks above, occasionally appearing beside them and climbing back up when their high road temporarily disappeared into another gully.

The third stage looked as if it might be the next to last. "There's a very bad patch of road ahead, but I could see the intersection," said John, when he climbed back up to get Diana. "Unless I'm suffering from highway mirages. I didn't quite get to it, although it was very tempting. Let's go."

They rounded the next curve and faced another precipitous drop. "Shit," said Harriet.

"It's not so much that it's steep," said John. "It's that the surface is terrible. But if I take her shoulders—"

"We'll fall," said Diana. "I'll walk. If you can hold me up on each side—"

"It's the only way we can do it," said Harriet.

John set her down and the three of them began the slippery descent. Abruptly, their painful concentration on the placement of every footfall was interrupted by a cry from above their heads. "It's the Jeep," said Caroline. "Hide."

Ginger was driving along the track with considerable care, trying to decide whether Carl Deever would be more enraged that the bus had been sitting precisely where he had said it would be, and that in two days no one had found it, or that someone had murdered Scotty without his permission. And to what extent would that rage be mollified by the knowledge that his wife, whom he had assumed was long gone, was still with the bus? Hell—why was she still with the bus? At that thought, he speeded up involuntarily, and the Jeep skidded around the next curve. Shaking his head, he slowed to a much more conservative pace.

A rattling of stones on the edge of the road behind him

made him slow even more, craning his neck around to the right in order to peer back into the canyon. Nothing. Probably an animal escaping from the menace of the vehicle. While his attention was directed toward the canyon, he failed to notice three adults plastered against the ground at the foot of the little gully wall. He drove on very carefully down the last steep, twisting section of road and onto the secondary highway.

It seemed to take them only minutes to get to the intersection once the Jeep had passed them by. The children forgot their exhaustion, thirst, and hunger in their elation and triumph.

"I threw an enormous rock," said Stuart. "I thought he'd never notice."

"That's because it landed miles behind him," said Caroline. "I threw two huge handfuls of stones. Right beside the Jeep." She giggled. "I almost hit him. Then we both ducked down."

"I read about something like that in a book," Stuart went on, managing to combine becoming modesty with looking extremely pleased with himself. "Where someone hid an elephant just by getting the bad guys to look the other way as they were walking by. He did it by throwing rocks, too."

"Thank goodness it worked," said Harriet. "Because you do realize that things in books don't always work in real life, don't you?" And then felt very mean-spirited. "But you really saved our lives," she added. "It was very clever of you."

"Of course we realize that," said Caroline haughtily. "But books give you ideas."

Then laughing out loud for the first time in a long time,

they ran, walked, limped, and hobbled their way to the crossroad.

And luck continued to smile on them when they hit the main road. A rancher in a battered-looking truck with a CB appeared almost at once, drove them ten miles closer to Santa Fe, and called the state police before dropping them off by the side of the road to await further rescue.

And so, when two cars filled with state police arrived, they found them sitting in the afternoon sun, waiting. Joe and Samantha Rogers climbed, white-faced, out of the second car, and stumbled in the direction of their waiting children.

"Mummy," screamed Stuart, and the twins launched themselves at their parents. In an orgy of hugs and tears and endless rapid speech they all moved toward the cruiser.

"Wait," said Caroline when they reached the cruiser. She ran back, flinging her arms around Harriet's neck. "Thank you," she said. Tears were pouring down her cheeks.

"Yes," whispered Stuart. He stood beside his sister in an agony of embarrassment, searching for the right words. "I don't know what . . ."

"Think nothing of it," said Harriet, and gave him a hug. "You made great camping buddies."

"Excuse me," said a voice from behind them. "But are you Harriet Jeffries?" And the questions and explanations began.

Fernando had left Kate half-asleep in the huge bed at four-thirty, promising to return within the hour. When Antonia roared into the house like a small tornado at precisely five o'clock, Kate was sitting in the living room. A Rottweiler stretched out on the couch beside her, its head in her lap, and she was apparently deep in a paperback novel in Spanish she had hastily picked up from the table beside her. She had one foot tucked under her, and the other one was on the floor, being used as a pillow by another sleeping dog. *"Buenos días, señora,"* she said, without a care for how miserable her Spanish might sound. After all, it was supposed to be miserable, wasn't it? She gently displaced both dogs' heads and rose to her feet, slipping into a pair of Consuelo's sandals at the same time.

"Buenas tardes, señorita," replied Antonia, chidingly. "But let's not force the child to practice tonight. She's just flown in and she's exhausted. Lola, my son, Roberto." Her eye fell on the two dogs, who were lying very still, trying for invisibility. "Okay, puppy dogs, outside. *Afuera.*" The dogs got up, cast a reproachful glance at her, and stalked majestically out of the room.

A thin, lively looking man, smaller than his brother but equally tense with suppressed energy, grasped her by the hand. "Thank goodness for that," he said. "There isn't space for all of us in the dining room now that Antonia has filled the house up with dogs. They're well trained, but large. Anyway, I'm glad we have a dispensation to speak English for this evening," he went on. "It never goes beyond the first day, you know, so don't get all comfortable. I take it you're another victim sent by our grateful government?"

"Commerce," she said, smiling. "Textiles. The first thing I'm going to have to do is find out how to say textiles in Spanish."

"And my son Guillermo."

When Kate looked up her breath caught in her throat

and she could feel herself change color. The resemblance between Guillermo and his brother was as overpowering as it was unexpected. It was not the same face; Guillermo had a fleshy sensual mouth and heavier nose and jaw than his finer-featured brother. He was also much fairer in coloring, and perhaps even bigger in size; and there was something slightly more relaxed about him. He lacked his brother's wary vigilance, perhaps. But his body, outlined against the light, and the way he moved through space, graceful and powerful as a tiger, bore such a familiar stamp that she stared at him in amazement and confusion. She felt stripped and vulnerable under his scrutiny. Fernando could have warned her, she thought crossly. But then he probably hadn't a clue.

"You are much more fascinating than the usual run of officials they send us from the Commerce Department," said Guillermo, taking her hand and forgetting to let go of it. He spoke in a soft, mannered voice, like someone with ambitions to be an actor, or an announcer on public radio.

"Given that most of them are fat men over forty, I should hope so," said Roberto.

Guillermo shot a nasty look at his brother and dropped her hand; he stepped back to examine her. "Local textiles," he said. "Very tactful. That's a beautiful dress," he said. "Where did you get it?"

"You know, I bought it in New York. Isn't that terrible? But I haven't had a chance to shop since I got here. I just arrived this morning."

"I love these designs," he said softly. "Exotic but familiar, if you know what I mean."

I should damn well hope so, thought Kate. They belong to your sister. But she nodded enthusiastically, like the good trade rep she wasn't. "I think I do. This is an excellent example of the possibilities you find in the top-end segment of the cotton market."

But she was torn from what was threatening to become a minute discussion of U.S. trade policy in the textiles industry—about which she knew nothing except that it was complex—by Roberto, who seemed just as determined as his more flamboyant brother to capture her attention.

"For God's sake, don't make poor Lola give a speech on American trade policy. It's bad enough that she's going to have to suffer one of Antonia's weeks." He smiled a shy sweet smile and she was drowned in panic again. Was that the treacherous voice that had called to her in the night, telling her that he was Bob Rodriguez? No. It wasn't possible. He couldn't be. Someone else had borrowed his name, thinking it would reassure her enough to bring her out. Surely, if he had been the person who had turned up at the cabin, who had tried to lure her out of her hiding place, he wouldn't be able to stand there chatting innocently. Because he'd know. He'd have realized she was there, listening, safe in his loft. He would have checked to see if the ladder was fastened in its "up" position. Wasn't he the mad inventor of the hidden ladder?

Just as she had convinced herself that she had nothing to fear from him, he tossed in a bombshell.

"Do you go in for photography?" he asked. "It would seem to go along with your job, I would think."

"A bit," said Kate, her heart racing again, and not quite sure of the safest line to take. Claiming not to know a lens cap from an f-stop could turn out to be as dangerous as admitting to expertise.

"I've been out all weekend photographing birds," he said. "Very difficult, but satisfying. Do you find it so?"

Kate looked confused. "I don't think I've ever photographed a bird," she said, quite truthfully. "They fly around so fast. I took some nice pictures of my dog once. Except he kept falling asleep while I was trying to get him to sit where I wanted him to."

"What kind of camera did you use?" he asked, staring at her in fascination.

"My dad's," she said. She was beginning to relax again. If this was designed to trip her up, Roberto was awfully clumsy at it. "It's one of those where you just point and push the thing. The button. Whatever it's called. In fact, he gave it to me because he's bought a video camera. But he's like that, you know. Gadget crazy. I could always try taking some bird pictures. While I'm traveling around looking at textiles."

"Do you travel much?" asked Roberto.

"Travel?" she said. Her knees were trembling slightly. "All the time. It's the job—death for your love life. I spend more time on planes than I do at my desk."

She could almost feel him checking off a long list of points he had been instructed to look for. What was next? An arm-wrestling challenge to check out the injured arm?

"Lola, my dear," said Antonia from behind her. "Lola, my son, Fernando."

Her heart raced, her stomach turned over, and she whirled around, her skirt—or actually, Consuelo's skirt— swirling wildly, showing off a considerable length of her elegant legs. She did her best to smile at Fernando as if she hadn't very reluctantly let him leave her bed not long ago. "What a lot of sons you have, señora," she said huskily, taking his offered hand and trying not to let it go. "Are there any more?"

Antonia grasped her around the shoulders, holding her for an instant in affectionate amusement. "No, Lola my dear, Fernando is the last of them. And as soon as Consuelo comes home, we will have dinner."

Guillermo looked thoughtfully at the three of them and walked over to the window. "There she is," he said. "Speak of the devil—"

"Don't say that about your sister," said Antonia and led the way into the dining room.

At that same moment, Walt Frankel was watching the ringing telephone and considering whether it was worthwhile answering it. Or should he simply pack up now and hitchhike to Oregon? He shook his head and picked it up. And groaned internally. "That's wonderful news, Mr. Deever," he said. "I'll contact the governor right away. He'll be very pleased."

"Not yet, you stupid little bastard," said Deever. "I want someone to go out to the bus with me from the Sheriff's Department—"

"That would be the state police, Mr. Deever— I mean they've been in charge—"

"No, it wouldn't. I'm having trouble with them right now. I want someone trustworthy from the Sheriff's Department to drive out there on a tip. Just a wild tip he's being asked to check out discreetly. But I want it to come from the governor's office. Ginger will show him the way, and I'll be along. And then you can go to the movies or something and stay out of the whole thing. The cops will let the governor know."

Frankel's mind raced furiously as he checked over his little list of personal favors owing. Little list described it all right. Small, and getting smaller by the minute. Chewing his lip, he pulled the telephone toward him. Tomorrow, he really was going to do it. Off to Oregon. He couldn't stand one more day of this.

As the day wore on, the remaining passengers on the bus had spread themselves as far apart as they could until night and darkness drove them together again. Rick and Suellen were back up on the mountain, where they could talk in privacy but keep an eye on what was going on.

Teresa Suarez had broken out a deck of cards and was sitting in the bus playing solitaire with as much intensity as if the game was at a hundred dollars a card.

Rose Green had exhausted her own life history, and was now pumping Karen Johnson for hers, as they walked gently back and forth on the road close to the bus. "The doctor says I have to exercise every day," she had said. "And I don't think sitting in a bus counts as exercise." And so they strolled at a comfortable pace, searching amicably for interesting things to talk about.

And that meant that it was the Kellehers, sitting up on the rocks, who saw the car arrive. And who saw that it contained two men, one in uniform, one not. And that the man not in uniform was Carl Deever.

The deputy sheriff braked with a flourish and got out of his vehicle right in front of Karen and Rose. "Thank God," said Rose. "We thought no one would ever come. Are the others all right?"

"What others?" asked the deputy.

"Is my wife all right, deputy?" asked Deever, climbing slowly out of the car. "Where is she?" He spoke in a troubled, unhappy voice.

"Is Mrs. Deever on the bus?"

Karen shook her head. "Mrs. Deever? There's no one

called Deever on the bus. Or on the trip. I mean there never was a Mrs. Deever among the passengers. I'm sorry."

"Your wife isn't—"

"The hell she isn't," whispered Deever vehemently at the deputy. "She may not be calling herself Mrs. Deever, but she sure as hell is on that bus. She was seen. Goddammit, man, go in there and get her. A tall blonde. How many tall blondes can there be?"

"Well—I can't go in there and arrest her just for—"

"That woman has stolen half a million dollars from me, Deputy, and she's carrying it with her. I want her arrested."

The deputy stood in the doorway to the bus, where Teresa was just turning over her last card. "Mrs. Deever?" said the deputy.

"Certainly not," she said. "Teresa Suarez. Can I help you?"

"There's a Mr. Carl Deever out here who says you're his wife, ma'am, and claims that you possess stolen property. Of his, that is. Stolen from him, I mean." His syntax was falling apart under Teresa's cool stare.

"Oh, really, such a fuss," said Teresa. She stood up and walked over to the window with its lightly darkened glass and looked out. Carl Deever was getting back in the car from the Sheriff's Department. "And I don't see how a wife can be accused of stealing anything from her husband when she's simply gone on a little vacation with some spending money and things like that." She turned back and glared at him, splendid in her anger. "I think this is completely ridiculous. Anyway, go on out. Tell him I'll be there in a minute. I just have to pack up my things." And she began slowly, very slowly to put herself together. Suitcase, overnight case, hiking gear, handbag. "Could you help me with these, Deputy," she called.

"Certainly, Mrs. Deever, ma'am." He climbed into the

bus and picked up her suitcase and overnight bag. "I'm sorry about this," he muttered. He hated domestic complaints. Even rich ones.

"Don't worry about it, Deputy. It'll all work out in the end."

And Teresa Suarez strode out of the bus, long-legged and beautiful, in spite of their forty-eight-hour ordeal. She waved merrily in the direction of the car just as its door flew open and Carl Deever burst out. "Who in hell is she?" he screamed. "That's not my wife."

"There wasn't anyone else in the bus," said the deputy. "And she's a tall blonde," he added, as if he expected Deever to take another look at her and change his mind. Teresa glanced over at him and winked.

It was a curious dinner, one that Kate would remember for a long time. Roberto and Guillermo sat on either side of her and plied her with wine, which she accepted and didn't drink. They, on the other hand, were pouring generous quantities into their own glasses, and a sense of strain surfaced rapidly.

Consuelo sat quietly, eating little and watching her brothers. At the end of each course, she cleared away Kate's nearly full wineglass with rapid movement of the hand. "Let me help you," said Kate, clearing plates filled with untouched casseroled chicken.

"You're Kate, aren't you?" said Consuelo, once the kitchen door was safely closed. "Fernando told me about you. Don't worry—I know how to keep quiet. But look—you have to watch my brothers. Don't say anything to them—well—you can see why. They get drunk and can't keep their mouths shut." She sat down at the kitchen table as the voices rose in the dining room. "Have some more chicken," she said. "Or I should say, have some chicken. It's really good, and I couldn't eat in there. I knew there was going to be an explosion. I could feel it building up as soon as I walked in the door. It's better to leave them." She took down two clean plates, put a piece of chicken on each one, grabbed two knives and forks, and put one plate in front of Kate. "Bread?" she asked. "It's from our local bakery, fresh today. And salad." She took a pitcher of lemonade from the refrigerator and poured some for both of them. "Fernando told me about your injury and how you're not supposed to drink. He asked me to help get the booze out of your way so you wouldn't be embarrassed."

What else has Fernando told you, I wonder? thought Kate, and tried the chicken. It was a revelation, like everything else she had eaten in this house. "Will they get anything to eat?" she asked, pointing at the dining room, worried about Fernando, who must have been starving at that point.

"Oh, sure. They'll come out eventually and get something in here, together. Or at least Antonia and Fernando will. And maybe the others if they're not too trashed to see their plates."

"No wonder Fernando gets upset about drunks," said Kate.

"Oh, yeah," said Consuelo. "He's a real one-man band on the subject." She grinned. "That dress looks great on you. I knew they wouldn't recognize it."

"It's gorgeous," said Kate, absently. "Did you have a cousin who was addicted to pills and alcohol?"

"A cousin? An addicted cousin? Here in Albuquerque?"

"I think so."

"We don't have any cousins over the age of eight, except

in Mexico, and we've never met any of them. Antonia doesn't speak to her family, except for her two younger brothers who live up here now. And their kids are all little. What are you laughing at?"

"Me. Believing your brother." She saw the look on Consuelo's face and hastily reached over to pat her hand. "It's okay," she said. "He was just trying to encourage me. Talking about people who had overcome worse problems, shall we say. It was probably an old girlfriend, and he turned her into a cousin."

"I don't know," said Consuelo, staring intently at her.

"What's wrong?" asked Kate. "What are you looking at?"

"Nothing. I just wish I had blue eyes, that's all."

"I don't see that I have anything to apologize for," said Teresa Suarez. "A great big deputy came charging in here and accused me of stealing a whole lot of money or something from a man out there who claimed he was my husband. The deputy said I had to go with him, so I did. I didn't want to be accused of resisting arrest or something like that."

A large state trooper, larger than the sheriff's deputy, was looking down at her appreciatively and nodding. "Sounds reasonable to me, miss. And we're very glad to find you folks here in good health. People have been worried about you."

"Why thank you," she said sweetly. "What a gracious thing to say. I'm afraid our bus is inoperable—"

"Did it crash, miss?"

"Not really. It skidded and stalled, and when they started it up again, it ran out of fuel. It's probably not really damaged at all."

"Now, is this everyone? We heard about Mr. Donovan and Mrs. Nicholls, and the five who went on ahead to get help were the ones who got in touch with us," he said, turning to glare at the hapless deputy. "We can drive the three of you out right now and take you to your hotel. But weren't there two more people here at the bus?"

"Rick and Suellen," said Teresa. "They were here just a minute ago."

"There'll be lots of people coming out," said the trooper. "We'll make sure they get back to the hotel as soon as they return to the bus."

"Hotel?" said Teresa. "You mean a real hotel with bathrooms and running water? Oh, joy. I can't believe it."

"We are apparently guests of a Mr. Andreas," said John, as he dropped the duffle bag on the thickly carpeted floor and looked around their luxurious hotel room.

"Who's he?" said Harriet, as she pulled off her sweatshirt.

"The owner of the tour company, and a very good friend of Joe and Samantha, parents of Stuart and Caroline. He puts his tours in this hotel when they stop in Santa Fe." He looked at Harriet, who was now standing stripped and beautiful in the middle of the room. An onrush of desire reminded him forcefully of how long they had been apart, and then, once together again, never alone. "Harriet," he said thickly, reaching out his arms. She glided silently toward him over the yielding rug and buried herself in his grubby sweatshirt. "Harriet, this has been agony. God, how I've missed you. I don't know which was worse," he said, kissing her, a long slow exploratory kiss.

"What do you mean worse?" she murmured when she finally broke away and looked up.

"Missing you when you were half a continent away from me, or when you were right at my fingertips," he said, running his hands delicately over her back.

"And?"

"I decided I'd rather spend ten years in the same room with you with one of those swords between us than have you gone," he said. "I really would. Life was very bleak without you." He paused to nibble gently on her neck. "Of course, the perfect solution is the room without the sword . . ." He broke off and began pulling off his sweatshirt.

She stepped back. "I'm going to take a shower," she said firmly, "before you make me forget what my name is. And rinse the sand and dust off me and my hair, and then I'm going to take a bath, and soak the stiffness out of my limbs. You want to join me? Maybe I can fit you in between the shower and the bath," she added lasciviously and giggled.

"Showers for two," he said, walking into the bathroom and turning on the water.

John ran his hands over Harriet's damp hair and then bent over and kissed her. She stretched luxuriously and curled up under his arm. "How about getting into the fluffy white robes supplied by the management and ordering something extravagant from room service?" he said. "And shall I shave? Or do you think I should grow a beard and horrify my colleagues?"

"Yes. And you can shave during my hot bath." She ran her hand over his stubbly cheeks. "Although you do look dashingly tramplike at the moment. What shall we have for dinner?"

"What about Kate?" said Harriet suddenly. She had finished shrimps in a garlic and hot pepper sauce, a filet stuffed with crab, vegetables, a large salad, and was now tackling the fruit bowl that arrived compliments of somebody.

"What about her?" asked John sleepily.

"Well—she was expecting us around eight on Friday. It is now well past eight on Sunday. Don't you think she might be a little worried?"

"No."

"Why not? I would be."

"Harriet, my love, we have been the hottest piece of news in this entire area for the past three days. She probably knows more about what's been happening to us than we do. She's been reading the papers and watching television. We were just living through it."

"Of course. Do you think my brain has been permanently affected by this experience? I don't seem to be able to think anymore."

"I believe it has more to do with lack of sleep and a definitely peculiar diet over the past few days. You'll recover. Now—if you've finished with all that food, I'll get them to come and take away the dirty plates. And then," he said, leaning over the back of her chair and rubbing her shoulders, "we can pick up where we left off a couple of hours ago."

"You mean you're willing to forgo watching yourself and your great adventures on the evening news?"

"You're damned right I am."

If they had been watching, they would have heard that two people were still missing from what was now being referred to as the "fatal tour." Searches had been organized to try to discover the whereabouts of Mr. and Mrs. Rick Kelleher of Amarillo, Texas.

CHAPTER 14

Kate leaned heavily on the banister as she came down the stairs, trying hard to walk like a vigorous woman of twenty-nine instead of the very aged lady she felt like. Fernando had been gone since long before dawn, filled with worried exhortations instead of words of passion. When she eased herself out of bed, every muscle in her body had been stiff and sore, and a hot shower had done little to alleviate the chill in her soul or the acute discomfort in her body. But pride and the smell of coffee got her moving, and she forced her spine erect as she neared the kitchen. Two gigantic Rottweilers did what they could to help, converging on her, one on each side, as if they were trying ineptly to hold her up.

"Thanks, fellas," she said, giving them a pat for their efforts. "But I don't think it'll work." She had a sudden urge to get outside and walk until her muscles loosened up. Maybe if she took these two beasts with her . . . Probably not. Fernando had been very insistent that she stay indoors.

Antonia was in the kitchen, pencil in hand, reading something that looked like a student paper. "My dear," she said, pushing it to one side and rising quickly. "Let me get you some breakfast. No protests. I promised my son that I would fatten you up. Have some coffee," she added, getting another cup and filling it.

And Kate watched her once more move rapidly and smoothly through the process of putting a meal together. "You make me feel completely incompetent," said Kate. "It seems impossible that anyone could be so good at so many things at once. I'm good at what I do, and I can actually cook a few things—but compared to you I'm a moose in a kitchen."

"It's nice of you to say that," said Antonia, her voice curiously neutral, "but it's not really a compliment. You might as well praise a slave for being good at working in the mines. At one time, I had no choice. I had to be competent and efficient, and since the old skills stay with you, you use them."

"I don't understand," said Kate. "When you say you had no choice. We can all choose to remain unskilled and ignorant, can't we?"

"Perhaps. It depends on what you expect from your life. I was married when I was sixteen," she said, turning over the bacon and taking the eggs out of the refrigerator. "My parents were farmers—poor landowners—in Mexico. They believed they had come down in the world. We had little money and a lot of debt, and when our neighbor's rich American cousin turned up and said he wanted to marry me, they were completely dazzled." She paused. "He was offering to buy me, if you want the truth," she added reflectively. "He helped pay their debts in exchange for a wife."

"Did you want to marry him?"

"Very difficult question." She shook her head. "I don't know. How do you decide? Human beings are driven by so many different forces and desires that it's hard to isolate the most compelling one. It would be easy to say that my parents forced me into it, but that wasn't true. A sixteen-year-

old girl always thinks it would be very nice to be rich, and
have lots of clothes and to live in the promised land, and
anyway, it made me feel important and beautiful that he had
chosen me out of all the girls he could have had. Good for
the ego. On the other side, I didn't love him, and I didn't
want to marry anyone. I dreamed instead of going to university." She stared out the window into the yard filled
with dogs. "In those days, in my village, it was a fairly
remote dream, but not impossible. Not at all impossible. But
my parents were wildly anxious to get rid of me safely and
prosperously, to have more money to spend on my brothers.
I listened to them and married him. More coffee?"

"Please. Look—I can do my own eggs. Are you sure I'm
not keeping you from your work?"

"No. No one can do *that* any longer," she said, smiling
with a hint of malicious triumph. "Although my husband
tried, very hard. And marriage to him was as terrible as I
ever could have imagined it in my gloomiest moments. At
eighteen, I had three sons and a husband who was a pig and
I thought my life was over. Clearly, he had come looking
for a bride in his grandparents' village because he thought
he could find someone who was so young and naive and
ignorant that she would tolerate much more than any
American girl ever would. But I had grown up in a village,
after all, not a tower or a cave, and I had some ideas about
a woman's rights in marriage. Then I discovered that the
company he worked for was heavily involved in illegal
operations—"

"What kind of company was it?"

"Trucking. He was a driver. Earning good money, as they
say, but not the plutocrat of my parents' dreams. You can
imagine how many different kinds of profitable traffic

there could be between Mexico and the United States. I
didn't like that. At home, we may have been poor, but my
parents were at least fairly honest. I decided that independence was the only rational course. I tried to make sure
that I did not get pregnant again, and I worked very hard
to perfect my English. I finished high school and began to
take a few courses at the University of New Mexico. My
husband was furious—he didn't trust me around all those
students—but he couldn't stop me unless he gave up his job
and stayed home all the time to guard me and keep me
indoors. I'd taken eight courses by the time Consuelo came
along. I took two more after she was born—the boys were
old enough to look after her—and then my husband was
killed."

"In an accident?"

"In a manner of speaking." She paused, as if uncertain
whether to go on. "He had some insurance money," said
Antonia, slipping the eggs into the frying pan, "which I
used to buy this house. It was run down, but we repaired
it, and I was able to go to university full time. That was
when we started taking in people who needed to practice
Spanish. The boys took care of Consuelo after school and
helped around the house. I finished a Ph.D. and was hired
at the university here. Guillermo was twenty by then, and
chose not to go to college. Roberto and Fernando wanted
to very much, and did. We had five more years of hard
work and no cash, and suddenly, all the boys were working, we redid the house, and made it perfect." She set
Kate's plate in front of her.

"It is a beautiful house," said Kate, giving her hostess a
puzzled glance before tackling her breakfast.

"And now you are wondering why your comment produced this lecture. Aren't you?" Antonia filled their cups and sat down opposite Kate. She had not finished what she wanted to say.

"It was very interesting," said Kate diplomatically, having forgotten by now what she had said to trigger Antonia's speech. "But yes, I was wondering a bit."

"It's because my son has fallen in love with you," said Antonia in clear, precise tones, looking directly across the table at her. Kate felt like a laboratory specimen whose mind was being probed and assessed by those dark, inquisitive, and slightly hostile eyes. "I thought you should know something about us and how we function before either one of you is too badly damaged by the experience. Fernando does not fall in love easily. He is very intelligent, the most intelligent of all my children, except perhaps for Consuelo. He is also very—what is the word—reserved, I think, or perhaps controlled. I'm afraid that he finds his family a terrible burden."

"But he loves you all dearly," said Kate, horrified. "Everything he says about you shows that."

"I didn't say he didn't love us," said Antonia impatiently. "I said that we are a burden—on his spirit, perhaps. Not his pocket. Not any longer. I have achieved my wildest dreams of independence now, with tenure and a real salary. I don't have to look to any man to help feed me and my children and no man can tell me what to do. I'm talking about his father's legacy to his sons—that still haunts him. Do you understand what I am saying to you?"

"You mean your husband—his father—was a criminal as well," said Kate, who was beginning to understand where this conversation was going. "He was more than just an innocent employee of a dishonest company." She waited for a moment or two for a reply and then went on. "How did he actually die? Was he murdered?"

"In a sense. What you might call a legal murder. He was caught in a trap near the border and tried to shoot his way out of it. He was, in many ways, a stupid man."

"Is that why Fernando joined a police force?"

"Oh yes. That was why."

"All the rest of the passengers have had their clothes restored to them," said Harriet. "That's why they look so much more elegant than I do. And I'll have *huevos rancheros* and a very large glass of fresh orange juice," she added to the waitress without pausing.

"Sounds good," said John. "Or at least I think it does."

"Make it two."

"To get back to all these people in suits," he went on. "Have you forgotten that you didn't bring many clothes with you? Or at least that's what you told me. And if it bothers you, why not go out and buy a new pair of jeans? And even a sweatshirt. Unless you really want to eat breakfast in black high-heeled shoes and a white skirt. I'm sure you could get them here somewhere." He raised his hand and waved in the direction of the entrance.

"Who's that?" said Harriet, not bothering to look behind her.

"The investigating team. They said they'd drop by and pick us up, and here they are."

McDowell and Rodriguez threaded their way through the tables until they were standing over them, like a pair of grizzly bears watching a picnic. "Good morning, gentlemen," said Harriet. "Join us."

"We've already had breakfast," said McDowell. "Are you folks ready?" he asked abruptly. Now that he knew from the previous evening's interview that they weren't your ordinary rich civilians, he didn't feel he had to be excessively attentive to their tender feelings.

"You can't have too many breakfasts," said Harriet. "More coffee and one of those baskets of sticky things," she said to the waitress who wandered by to see what was happening. "You might as well sit down. We've only just ordered, and it's a much more comfortable way to drink coffee and eat Danishes."

"This is Sergeant Rodriguez," said McDowell, tacitly accepting their invitation by pulling out a chair. "He's been in charge of several aspects of the investigation, and I felt I should bring him in at this point."

Rodriguez sat down as well, and drew a deep breath. "There's just one small point where I think you can help me," he said politely. "Miss Jeffries, can you tell me when your friend Miss Grosvenor invited you to visit her in Denver? Precisely?"

"Precisely when?" said Harriet, looking oddly at him. "Are you sure you want the entire history?"

He nodded. "The whole thing."

"Okay. Don't blame me if you fall asleep. When she inherited that house in Denver about three years ago she invited me to come stay with her. Then every time she wrote, she repeated the invitation."

"So she didn't specifically invite you for a certain time?"

"Hang on a minute." Harriet, frowning in concentration, held up a hand to keep him from interrupting. "After she was injured, she sent me a postcard saying how much she needed company. I had been thinking about the Kansas project for a long time, vaguely, and it all fell together. I had nothing else to do. John was tied up with a case, and things are slow at home. I didn't write Kate that I was coming, because I hate tying myself down to specific times and places when I'm on a shoot in case I'm held up by the weather, and besides, I'm criminally disorganized about my personal correspondence. We set things up after I reached Kansas. Got that? After I got to Kate's, we organized the Taos expedition. All very last minute."

"So the dates and the times—when you were coming, when you were meeting her in Taos—they were *your* dates and times."

"Ah—I see what you're driving at. Yes, they were," said Harriet, with a hostile edge to her voice. "For the first time in her life, Kate had absolutely nothing to do, and she was perfectly happy to fall in with my schedule. Perfectly happy. She made no attempt to maneuver me into being at a certain place at a certain time." By now, Harriet was glaring at Rodriguez.

John offered him the basket filled with muffins and pastries; he took a particularly large and sticky Danish with a cheerful smile. "That's great, Miss Jeffries," he said, sounding both gleeful and triumphant. "I mean, thank you very much. It clarifies a few things for us." He turned to grin at McDowell, who glared back at him.

Obviously Harriet had just helped Rodriguez score a point in some epic battle between these two men. Maybe they had bets laid on who organized the hijacking. Bastards. "How is Diana Morris?" she asked, opting for a change in topic before she was arrested for cop assault.

"I beg your pardon?" asked McDowell. "Who's that?"

"The person on the bus we all knew as Diana Morris," said John impatiently. "The one we dragged, bullied, and carried for three miles or more out to the highway. We were just wondering if she was okay. When you've put all that work into someone, you like to know."

"I'm afraid we don't have any information on her," said McDowell stiffly.

"Look," said Harriet. "We all knew she was a cop. And either she was awful shy—which she didn't seem to be—or she was working undercover. She tried to tell us she was a librarian from Virginia. I suppose that means she was Washington-based."

"How did you all know—what made you all think she was a cop?" asked McDowell.

"Only because when the bus driver pulled out a weapon and started firing, instead of hiding under the seat, she took a round or two while casually saving the tour guide's life," said John. "I'm not sure I would have done that, but maybe she's better trained than I am. At any rate, it's not the automatic reaction of your average librarian."

"Sounds more like a royal bodyguard," said Harriet.

"All we know," said McDowell sourly, "is that when we got her to the hospital, this bunch of goons from the feds swooped down and carted her away. We don't know what happened to her. Or what she knows, which is probably plenty."

"And that means," said Rodriguez, "that when we've done all the dog work and have figured it all out, they'll appear again like magic and say, hey, friends, this is a kidnapping and a hijacking and it's federal. These guys are ours. This is our collar and you can go screw yourselves."

"How did they know that the bus was going to be hijacked?" asked Harriet. "You can't tell me that there's an FBI agent on every tour bus, just in case."

"Information received," said John.

"Or maybe they were watching someone on the bus and

the hijack was coincidental." McDowell used the word coincidental as if it hurt.

"Come on, McDowell." Rodriguez shook his head. "Deever is mixed up in it. He was convinced that his wife was on that bus, you know. Which means she probably was."

"Who's Deever?" asked Harriet.

"Rich man," said McDowell, "owns a ton of land and people here and there in the Southwest. He was under investigation a few years ago over a question of prostitution. Procuring underage girls by forcible means—mostly in Mexico—and transporting them across the border into Texas. There was an extensive investigation and then hearings. Dragged on forever. The Santa Rosa hearings they were. That's the town where a lot of the girls came from. He slipped out from under without a scratch on him."

"Hardly without a scratch," said Rodriguez quietly. "There's still a lot of suspicion hanging over him these days. And when he walks down the street, people cross over to the other side to avoid the smell."

"When you say underage," said Harriet, "just how underage are we talking here?"

"How does twelve grab you?" said Rodriguez. "There were a lot of twelve-year-olds. And two of the kids they found were only ten. That's even better."

"Ten," said Harriet. "My God. That's younger than the twins. That is absolutely disgusting."

"He is. Disgusting. Pond slime is lovable compared with Carl Deever." Rodriguez finished his coffee and pushed back his chair.

McDowell stood up. "I don't want to hurry you, but if you've finished your breakfast," he said, "do you mind coming over to my office? We have coffee there, too."

*   *   *

"What's new?" McDowell called out as he swept them into his small office. It did, in spite of its size, boast a window of its own to indicate his exalted status.

"The search party has located the van and a body tentatively identified as Jennifer Nicholls," said a young trooper, dropping a piece of paper on McDowell's desk.

"Good," said Harriet. "I don't suppose there's anything left of my camera and film. In the van," she added heartlessly.

"They said there was a great deal of camera equipment lying around there, and that some of it may have survived." The young man looked somewhat disapproving. "They'll collect it all for you and you can check."

"Thanks. Oh, just a minute," she called to his retreating back.

"Ma'am?"

"Could you ask them not to open any of the four by five film holders that might still be in one piece?"

"I don't think they're stupid enough to do that, ma'am. But I'll tell them anyway."

McDowell pulled up two extra chairs for Harriet and John. Rodriguez leaned on the windowsill, silhouetted against the brightness of the late morning. "One of the interesting things about all this was that a week before the tour left, the regular tour guide was bribed into calling in sick," said McDowell. "As soon as she heard about the bus disappearing, she smelled a rat, of course, and sat down and sketched the guy who contacted her. She's some kind of artist, apparently. The feds got to her as she was walking out the door to go to the local police, and in a rare show of cooperation, they have given us a copy of the sketch."

"Like hell they're cooperating. They don't know who it is and think we might," said Rodriguez.

"Well, I can't say I recognize him just like that," said McDowell. "But we're checking through Records. Meanwhile, we wondered if you'd seen him—at the airport, maybe. Anywhere." He handed the picture to John.

Harriet craned her neck to get a look at it as well. "My God, John," she said, "isn't that Jennifer's husband? It looks like him. I'd check with one of the other passengers, just to be sure, because by the time we got on the bus, it was pretty dark, but that's who he looks like. What was his name?"

"Brett," said John. "Brett Nicholls. And you're right. I'm sure it's him."

"Brett Nicholls?" asked Rodriguez. "Doesn't sound familiar. Is he one of Deever's men?"

"Can't be. At least, he sure as hell isn't any of the men they investigated for the Santa Rosa hearings," said McDowell. "The feds have them all memorized."

McDowell had dropped the copy of the sketch on the table, face down. "Mind if I look at it?" asked Rodriguez, strolling over and picking it up. He carried it back to his comfortable niche against the window. Harriet, her attention drifting from the scene in front of her, watched him move across the room, impressed in spite of herself. Then he turned the paper over and lifted it to the light. The change in him shook her; she caught one glimpse of his face, bleak, white, and strained, before he strode across the room again. He dropped the sketch casually on the table, and raised a hand in farewell. "Urgent call. Sorry. I'll be in touch." And he was gone.

*   *   *

"Maybe she went from the bus to the cabin."

"How?" asked Deever. "She doesn't even know there is a cabin. Or where it is. How stupid do you think I am?" The heavy draperies were pulled tightly across both sets of windows in his office, cutting off every last stray beam of light or breath of wind, as if only in darkness and fetid air could he be safe. He was sitting in the chair behind his desk, staring at Ginger in the semidarkness.

"Women always seem to find these things out."

Deever brooded over that thought. "If that's where she is, I want her out," he said at last. "We'll take her with us across the border and worry about her then."

Ginger sat and looked at him, waiting for clarification. "It would be easier to deal with her here. Leave her in the mountains somewhere."

Deever shook his head. "Too risky. Go and get her."

"The trouble is, Mr. Deever, I go out there in the Jeep and every cop in the state is on my tail, because they want to know where she is, too. Also they want to know what you're up to. I don't think it's a good idea. If she's there, I'd never get to her first. If she isn't, it's a big waste of time."

Deever whirled his chair around so that it was facing the curtained window and leaned back in it. "Shit," he said. "You're right." He drummed his fingers together as he thought. "I think we'd better get out of here and stay out for a while until things calm down," he said at last. "We'll fly in, pick her up, and get the hell out of the country. Leave the fallout for Harper to handle. That's what lawyers are for, isn't it?"

"What about that photographer? Grosvenor."

"There's not a hell of a lot she can do if we're in Mexico. And after that, well—it's her word against mine. No one made her come out here, did they? And who's going to believe a lush like that?" He considered that a moment longer. "Tell Harper to write her a letter, sort of apologizing for any misunderstandings, but not admitting liability, of course. And then offer her a few thousand."

"I don't know, Mr. Deever. She's a famous woman. Rodriguez said—"

"Fuck Rodriguez! I'm sick of the sound of his name. She's a neurotic bitch and a lush and she needs the money for booze. And if she's too fucked up to work, like they say, she isn't much of a threat," he added, an edge of doubt creeping into his voice. "Anyway, by the time we're ready to come back, she'll have drunk through the money and be brain dead."

Kate was being driven mad by inactivity. Antonia had disappeared into her study to work; Consuelo had rushed downstairs for a hasty breakfast and then hurried out of the house, late for school; a woman whose name Kate did not catch turned up and began to clean very energetically. Every time she found a quiet corner to sit down in, she was chased from it by an orgy of mopping and dusting and wiping.

But after a couple of hours, even that game was over. Antonia emerged from her study, pointed out the cold lunch waiting for Kate in the refrigerator, and rushed off to teach her first class of the day. "Don't go outside," she called, as she headed for the garage. "Don't answer the door or the telephone." And she was gone.

It was still much too early to eat lunch. She helped herself to some fruit in order to pass the time, and paced back and forth between dining room and living room. Her constant headache had been receding slightly. She'd been able to ignore it for hours at a time while mind or body was engaged in other things. But now, with nothing to occupy her but a returning sense of self-pity, it resurfaced, preventing her from doing anything that required concentration and thought. She looked at the bookshelves, with their rows of novels in Spanish, and tomes of philosophy and criticism, and gave up the idea of curling up with a book. The phone rang. Once. Twice. And stopped. Of course, the energetic housekeeper was still around. She went back up to her bedroom and stared out the window at the dogs. There were six of them outside, almost the entire complement of Rottweilers except for the pups. The housekeeper must have put all the dogs outside so she could clean. They were sleeping in the cool shade of a pleasant arbor, and she envied them their ability to fritter away the day. Perhaps she should emulate the dogs, and give herself over to sloth.

As she watched, one of the puppies, fat, huge-pawed, and awkward, stumbled out of the kennel. It blinked, surprised, at the brightness of the day. In the opening of the kennel, she could just make out the seventh dog crouched, vigilant, watching her venturesome young. Calendar stuff, thought Kate contemptuously, and walked over to the chair where Fernando had set her camera bag. She took out her OM 4 and regarded it critically. It was just as it had been when he'd picked it up from the floor of her motel room. In a spiteful gesture, whoever had searched her room had wrenched open the back and exposed the film. Not that it mattered a damn. She had put the film in the camera after throwing away the roll with the accursed shot of the murdered child on it, and hadn't touched that, or any camera, since. She tossed the useless film in the wastebasket, found another roll of HP5, and went to work on the camera. With absolute concentration, she took out her blower and delicately removed each visible speck of dirt or dust from the open parts of the body, and then set to work cleaning the lens, checking that everything was still functioning, and loading the film.

Out the window, the puppy had been joined by two others, and all three were rolling ferociously about on the grass and dirt, in a magnificent play fight. With the rapidity that was her trademark, she flew through a half roll of film catching the battle. Roaming through the viewfinder beyond Antonia's fence, she saw in another yard a girl in short shorts and a halter top swinging on a child's swing set in desultory fashion. She appeared to be waiting for something she feared would never happen—to grow up, perhaps, or for a boy to come along and release her from the slavery of boredom. As Kate switched lenses and shot the other half roll of film, she realized that she was humming to herself.

But then the roll was finished and she lacked the will to find another in all that mess in her camera bag. She stared at the camera in her hand as if it were an alien creature. Without thinking, she slipped the rewound film back into its container, and marked it with time and date. She put the camera away and sat down, exhausted and deflated. Her head pounded; her back and chest and shoulder ached miserably. Her legs felt stiff and awkward.

What she needed was a hot bath. She hurried toward the bathroom as if it might disappear in the length of time it was going to take her to get to the taps and turn them on. She tossed a bubble of scented bath oil into the hot water and looked down at her working jeans. Silk negligees, that's what you need, Kate, she thought, and little feathered things to throw over your shoulders; then you might feel like lazing around all day. It was a strange sensation, to be enveloped in fragrant steam with nothing to do but enjoy it. She went back into the bedroom and stripped off her practical, working clothes, heedless of the open curtains, and then, in spite of protesting leg muscles, stepped into the tub.

The fragrance of orange and the lapping of water calmed her head and soothed her body. She drifted, in a beautifully semiconscious daze, thinking of very little, but remembering with startling clarity every gorgeous erotic feeling Fernando had aroused in her. As she ran her tongue lightly over her bruised and swollen lips, she could feel his lips on hers, and the delicate play of his tongue, darting between her teeth. The warm rippling water brought back long, slow caresses on her earlobes, her neck, her breasts and belly, awakening her body until it vibrated in sympathetic harmonies with his. And now that she had been brought to such a glorious pitch of arousal, she thought happily, nothing could send her back to her old state of numb indifference. He was, she decided, falling abruptly from the poetic to the pragmatic, really something else. Where he had learned his extraordinary skill was another and more interesting question; but she'd leave that for another time.

She was amazed at how easily he had walked into her life and turned it over; or had she been the one to walk into his with arrogant certainty and upset his existence? That was another question to be answered later. Much later. All she knew was that for the past four months her body had been trapped in an irritable drug-hazed stupor, capable of feeling two things: pain and absence of pain. He had reached out a hand and she had broken free. She would never go back there again; she was serenely confident of that.

She wondered, idly and unworried, where he was; he

had promised to be back as soon as he could, but had pointed out that if he started tearing off to Albuquerque every few hours, people would wonder why his attachment to his family had become so powerful. She smiled lazily and slid farther and farther into the tub, until the water rose and fell in tiny waves just under her chin.

And then, as though her dreams had the power to create their own reality, the bathroom door opened, just like the last time, and a puff of cool air blew in. She slowly turned her head. "I wasn't expecting you so soon," she murmured huskily to the dark shape outlined in the door.

"I don't suppose you were, Lola. I don't suppose you were."

The voice snapped her out of her daydream. She sat bolt upright, reached for a towel and clutched it to her chest. "My God. What in hell are you doing here? I thought you were Fernando."

"That's strange. Very strange. We don't look at all alike. And why expect my little brother to walk in while you're taking a bath?" he added maliciously.

"You do when you're standing against the light and I can't make out your face," said Kate, ignoring the last part of his remark.

"Perhaps. Anyway, I came to see you, Lola. Or should I call you Kate? After all, we both know who you are."

"You can call me Joe or Sam, if you want, as long as you get out of here." Her heart pounded with fury. "Right now. If you don't mind. I'd like to get dressed." The telephone began to ring again, its nagging call sounding over and over and over again.

He stopped to listen to the phone before answering, watching her carefully to catch her reaction. "Oh, but I do mind," he said, after the caller had given up. He sounded pleasantly amused. "At least, I mind leaving without you. Lola-Kate, my love, you and I are bound together absolutely and completely. I cannot do without you."

"What in hell are you talking about? You and I are not bound together by anything." She felt ridiculous, trying to carry on an argument from a bathtub, and that only made her angrier. "Now get the hell out of here."

"Oh, but we are, Lola-Kate. We are tied by the most powerful bond of all. The power of life and death, Lola-Kate, or to put it less poetically—my family has always had a tendency to be too poetical—in the relationship of fingerer and fingeree. You can get up in the box against me, Lola-Kate, and if you do, I will be screwed. I don't like thinking about that."

"You're wrong," said Kate. "In fact, you're crazy. I know nothing about you. I've certainly never seen you do anything but eat dinner and get drunk."

"You're lying, Lola-Kate," he said in a sad voice. "It's not surprising, but I had thought you were tougher than that. You disappoint me. You really do." He had moved into the room and was lounging against the counter, a study in relaxation. A dog barked in the backyard, and another one answered it from closer by. The house creaked and moaned, in the manner of old houses. "Where are the goddamned dogs?" he asked edgily.

"They're all outside," said Kate, and then realized it had been a stupid thing to say. The thought of a pack of dogs outside the door might chase him out the window. Too late. "In the back."

"Good." He turned his attention back to her. "Lola-Kate, I saw you. When you walked in here yesterday and took one look at me and freaked. Because we'd met, hadn't we? At Deever's. When I came to collect my money."

"Rocco?" Disbelief was written across her face. "Are you Rocco? No. You can't be."

"Don't call me that, Lola-Kate. It's not my name. I hate it. Deever does that to people. He takes away their names and then sneers at them for not having any. I have my father's name, goddammit. It's an honorable name and it's mine." As he straightened up, his right hand darted to one side and back again. He held it out to show her. A knife lay across his palm; a stray beam of light hit it and was reflected for a moment into Kate's eyes. "It's sharp, Lola-Kate," he said, in a soothing, gentle voice. "I keep it very sharp. It won't hurt."

She froze, trapped by the menace of the honey-sweet voice.

"Now," he went on briskly, "get rid of that towel. Go on. I don't give a damn what you look like. The towel's in my way." Before she had time to react, he grabbed it by a corner, ripped it out of her hands, and tossed it aside. With his left hand he slid his fingers onto her scalp and grabbed a fistful of her newly cropped hair. Then he jerked her head fiercely back.

And in one spasm of terror and infinite regret, she knew this was the end. The world went black.

And then it went white, with black spots. "Put that knife down and let go of her," said a very familiar voice. "Before I blow the back of your head off. I'm right behind you. At this range I can't miss."

The pressure on the knife eased slightly. "You wouldn't shoot me, little brother. I know you. You haven't got the guts. Remember last time? You wouldn't do it then—you won't do it now."

"You fool," said Fernando steadily. "I was fourteen the last time. Or was it fifteen? I'm smarter now. And if you must know the truth, old pal, I care a hell of a lot more what happens to her than what happens to you. After a while you can even wear out family loyalty."

Kate kept her eyes tight shut. It seemed crucial that neither of them should notice her; she clasped her arms over her chest and tried very hard not to move or speak or think or feel.

"Give me the knife," said Fernando, "and let her go. You can have five minutes' start to get the hell out of here before I call in."

"That's a laugh."

"Maybe, but it's better than nothing."

"I have a better idea. Come on, sweetheart. We're leaving."

Kate was suddenly jerked to her feet by her hair. It was another revelation in new and painful experiences. Then, pressing the knife against her throat again, he grabbed her around the waist and heaved her with no difficulty out of the tub. The Rodriguez brothers were strong. "We're walking out of here, little brother, and if you shoot, the chances are maybe fifty-fifty that I will slit her throat going down. You want to risk that? Now get out of my way. Stand back."

Fernando didn't move.

His brother drew the edge of the knife delicately across Kate's chin, and she could feel the warmth of blood that trickled down her neck. "I have no trouble cutting someone's throat, little brother. Do you want to watch?" He shoved her, holding her tight against him with an arm around her waist and a knife at her throat, like a shield, and this time Fernando stood aside, his weapon still raised. They moved in a dreadful parody of some mad dance routine through the bedroom, around the huge bed, and out the door into the hall. At the top of the stairway, they stopped abruptly. Directly ahead of them, Kate heard the click of claws on the wood of the stairs and a deep-throated sharp warning growl. The knife loosened and then tightened its pressure on her throat.

"Careful, Lola-Kate, because if anyone tries anything, your little throat goes first," he murmured in her ear. The growling started again, low and long and menacing. "Shut up, you fucking miserable hound," he said. "Get the hell out of my way." A huge, broad-headed dog with a gleaming brindled coat stood in the middle of the stairway, legs set apart, head slightly down, defying anyone to pass.

There are only seven dogs, thought Kate, unable to think of anything else, and they are all outside. I counted them. Six in the yard, and a mother in the kennel. Seven.

Then she heard a key in the lock and felt the change in atmosphere as the door opened.

A horrified and powerful voice screamed so loud the entire house echoed with the name. "Guillermo!"

Fernando yelled, "Hold him, Prince!"

And Prince sprang up the stairs. At the same moment, Guillermo Rodriguez flung Kate's still wet and naked body at Fernando, immobilizing him for a brief slice of time. As the dog's teeth sank into Guillermo's knife arm, he put both hands on the banister and vaulted it, sliding down for a foot or two before falling to the ground floor, leaving cloth, skin, and blood behind him. He landed in an awkward crouch, but one millisecond of rebound carried him to his feet and, knocking his mother out of the way, he threw himself out the door she had left open. He was in her car with the door shut before Prince hit the metal with an echoing thump and fell back. Guillermo reversed and turned in a shower of gravel, knocking the dog out of the way. As the car disappeared around a corner, Prince scrambled to his feet, shook himself, and walked soberly into the house.

Antonia ran up the stairs, tearing off her jacket as she moved. Fernando was standing rigid in the hallway, white-faced and shaking with rage, clutching Kate by the arms in a fierce grasp, and staring after his brother. Antonia took her, wrapped the jacket around her shoulders, and held her tightly, patting her on the shoulder. Fernando began to pace back and forth along the hall. "Thank God I came home when I did. Otherwise I'm not sure what he would have done," she said at last.

"And that the dog was in the house," added Fernando grimly.

"I don't know where he managed to hide. The first thing Juana always does is put all the dogs out."

"Why did you come home?"

"I wanted to check that Kate was all right, and I remembered that I'd told her not to answer the phone. I felt very uneasy for some reason and so I came back after my class to check, that's all." With her arms still tightly around Kate, she watched her youngest son closely.

"If you hadn't walked in, he would have killed her," said Fernando. "A hell of a lot of good I was doing, just standing there, watching, waving a gun around."

"If you hadn't come in when you did, I would have been dead long before Antonia made it home," said Kate. "He was about to kill me then."

Fernando walked with deliberation down to the end of the hall, sat down at the little desk, and punched numbers rapidly into the telephone. "You're calling them?" his mother asked.

"I have to, Antonia. And then Kate must get dressed and

go to Santa Fe to make a statement. I should have taken her yesterday, but I was afraid that would put her in greater danger. I was worried that we had Deever people in the department. That's a laugh," he added bitterly. "But you begin to believe that he has them everywhere."

"He does," said Antonia sadly.

After a long, murmured conversation, Fernando put down the telephone receiver and stood up abruptly. "Come on, Kate. We're off to see McDowell in Santa Fe. Apparently your friends are still there."

"My friends?" asked Kate, puzzled. "Do you mean Harriet? You've actually found her?"

"Yes. She was spending her time looking after a pair of twins and a wounded FBI agent. Except no one is supposed to know she's an agent."

"Do you know what this means?" said McDowell, from the comfort of a chair in the bar at the hotel in Santa Fe.

"Sure. It means," said Fernando, "that we can get Deever on something so tight he won't be able to slip out from under it." He was beginning to regain his normal color after a drive to Santa Fe that Kate was not likely to forget soon.

"What's that?" asked Kate, who was drinking super sweet Turkish coffee on the theory that it was good for shock.

"Kidnapping. Forcible confinement. In short, you, Kate. You're the perfect witness. Respectable, honest, virtuous, intelligent."

"Ooh," she said. "I like the sound of that."

"And with you up our sleeves, we can keep him locked up until we pin down the connection between him and the hijacking. The other passengers said that the hijackers were told there was something on board worth a million bucks and they wanted it. They were looking for gold bars or something like that, but we know what was worth a million to Deever."

"Getting off," said another voice.

They all looked up. "Harriet," said Kate, trying to rise from the low, comfortable chair and falling back again. "Am I glad to see you. But I absolutely can't get up. Come here." She reached up and gave Harriet an enormous hug.

"And this is John," said Harriet, startled. Something had happened to Kate since she'd seen her last. Besides the fact that she had cut off most of her hair. "Remember? The cop. Ever since I was on that bus I've been wondering what could be worth a million. Because it takes a hell of a lot of jewelry to be worth that amount to a thief, doesn't it?"

"After it's fenced, yeah," said McDowell.

"So you have this guy that the whole world is after for something he's actually done, and I would bet that evidence—proof that he's innocent—would be worth a fortune to him."

"How about lack of proof that he's guilty?" asked Kate. "Isn't that just as important?"

"So what was he looking for?" asked McDowell lazily, willing enough to play games with a couple of interesting women over a beer.

"His wife," said Kate. "That's what he said. And she was on the bus."

McDowell looked unimpressed.

"What does his wife look like?" asked John.

"Victoria Deever?" said Fernando. "Can't miss her.

Classy. Expensive. One of those tall, leggy, long-haired blondes. They've been married for maybe five years. She's certainly seen enough by now to testify against him. I'd be surprised if she did, though. I would guess if she opened her mouth to say anything, that would be the end of her."

"But it's irrelevant," said McDowell, pulling out his trump card. "She wasn't on the bus. The only tall, leggy blonde on the bus was named Teresa, not Victoria. And she's a Latino from New York, not a Southerner from the Carolinas or wherever and she didn't seem to have any connection at all with Deever, although we're still checking on that."

"Then it has to have been Suellen Kelleher," said Harriet.

"But she's not a tall, leggy blonde," said John.

"It only takes a couple of hours to turn a long-haired blonde into a short-haired brunette," said Harriet. "And I bet if you put Suellen into better fitting clothes—remember on the trip she was wearing very bulky outfits that hid her shape—she'd be tall, and slender, and long-legged."

"It's possible, I suppose," said McDowell, grudgingly. "She's the only one to have disappeared. I wonder if he got rid of her?"

"She'll be at the cabin," said Fernando. "Hiding." He spoke softly, and his face had turned ashen in color.

Everyone turned in his direction in silent astonishment.

"Cabin? What cabin?" said McDowell, at last.

"Deever's cabin," said Fernando.

"Deever has a cabin," said McDowell softly. "And why is this the first time anyone's heard about Deever's cabin? Since you seem to know about it. Whose side are you on?"

Fernando pushed his untasted beer to one side. "I haven't said anything partly because I only figured it out in the last twenty-four hours. And once I figured it out, it's taken me this long because my brother is probably there as well. Hiding." He stopped, as if going on was causing him physical pain. "That's why I know about it. Because of my brother. He took me there once, fourteen—fifteen years ago. He said it belonged to a powerful and important and rich friend of his, and he was allowed to use it whenever he wanted. He had a key. Guillermo never had any powerful, rich, important friends except for Deever that I knew of."

"Well—you'd know, Rodriguez," said McDowell grimly. "Better than I would."

"I thought he'd outgrown him, you know, gone on to other things. And that he had a real construction business, not just another Deever front operation." Kate watched his hands. His nails were digging deeper and deeper into the flesh of his palms until she was afraid he would start to bleed. "But I never asked in case I found out—I was always very good at kidding myself when I wanted to."

Fernando took four of them along the mesa road to the path, McDowell and three troopers from Santa Fe, including one who had been introduced merely as "being good with a weapon just in case." "We could drive in much closer by going around and over the mesa," he said. "But there's no cover that way. They'd be long gone before we got there. It's not that far by the path as long as the climb doesn't bother you."

"Go on, Rodriguez, and stop trying to pretend you're the wild man of the woods," said McDowell, looking at the slope and wondering if perhaps he should have sent someone in his place.

"Anyone bring a compass and emergency rations?" said

a wit from behind, and the party began to scramble energetically up the hill.

Deever's beautiful new Piper Cheyenne IIIA had taken off
from an abandoned section of county road—now his private airstrip—conveniently located behind the adobe man-
sion exactly ten minutes before another four men arrived
at his gate with arrest and search warrants. Both birds had
flown, leaving only a jaded and unsurprised Pedro and
Maria behind. Jaded and unsurprised and ignorant.

Deever landed with more haste than elegance on the
mesa and taxied bumpily along to the far end. Here—if
one looked carefully—was a well-tended path not broad
enough to show from the air. He climbed out and headed
purposefully for the path.

Inside the cabin, Victoria Deever and Rick Kelleher sat
on a camp bed, holding hands, and staring at Guillermo
Rodriguez. He was sitting on a hard chair, with a clean
handkerchief wrapped around the spot where the dog had
marked him, and the blood was slowly oozing out and
dripping onto the floor. In his hands and across his lap he
was holding an assault rifle. "I don't see what good this is
going to do you," said Rick.

"Deever wants her," said Guillermo simply. "He wants
her so bad he was willing to have that whole goddamned
bus hijacked to keep her out of the hands of the feds."

"I wasn't going to the feds," said Victoria. "Do you think
I'm crazy? I was too scared to go to the feds. I just wanted
to get out of there and settle down with Rick, that's all.
They asked me, and I told them I'd never live long enough
to testify for them, so what was the use?"

"They were there," said Guillermo. "On the bus. I can

smell cop. They were going to snatch you and force you to testify. Otherwise they'd charge you along with him."

"Bastards," said Victoria.

"I wouldn't necessarily believe everything he says, sweetheart."

"Some of what he says is so obvious it can't help but be true," she replied.

They sat and waited and looked at each other and at the rifle in Guillermo's hands.

"So now what?" asked Victoria. "You're gonna turn me over to Carl. He kills me, and then he kills you and Rick, and then where are we?"

"Come on, Mrs. Deever—"

"Whatever you do, just don't call me Mrs. Deever. It makes me sick."

"Okay. Victoria. You didn't think that I'm stupid enough not to have a plan to get us all out of here, do you?"

"I wish I didn't," she said. "But I do."

Then the cabin was filled with the baby roar of the Piper Cheyenne. "That's Carl," said Victoria. "Rick—I love you, and I wish you'd go out and hide in the bush somewhere. Because once he has me and Rocco, he'll stop looking."

"No, sweetheart," said Rick. "I'm staying."

"They've landed," said Victoria. "They'll be taxiing down to the path. That's that funny sound. Then it's just three or four minutes to here."

"Not a hell of a good idea to meet them here," said Guillermo. "Come on, friends. Out to the path."

CHAPTER 15

Deever walked with the arrogance of the invulnerable toward the path, resplendent in tooled leather boots and expensive checked shirt. But as he moved into the shadow of the woods, his stance altered; he became a part of his landscape, melting into the trees, with only his eyes, flickering back and forth in nervous haste, betraying his humanity. Ginger followed him to the beginning of the path, paused for a moment to consider the situation, and sat down to wait on a convenient piece of rock.

A flash of movement somewhere had caught Deever's attention; one jump and he was behind an inadequate tree, absolutely still. Whether the stillness was of watching predator or terrified prey was difficult to determine. The group of men at the top of the ridge observed him in silence, waiting.

Then a voice rang out, relaxed and half-amused. "I have her, Carlos," said Guillermo. "With her boyfriend as a bonus. You can do what you like with them once I get the rest of my money." He was standing in front of the cabin. "You can even come out from behind that tree," he added, spreading his hands in a gesture of peace.

"That's great, Rocco," said Deever, stepping back onto the path as soon as he had located the head of soft brown hair.

Guillermo moved closer to him, smiling confidently.

"You fucking idiot." Deever fired before Guillermo had time to focus on his weapon, and caught him straight in the chest. The force of the blast threw him to the ground; he lay on his back on the soft forest floor, his body twisted slightly toward the west.

McDowell grabbed Fernando by the shoulder in a grip of steel. "Don't you move, Rodriguez," he whispered in his ear. "If your brother's alive, we'll be there in time to help him. If he isn't, there's nothing you can do. But I want Deever alive and I want for us to be able to prosecute him. No matter how many expensive lawyers he has. So you behave yourself." He beckoned to the slighter and faster of the two juniors with them. "See that guy?" he said, pointing. "His name is Ginger. Now you go up to him real careful and quiet and get him. And then hang onto him. Got that? You," he added to the man beside him, "go along and make sure there aren't any surprises."

Ginger was a realist. When the inevitable turned up, his creed had always been to accept fate with grace. A gun barrel next to his ear in the hands of a state trooper was, in Ginger's rule book, the inevitable. He spread his arms in a gesture of submission and sat tranquilly on his rock to watch the rest of the spectacle.

McDowell, Fernando, and the last trooper, armed with a sniper's rifle, had separated and were working their way down the slope as unobtrusively as they could. McDowell checked the positions of his two men, raised his pistol to slightly above firing position, and stepped out from behind the tree that sheltered him. "Drop your weapon, Deever," he said, in a conversational tone. "We have you surrounded."

Carl Deever whirled 180 degrees to face this new threat.

As soon as he began his move, McDowell called out, "Now!"

The trooper who was good with weapons made a minute final adjustment to his aim and shot Carl Deever in the right shin, just above his beautiful boot. He screamed and dropped to the ground like a dead bird, crippled and impotent from the pain and shock of the blow. McDowell walked over and picked up his rifle before he had time to develop any ideas about reaching for it. "Good work, trooper," he said. "A nicely placed shot. Carl Deever, I have right here in my pocket," he went on, patting his chest, "a warrant for your arrest for the kidnapping and attempted murder of Miss Katherine Grosvenor. And just so's you know, when you're booked we'll be adding in the murder of Bill Rodriguez. You have the right—" And his voice droned on, scarcely audible over Deever's moans and curses.

Fernando Rodriguez stooped over his brother's body and gently closed his staring eyes, in defiance of all regulations and the established practices of his department.

"Where's his wife?" asked McDowell, after calling for a helicopter and medics. The quiet marksman had bound up the wound he had left in Deever's leg, and was standing over him until transport arrived.

"I don't know," said Fernando, pulling himself together and heading purposefully into the cabin. "Mrs. Deever? You in here?" he called. He looked around. It was smaller than he remembered, and very spartan in amenities for someone of Deever's wealth, but perhaps that was the idea. No one who stumbled across it would suspect that it belonged to a rich man, and that, no doubt, was why its existence had remained a secret. Except that Deever had given Guillermo a key on his sixteenth birthday. And Guillermo had taken him there. With a deliberate act of will, he put the memory of that day out of his mind, and concentrated on his task. A rear window was wide open, and Victoria Deever was not in the cabin.

"Mrs. Deever?" he called through the window. "It's safe to come out now," he said. "Your husband is under arrest. So's Ginger."

He was rewarded by a rustling in the bushes behind the cabin. He headed outside just as a tall woman with short, dark brown hair, followed by a broad-shouldered, sheep-ish-looking man, came around the corner. "Hi," she said, brightly. "I'm Victoria Deever. I apologize for the disguise and hiding from you and all. And this is Rick Kelleher. He wanted to stay out here and tackle Carl, but I wouldn't let him."

"Good decision," said McDowell.

"Well—I'm glad y'all didn't get shot. I was worried for a while." She caught sight of her husband, handcuffed and wounded, lying on the ground. "Hi, Carl, honey," she said, with a broad grin that ill-suited her pale elegant features. "It's me, little Vicky," she went on, nudging him sharply with her foot. "Your wife. Remember? And now, for just this one time in your life, you pay attention to what I'm going to say."

"Get that fucking bitch away from me," screamed Deever.

"Not yet, Carl, honey," said Victoria. "You listen to me first. I never was going to testify. That's what gave me the guts to finish packing and go to the airport this time—so they couldn't pressure me into it. And I wanted to be with Rick. I just don't feel they ought to ask a wife to do that, no matter how much she hates her husband. 'Specially when she knows he'll have her murdered if she does. That was a real stupid move on your part, sweetheart. Hijacking a whole bus just to get rid of me. You should learn to trust people once in a while, you filthy little prick." Her light, fluting voice had turned dark with hatred. "I hope your leg hurts like hell, asshole, and I'll see you in court." And she turned and walked with great deliberation into the waiting arms of Mr. Kelleher.

The survivors of the hijacking who were availing themselves of Mr. Andreas's hospitality wandered one by one into the bar, as if the prospect of spending the evening alone with their thoughts was unpalatable. When John and Harriet came in after a late dinner, three of them were gathered around a low table, chatting quietly.

"May we join you? As honorary members of the tour?" asked Harriet.

"Surely," said Rose Green. "Weren't you the ones who got us out, after all? Did you rescue your equipment from the van?"

"They say they've found some of it," said Harriet. "I'll probably have to shoot the project over again, though. But that's okay. I like Kansas. Why are you people all still here?"

"When you've come all the way from New York on Friday for a vacation, it seems silly to go home on Monday," said Teresa. "If the tour company comes up with something interesting for the rest of the week, I'll take it. Otherwise, they've promised me a rental car. Karen and I are going to kick around in New Mexico. It's about time she got acquainted with the Southwest if she's going to be conducting tours through it. Just think about it. The only Mexican food she's ever eaten was in bars in Maine."

Karen smiled in confusion. "I haven't had enough money since I got out here to eat in restaurants," she said. "I'd really like to see the pueblos, too. And some of the museums."

"I'm doing the same thing," said Rose. "Mr. Andreas of the tour company says he's going to arrange at least another week's holiday for me. I like the place."

Harriet deduced that Mr. Andreas had spent the day energetically mending his public relation fences.

"How nice," said Rose. "It's the Kellehers. I wonder where they've been?"

The arrival of Victoria Deever and Rick Kelleher altered the atmosphere. Out of her hiking-boot-and-heavy-sweater outdoorsy clothes and back into shimmering silks, she was a different woman. Teresa Suarez looked narrowly at her as if to satisfy herself of something and then sat back in her chair. "It is Victoria Deever, isn't it?" she asked. "I reckoned it was you Deever was searching for when he came out to the bus."

"I don't know how to thank you," said Victoria with a return of the nervous twitch that Deever induced in her, "but I surely do appreciate what you did out there at the bus. It gave us time to get away. Otherwise he'd have killed me."

"Why?" asked Rose, more curious than shocked.

"Because the next time he's in court, I'll be up there in the witness box, testifying," she said simply.

"Did your husband actually pay Gary and Wayne to kidnap you?" asked Karen.

"It looks like it," she said, trying to smile. "I thought I'd been so clever. Making reservations and all for a week in

New Orleans, while Rick signed us up for this tour, but Carl found out anyway. Only one person besides us knew, and I guess that was one person too many. I'm sorry for ruining your vacations. I never meant for anyone to get hurt."

"Don't worry, my dear," said Rose. "It wasn't your fault, I'm sure. But it is getting late, and I'm too old a woman to sit up all night in bars. We'll meet at breakfast."

Karen and Teresa exchanged glances and rose to their feet. "We have planning to do if we're to hit the road tomorrow," said Teresa. "See you at breakfast."

"I certainly cleared the room in a hurry," said Victoria wryly.

"They've figured out from experience that you're dangerous to sit beside," said Rick, his face in its usual deadpan expression. Whether that was intended to comfort her or not, Harriet was not quite sure.

But Victoria laughed, a hearty, earthy laugh, and ordered a margarita.

In the pause that followed, Kate came in, half-rushing, half-limping, and eased herself into one of the chairs recently abandoned by the tour victims. "Am I glad to get away from there," she said.

"From where?" asked Victoria.

"The police station. Cop shop. Whatever. Where I have been giving evidence, deposing, witnessing, all those things, while people slowly recorded everything I said, and checked it, and double-checked it, and sent out for sandwiches, and checked it some more. Tomorrow—the FBI," she added, in thrilling tones. "And I'll have mineral water with a twist," she said to the waitress. "Is there anything to eat here?"

"Sure thing," said the waitress and disappeared.

"I'm Kate Grosvenor," she said leaning over the table and shaking hands with Victoria and Rick. "Girl photographer extraordinaire. Since no one is going to introduce us."

"Victoria Deever," she murmured. Rick added his own name and leaned back again. He looked like a man who was enjoying himself immensely.

"Actually, I knew that," admitted Kate. "I've taken and developed an awful lot of pictures of you. Can't miss those fabulous cheekbones even under that weird hairdo."

"It was the best I could manage at short notice," she said apologetically. "But you know, between the hair, and wearing jeans, and sort of changing the way I moved, I think I fooled just about everybody."

"What are you going to do now?" asked Kate, settling in for an interesting gossip. "Back to experimental dance?"

"I don't think so," she said. "To be brutally honest, my career was stalling out when I met Carl. Rick has a wonderful spread up in Colorado, and a business in Texas, and I think I'll just settle in and help him."

"Victoria has a fine head for business and accounting," said Rick admiringly. "And a great memory for figures. That's what makes Deever so nervous."

It was very late when Fernando Rodriguez, drained by now of all feeling, walked into the hotel to find Kate. His heart sank when he saw who was with her. He'd expected Harriet and John, but to discover her in the middle of an animated conversation with Victoria Deever was a shock. Kate caught sight of him wavering in the entrance, and beckoned. He moved a chair next to her and sat down. "Were you waiting long?" he murmured.

"A while," she acknowledged. "I was hoping they might let you off early—"

"It's better this way. Roberto has gone to Albuquerque. He'll stay with Antonia."

"How is she?"

"She said on the phone that Guillermo died ten years ago, and that she's been waiting a long time to bury him. Don't ask me what she meant."

"You know damn well what she meant," said Kate.

"Okay," he said. "I know what she meant. For me it was fifteen years ago. But for Roberto it only happened today. He's taking it hard. They were still pals." He was desperately tired. He wanted more than anything else to climb into bed, clutching Kate to him as hard as he could, and sleep until he was ready to face the world again.

Victoria Deever leaned across the table, looking intently at him. "Sergeant Rodriguez," she said. "I want you to know how sorry I am. I only realized Rocco was your brother a few minutes ago. That must have been hard for you," she added with delicacy.

He nodded, too tired for words.

"He hated being called Rocco," said Kate. "Why did Deever insist on doing that to people?"

"Carl invented names for everybody. I was lucky to get Vicky, which I hate. Of course, if I hadn't minded, he'd have called me something worse. He said Mr. Rodriguez had a body like a fighter and so he called him Rocco. After Rocky. God knows where poor Ginger's name comes from. Someone told me he used to have a guy named Fred around as a general watchdog. You know, Fred and Ginger? That sounds disgusting enough for Carl. Scotty he named from 'Star Trek'—and so on. And tough shit if you didn't like what he called you. He claimed it had something to do with his phones being tapped all the time. I think he liked forcing people to answer to any name he wanted." She finished her drink with a grimace, as if the thought of Deever had spoiled its taste. "A power thing."

"But it worked," said Fernando, with some animation in his voice. "We knew someone up here looked after his interests. I thought he was in our detachment, because Deever knew exactly what was going on. I didn't think of my brother and all his friends and drinking buddies."

"Well," said Victoria, "like I said, I'm sorry. Because a brother is a brother. Even if he did try to kill us."

"You had no way of knowing it, but you were perfectly safe as long as he was just waving a rifle at you," said Fernando. There was pain in his eyes, and Kate caught his hand in hers. "He hated guns."

"I can't say I felt safe," said Victoria. "Looking into the business end of a firearm is rather unsettling, I find."

"I don't think he ever fired a gun in his life," said Fernando. "And when our father was shot, Guillermo told me only fools carried guns. Guns were for scaring people, and if you did that too often you'd get shot yourself. But he had knives, a lot of knives, all razor-sharp. Jesus," he muttered, and ran his hand through his hair. "All those people."

Victoria shuddered and stood up. Kelleher scrambled to his feet at the same time. "I'm dead tired," she said. "I could use about three days' sleep. I was too strung out before, so we came down here. It was real nice talking to you. It helped." And they swept out.

"I'm glad," said Harriet. "I found listening to her unsettling."

"It's from being married to Deever for five years. She'll recover," said John.

"Come on, Kate," said Fernando suddenly. "It's late. Let's go."

"Where to?"

"I got us a room in a smelly, flea- and rat-infested boardinghouse. Ready to chance it?"

"Is it cheap?" said Kate, getting to her feet a little stiffly.

"Damn right." He helped her up the last bit and they walked out of the bar, hand in hand.

As they disappeared into the lobby, Harriet heard Kate moan, "I'm starving. I won't last for another ten minutes."

"Now there's an interesting development," said Harriet. "I knew something drastic had happened to her. It has. Sergeant Rodriguez. I like him," she added sleepily.

"Shall we retire to our palace on the fifth floor?"

"By all means."

"John—"

"Yes?"

"What are we going to do?"

"Now? Tomorrow? Or for the rest of our lives?"

"It scares me to hear you say that. It sounds so final. Like death."

"The cure for death is love," said John, running his hands down her back. "Now and for the rest of our lives. I'm not sure about tomorrow."

"Say—I'm beginning to like this place for breakfast," said McDowell, looking up as the others trailed in to join him.

"A man could get used to doing this every day instead of sleeping."

"Have you eaten?" asked Harriet.

"Yes," he said cheerfully. "And I've ordered continental breakfast for four. Don't want to waste a lot of time this morning, do we? After working all night, I needed something substantial, so I came early."

"What have you been doing all night?" asked Kate.

"Talking, and listening. Mostly listening. Ginger—whose name, by the way, is Giancarlo Giovanni Cardone—wants to cut a deal and he's talking to anyone who'll stand still. The guy from the feds has him now, trying for bigger, more important stuff than just plain little murder."

"Can I just ask what was supposed to happen?" said Harriet. "I mean what in hell did they think they were up to?"

"Sure. As far as I can tell, it goes something like this. Deever suspected his wife was cheating on him, and he figured she'd try to get rid of him by going to the feds. So he'd been watching her for more than a year. Ginger says she got ready to leave at least three times before, but chickened out—she knew what he'd do to her if she walked. Then she tells him she's taking a vacation with this friend, Jessica, and she buys the tickets and everything, but Kelleher—the boyfriend—is also buying tickets and Deever is also watching him. So he knows. And they're all waiting around to see if she'll do it this time."

"Why not just get rid of her?" asked Harriet.

"No need if she isn't going to leave him," said McDowell. "And it'll look suspicious. So Deever offers Bill Rodriguez a million bucks to get the bus hijacked and Mrs. Deever killed in the process, because by this time he knows the feds are pushing her hard, and he wants her dead in a way that leaves him absolutely clean. Bill hires the King brothers and books a spot on the tour for himself and his girlfriend, as Brett and Jennifer Nicholls, so he can manage the operation. The King brothers are supposed to sandbag the driver, pick up the passengers at the airport, drive them to some remote—but prearranged—location and abandon them there, unharmed. Except for Mrs. D., who's being taken care of by 'Brett Nicholls' in a sad accident. The two guys get their twenty thousand bucks and disappear. No one said, but I suspect Guillermo was planning on a brave rescue attempt in which Victoria *and* the King brothers would get shot."

"But the brothers thought something on the bus was worth a million and they wanted it. How did they find out?" asked John.

"My brother no doubt got canned one night and told them," said Fernando.

"Then everything went wrong. The bus took off in the wrong direction and disappeared. Deever found out you two had been following it and figured you were feds. The only person you had contacted was Kate, so he went after her. I guess Bill decided it was time to look out for himself; he started getting rid of everyone who could finger him, the two hijackers, Jennifer, and Donovan. Donovan was on the bus as a backup. Catching Victoria was real important to Deever."

"I still don't see why he didn't just hire someone to put a bullet through her as she walked down the street," said Kate. "People aren't that hard to get rid of in a place like Dallas."

"I'm sure he thought of it, and reckoned it was too risky. When the wife of a crime boss is gunned down in the street, people think contract. And from there it isn't too far to a contract put out by the husband."

"Who was Jennifer?" asked Harriet.

Fernando shook his head. "I didn't keep up with my brother's love life."

"Anyway, Deever didn't know about the kids. That also screwed up the operation. You see, once he knew she was going, he canceled the hotel reservations, and no one should have missed that bus for two days. Maybe more." McDowell yawned. "But what happens? There are kids who are supposed to be on the bus, and hysterical parents demanding action within minutes or maybe an hour from the time it disappeared. That was pure bad luck for Deever, and can only be counted as counterbalancing his extraordinary good luck so far."

A tall, thin, limp man with small eyes, dressed in a suit that hung loosely on his frame and a tie that drooped from his curling shirt collar, materialized at their table, unobtrusively, like a waiter. "They told me you'd be here." His reproachful voice chided them for looking happy and comfortable. "Morning, Ed, Rodriguez," he said, and sat down. "And Harriet Jeffries, John Sanders, Katherine Grosvenor. Am I right?"

"So far," said John. "Who are you?"

He flipped a black wallet open and shut, displaying a blur of color picture and print. "Fred—" he muttered, adding a mumble that might have been a last name. "I'll have coffee," he said to the waitress, "and some of those pastries." He turned back to them. "I've just finished talking to Mr. Cardone," he said. "Most interesting. And I'm about to meet with the district attorney. Our feeling at the moment is that it might be awkward if a trial for murder here in New Mexico were to take place before existing federal charges could be heard . . ."

"Come on," said Fernando. "This is McDowell's turf. Let him deal with it. Let's go."

They left Fred and McDowell deep in conversation and strolled out of the dining room. "Why don't we go for a coffee somewhere where the feds aren't polluting the atmosphere with gray suits?" said Kate. "I never got my second cup, not to mention my third. And I'm still hungry."

"Good idea," said Harriet.

"How about a real breakfast?" said Fernando. "Follow me."

Several corners later, they came to a small restaurant, bright and noisy with tiles. Fernando walked briskly through the indoor section, stopping to speak briefly to the waitress in Spanish, and out the other side onto an almost deserted patio, hung with vines and filled with birds, singing and quarreling with each other. They sat down at a brightly painted table and looked around them. "She'll be here in a minute with coffee. Proper coffee. None of this international hotel school shit."

"Did you know Deever?" asked John, as he finished off his very large breakfast. "Before all this?" A sparrow was making dashes for crumbs under his feet and he moved aside to give it more scope.

"Yeah. I've known Deever forever. He's the curse that hangs over my family. My father was killed smuggling illegal aliens for Deever. In a shoot-out with the feds. Can you believe it?" he asked bitterly. "Just like the movies. Anyway, I sort of grew up at Deever's ranch. Pedro would be out teaching me to ride, and Deever would be working on multimillion-dollar deals inside with my father. But I wasn't the reason he took us kids out there with him all the time. It was Guillermo. Deever was crazy about Guillermo. He wanted to adopt him after my father died and Antonia freaked. Screaming about not selling her child to a pervert."

"Was he?"

Fernando looked extremely uncomfortable. "I don't know," he said. "As far as I can tell, he's not homosexual. But maybe he likes boys. The trouble is that my evidence is lousy." He shook his head. "Guillermo was furious with Antonia. He was dying to be rich and live like Deever. He didn't give a damn if the guy ruffled his hair and patted his bum and worse, for all I know. Deever used to give him money, and Antonia would find it and make him return it. She swore we'd make our own way without using blood money. But then he said he wasn't going to see Carlos any more and we believed him. Or I did until he took me up to Deever's cabin."

"What happened at the cabin?" asked Kate.

Fernando's cheek darkened with blood. "I don't know if— What the hell—it was probably all bullshit anyway." He stared down at his plate and began speaking in a low monotone. "Guillermo told me he'd promised Deever he'd bring me to the cabin that day. And then he told me why, and how much money he'd give us, and that Deever wanted to pay for me to go to college, and that we wouldn't have to slave at home to try to make ends meet. He said Deever was willing to marry Antonia, if that was what we wanted, so that I could live at his house. My brother said—" And Fernando stopped. The color had drained out of his face once more. "My brother said," he went on, "that he was getting too old for Deever."

"What did you do?" asked Kate.

"I freaked out. There was a hunting rifle on the wall of

the cabin, and I grabbed it and pointed it at Guillermo, and said I was going to kill him. He said I didn't have the guts, and I just ran. He was right. I didn't."

"That's awful," said Harriet. "Not that you ran, but that Deever—"

"Wait," said Fernando. "The next day, Guillermo said that none of it was true. He'd only wanted to see how I'd react and then he said it was the funniest thing he'd ever seen. And he did do things like that. And so I don't know, and by now it doesn't matter."

"What are you two going to do now?" asked Harriet, in a determined attempt to change the subject.

"Eat," said Kate, "and get fat. But aside from that—" She paused. Not being quite sure whether she was taking entirely too much for granted.

"We have to go to Albuquerque, and then I thought we might take a few days and go up in the mountains. How does that sound?" Under his serene assumption of agreement, his eyes looked sharp and uncertain.

"Sounds marvelous. What about you two?"

"We have to stick around and see about my equipment," said Harriet, "and then—I don't know. We have almost a whole glorious week with nothing we have to do. Except give ourselves over to complete abandonment."

"If we're going to do that," said John, "we'd better rent another car."

The rain started south of Eugene and hadn't let up. The countryside was silvered over with rain and mist; every shape was soft, vague, indefinite. Walt Frankel smiled. Fifty miles from Portland and the downpour increased in intensity. He turned his windshield wipers up to maximum and eased his foot off the gas to compensate for the lack of visibility. Here it was, May, and the world was cool and brimming with moisture. The leaves were bursting with it, the grass was green and rampant with it, every ditch and stream and hollow was overflowing with it.

Frankel's request for a six-month leave of absence from his position as personal assistant to the governor—for medical reasons—was lying on his boss's desk. It had been placed there, accompanied with an authentic-looking doctor's letter, several hours before the story of the collapse of the Deever empire reached the press. Because as soon as word of the imminent arrest hit the governor's office, Frankel had begun to count up every traceable action he had taken on Deever's behalf. It was time to leave. He cleared Deever's money out of his safe-deposit box and packed it away. With a valedictory wave at the clear, deep blue sky and bright sunshine, he jumped into his car and headed for Oregon.

As he edged his way happily around a three-car collision caused by wet roads and poor visibility, he wondered what kind of job he might be able to get in Portland. Because he was home at last.

Harriet parked the car well past the bridge over the Rio Grande and they walked slowly back. The flat mesa covered with gray-green sagebrush looked like a calm sea trapped in a circle of mountains, except for the stark brown slash of the river gorge cutting through it. Small clouds darted across the sky, casting their shadows on the gray-green sea as they moved. The air was clear and cold. They stood close to the edge of the canyon and stared down into the river below. The steep layered rock was frantic with life, home to a countless host of small birds who were unendingly busy with the labor of spring. Otherwise the land was quiet and serene. A car stopped illegally on the bridge to allow its passengers to disgorge, take a picture, and leave again. A rabbit hopped by them, apparently assuming they were some kind of exotic bush, not to be included in its scheme of things. It nibbled on a small plant, gazed around suspiciously, and hopped on to the next likely looking edible object.

"Kate was right," said Harriet. "There is something compelling about the land out here. And the tourists and all their shops and restaurants are just accidental pimples, here and there. Ugly, but in the long run, temporary."

Harriet shivered and John stepped behind her, wrapping his arms around her and pressing her chilly back up against him to warm her. "What shall we do?" he asked. "Look at this. It's forever. Look at it and tell me honestly what we should do."

"I think we should get married," said Harriet soberly. "Even though it frightens me to think of it. We can't go on like this, can we, and I can't do without you, and so I think I should marry you. What do you think?"

He turned her around and kissed her.

The rabbit stopped nibbling and looked narrowly in their direction. Another passing car slowed; its occupants lowered their windows and cheered. The rabbit hopped slowly away, intent on its own concerns.